About th

Scott Hunter was born in Romford, Essex in 1956. He was educated at Douai School in Woolhampton, Berkshire. His writing career began after he won first prize in the Sunday Express short story competition in 1996. He currently combines writing with a parallel career as a semi-professional drummer. He lives in Berkshire with his wife and two youngest children.

WHEN STARS GROW DARK

Scott Hunter

A Myrtle Villa Book

Originally published in Great Britain by Myrtle Villa Publishing

All rights reserved
Copyright © Scott Hunter, Anno Domini 2021

This book is sold subject to the condition that it shall not, by way of trade or otherwise, be lent, resold, hired out, or otherwise circulated without the publisher's prior consent in any form of binding or cover other than that in which it is published and without a similar condition including this condition being imposed on the subsequent publisher

The moral right of Scott Hunter to be identified as author of this work has been asserted in accordance with Section 77 of the Copyright, Designs and Patents Act 1988

In this work of fiction, the characters, places and events are either the product of the author's imagination or they are used entirely fictitiously

Acknowledgements

Thanks to Stuart Bache (Books Covered) for the cover design, and to my insightful and excellent editor, Louise Maskill

For those who suffer

*Remember your Creator
in the days of your youth,
before the days of trouble come
and the years approach when you will say,
"I find no pleasure in them"—
before the sun and the light
and the moon and the stars grow dark...
--Ecclesiastes 12*

Author's Note

This is the seventh book in the DCI Brendan Moran series. I try to write each one so that it can be read in isolation from the other books in the series without troubling the reader too much about past events. In the case of *When Stars Grow Dark*, however, I do think that it would be beneficial for the reader to have read the previous book, *The Enemy Inside*. SH, December 2020

CHAPTER ONE

Fabrice Cleiren was tired. Not the sort of normal tired-after-a-hard-day-in-the-office tired, but tired to the core of his being. He'd made himself stop just once *en route* from Fishguard, wearily guiding the 13.5-metre Scania into the truck park at the services and allowing himself – reluctantly – a ten-minute comfort break with coffee to go. Reluctant because time was money, and money was a dwindling commodity in his life right now. Was he nervous too? Yes, maybe a little. All had gone smoothly so far. And that was the issue – too smooth was worrying.

He felt under his seat, found what he was looking for, felt reassured. He had to make Dover by ten, at which point he could rest for the duration of the crossing. He rubbed his eyes, squinted at the console satnav. It told him he had around three and a half hours to go. It was rush hour on the M4, and the clouds were beginning to deliver on their earlier promise of torrential rain.

Cleiren flicked on the wipers, grunting with irritation as the giant arms arced across the expanse of glass. Rain meant delay. Delay meant an angry boss – van Leer, the officious transport manager. He could picture him pacing up and down the lorry park with his clipboard, bending to inspect tyres, obsessively checking for faults – faults he inevitably attributed to the driver. Cleiren maintained a steady sixty-five, chugging along behind an *Eddie Stobart* transporter which was doubtless heading for the same destination. If he ever achieved financial Nirvana, like winning the lottery or inheriting a fortune from some long-lost uncle, he'd take great pleasure in telling van Leer what he could do with his clipboard – that would be deeply satisfying. But even though these special trips weren't doing his finances any harm, it was still early days. And there was always the element of risk playing on his mind, a constant drumming in his subconscious, like the bloody British rain.

He sighed. Whatever lay ahead, it wasn't going to happen fast. For now, and the immediate future, it was business as usual: eyes front, concentrate on those three lanes stretching ahead like a life sentence.

He felt the beat of the huge diesel engine begin to labour as the truck reached a slight incline. He changed gears, settled back in his seat. The cabin was comfortable, a home from home. Too comfortable, maybe. It was easy to drift. First your thoughts, and then, if you weren't careful, your eyes would start to close. It had happened more than once. The most recent time he'd snapped awake as the truck drifted across the carriageway, way too far into the middle lane. He'd yelled aloud, hauled the rig back on course. It had been three in the morning, no one else on that stretch that particular night. *Lucky, Fabrice...*

He clicked a button on the screen. Audio. *Pearl Jam*. And make it loud. Cleiren tapped the steering wheel as

Matt Cameron's drumming did its damnedest to drown out the battering downpour. Fifty-mile- an-hour speed limit coming up. Now what? Ah, of course – how the British love their road works. More delay. Cleiren clucked his tongue – the limit was imposed all the way to the M25.

He touched a pedal and felt rather than heard the hiss of the air brakes as they slowed the truck down from seventy-and-a-bit to the required fifty. No hard shoulder. *Great. Let's hope we don't get a puncture like last month.* The *Stobart* in front was obscuring his view. No chance to overtake at this speed.

Cleiren drummed his fingers on the wheel, squinted through the wet glass. The concentration required to deal with the combination of poor light and heavy rain was beginning to give him a headache. His eyes flicked to the recess beside him where he kept his cigarettes, chewing gum, assorted loose change. He had some paracetamol somewhere. His fingers fumbled in the plastic hole, drew a blank. He switched hands, tried the door's side pocket...

Without warning the truck ahead slewed snake-like into the centre lane, dragging its rear end in a lazy swing behind it. Cleiren blinked. During the three seconds that followed, his first instinctive question – *why?* – was swiftly answered by the frozen-framed image of a stationary vehicle just a few metres ahead, red hazards blinking impotently like the trembling eyelids of a condemned man.

The impact shunted the Vauxhall Astra a hundred and fifty metres along the carriageway until its carcass came to a spinning standstill facing the way it had come. By then, Cleiren's amputated cab had also come to rest – upside down, twisted, but more or less intact. The Scania's detached trailer and container, however, were still in motion, following the same trajectory as their displaced parent. In excess of six tons of hurtling metal slammed into the cab's rack-mounted fuel tanks with a sound like a muffled thunderclap.

The explosion was heard on the other side of town. Remarkably, just the two vehicles were involved, the accident having been, by some miracle of physics, confined to the slow lane. By the time emergency vehicles arrived, traffic was backed up all the way to Junction 13 as motorists slowed ghoulishly to survey the damage before moving on with a muttered prayer to whichever god seemed best placed to see them safely home.

'It's an RTC,' DCI Brendan Moran protested. 'Can't Traffic deal with it?'

He'd literally just walked in the door, hung his coat on the hook and bent to ruffle his Cocker Spaniel's furry head when the phone had begun its urgent jangle.

'They are, guv, but there's something … odd about one of the casualties.' DC Bola Odunsi's sonorous tones were full of urgency, and something else; curiosity. Something had piqued the big detective's interest.

'Odd? Like how? Has he two heads, or what?'

'No, no. Nothing like that, guv. Doc on the scene seems convinced, though.'

'About?'

Bola took a breath. 'So, this is what we have. Three fatalities – truck driver wasn't paying attention. You know the roadworks at Junction 12?'

'Yep, the smart motorway improvements.'

Moran's emphasis of *improvements* left Bola Odunsi in no

doubt concerning Moran's view of the whole smart concept. Smart? What, in the name of all creation, were the government thinking? No hard shoulder, automated signs – swift response to breakdowns? You must be joking. In an ideal world maybe it would have worked, but so far the stats just showed an increasing number of fatalities. Added to which, the regular lay-bys that had been part of the original plans hadn't been implemented correctly. There was supposed to be a 'refuge area' every eight hundred metres, as recommended by the Transport Select Committee, but the brief hadn't been followed; there were long stretches of so-called 'smart' motorway where no such refuge had been constructed, which meant that accidents such as this were becoming more and more commonplace. Having had personal experience of a serious RTC, this was a subject close to Moran's heart.

'That's it,' Bola confirmed. 'An Astra broke down. No hard shoulder. Bad weather. Poor guy in the truck didn't see it until it was way too late.'

'So what's the doc convinced about?' Get to the point, Bola.

'Ah, this is the interesting bit. Driver and one passenger in the Astra, both deceased.'

'Go on.'

'The passenger was a male Caucasian, late seventies. After the doc had examined his remains, he called us pronto.'

'Because?'

'That's the thing, guv. The doc reckons the guy was already dead – before the crash.'

'The driver had a dead body in the passenger seat?'

'Yep, that's about it. Seatbelt fastened and everything.'

Moran felt the old familiar tingle in his stomach. *Here we go again, Brendan…*

'Sit tight,' he said curtly. 'I'm on my way.'

CHAPTER TWO

By the time Moran reached the scene, traffic had thinned to a steady trickle; rush hour was over, but not for the emergency services. He was guided into the area by a stressed traffic policeman in a chequered hi-vis waistcoat. The powerful lighting blinded him momentarily as he killed his car engine and stepped out. DI Charlie Pepper had already clocked his arrival and was on her way to meet him.

Moran shielded his eyes. 'What a mess.'

'It sure is. Smart motorways, eh?' Charlie grimaced.

'Don't get me started,' Moran growled. 'Just lead me to the bodies.'

Charlie guided him to the remains of the Astra. The corpses had been extricated – with some difficulty – by a cooperative of fire and police personnel. From the start it had been clear that medical attention was not required. The corpses lay together on the tarmac, side-by-side, zipped into body bags.

'Doc still here?' Moran craned his neck for Sandy Taylor's familiar profile.

'Dr Taylor's with the ambulance crew, guv. They offered him a hot drink.'

'Good. I want to quiz him while it's still fresh in his mind.' Moran approached the first bag. 'Which is which?'

'Passenger on the left, driver on the right.' Charlie stood back.

'Bad, is it?' Moran bent to unzip the first.

'Pretty bad, guv.' Charlie's hand was over her mouth. 'Put it this way, the doc could have done with something stronger than tea.'

Moran hesitated. 'Right. Thanks for the warning. Do we have names?'

'We have an *address*. Label on his keyring. Lorne Street, Reading. Lantern showed negative on the prints, but–' Charlie held up a clear plastic bag.

'Smartphone?'

'iPhone 6, so we're in with a chance. Might as well do it now.' She bent, started to unzip the body bag, exposed the driver's head. The zip stuck.

'Let me help.' Moran straightened the offending area, jerked the zipper down smartly.

'Thanks.' Charlie gingerly withdrew an arm, splayed the fingers on the right hand.

'Might be a leftie.' Moran made a face.

'We'll soon know. Hang on a mo' – God, he's stone cold already. I'll need to warm him up a bit first.'

Charlie took the corpse's index finger, rubbed it between her own hands. 'My hands are almost as cold.' She continued to massage the finger.

'You know what they say,' Moran smiled. 'Cold hands–'

'Yeah, yeah. Not sure where my heart is these days. Let's not go there, eh?' She continued with the massage.

'OK, that'll do. Here's hoping.'

Charlie took the smartphone out of the bag, pressed the driver's finger to the touch button. For a moment nothing, but then the screen lit up. 'Bingo.' She let the corpse's arm drop, and her own fingers moved nimbly over the iPhone's screen.

'Here we go. Mr Isaiah Marley.' She stabbed the screen again. 'Aged thirty-eight. Single.'

'Facebook info?'

'Yep.'

Moran bent and quickly unzipped the passenger. Multiple lacerations, deep wound to the neck. Dislocated shoulder by the look of it, not that that was bothering him now.

'Ah, Brendan.'

Sandy Taylor's cultured tones interrupted Moran's train of thought. He straightened up. 'So, what's the issue, Sandy? Looks straightforward enough to me.'

'Indeed,' Taylor agreed. 'Until we examine the mirrors of the soul.'

'Bloodshot?'

'Take a look for yourself,' Taylor invited.

Moran bent again, lifted the eyelids. Sure enough, both suffused with blood.

'See the bruising around the nose and mouth?' Taylor went on. 'Also classic signs. I expect to find hypercapnia – high levels of carbon dioxide in the blood. I'll let you know as soon as.'

'And the driver?'

'Traumatic injuries to chest and skull. Killed in the accident, no doubt at all.'

Moran stood up, stuffed his hands in his pockets. It was

late March, but a winter chill still hung in the air. 'Satnav, Charlie?'

'Yep. Bagged up along with a few other bit and pieces from the Astra.'

Moran nodded. 'Good. I want to know where Marley was going – *and* where he was coming from. Get George and Bola onto it first thing. Let's find out all we can about Mr Marley. I want his life examined under the proverbial microscope.'

'Think *he* killed the old chap?' Charlie moved out of the way of a recovery vehicle, nosing its way towards the Astra's twisted carcass.

'Gut feeling?' Moran shot his DI a wry smile. 'Maybe. Or he may have been on a body disposal errand. We'll see.'

Charlie chewed her lip. 'Thing is, the old chap has to be, what, in his seventies? What kind of threat could he have been to anyone?'

Moran fished for his car keys. 'Old guys were young once, you know, DI Pepper.' He tucked his tongue firmly in his cheek.

'Sure, I mean – I didn't mean that–'

Moran let Charlie squirm for a second before allowing the corners of his mouth to rise. 'I know what you meant. I'll see you back at the ranch in the morning. Hopefully we'll have chapter and verse from Sandy and co by then.'

He was heading for his car when a thought occurred to him. 'Charlie?'

She turned, tilted her chin.

'The guy who hit the Astra. What do we have on him?'

'Dutch. Fabrice Cleiren. Twenty-five. Worked for some haulage company in Rotterdam.'

'Better not leave him out, eh? Tachograph readings?'
'Sure. I'll get on it.'

Moran drove home automatically, scarcely aware of the route he was taking. An old man, suffocated. A Dutch lorry driver. A fatal RTC. Connections? None apparent. But there always were, if you looked hard enough.

The canteen was rammed, the queue for decent coffee well into double figures. DC George McConnell cursed under his breath. The machine was broken – as usual. No choice, then. He couldn't contemplate starting the day without a serious boost of caffeine. His eyes stung from lack of sleep. Every night was the same – getting to sleep, no problem, but then in the wee small hours his eyes would open and his mind would replay a dream's subconscious images. He'd lie still, breathing hard, finding little comfort in the familiar contours of his bedroom, his mind insisting that he was standing in the entrance hallway of the High Nelmes Residential Home, a home for retired and injured police officers, at the foot of the wide staircase that led to the first floor, and to DC Tess Martin's bedroom.

He wanted to go up, but his feet refused to move. He heard footsteps, and there she was, looking down at him. Tess smiled, took two steps down. There was something wrong. She stopped, her hand went to the banister to steady herself. He wanted to help her, but he was frozen to the spot. He watched helplessly as Tess' head bowed and her body shimmered, became insubstantial. He reached out, tried to make his rebellious limbs move. He had to help her. She would be fine, if only he could just–

'Are you in the queue, or what?'

The voice dragged him back, made him jump as though stung.

DC Chris Collingworth raised a hand in mock defence. '*Woah*, steady, now.'

George glowered, moved forward in the queue.

'Nerves bad?' Collingworth enquired. 'Take a break, George. You're due a bit of leave, aren't you?'

George ignored the question. The last thing he needed right now was Collingworth. He shuffled forward.

'What can I get you, George?' The caterer grinned. 'Large one, as per usual?'

'He's always up for a large one,' Collingworth said. 'Several, if my sources are to be trusted.'

George felt his face reddening. It wouldn't take much, not the way he felt this morning. He nodded, scanned his card.

'Sleepless night, eh? Collingworth probed. 'Pining over a lost love? Now then.' He tapped his chin with his forefinger. 'Who might the lucky lady be?'

George felt his fists bunch. With an effort, he calmed himself.

'Here you go, George. Chocolate on top.'

'Thanks.' He accepted the coffee, walked away.

'Rude, I call it.' Collingworth's mocking voice followed him, but George kept going until his colleague's voice was lost in the canteen's hubbub.

'Over to you, DI Pepper.' Moran ceded the floor to his reporting officer.

'Morning, all.' Charlie's eyes swept the room. 'This is what we have so far – I know there's not much to go on, but you're going to change that.' She turned to the pinboard and tapped the first photograph. The passenger. Dead at the scene, but not killed *at* the scene. Unlike this guy, the driver.' Charlie tapped the second photograph, 'Isaiah Marley. Killed, we believe, on impact. Driving a stolen car, incidentally. Owner reported it missing yesterday afternoon.'

She faced the assembled officers. DCs Bola Odunsi, relaxed and amiable as ever, George McConnell looking like death warmed up, Chris Collingworth and, at the back, DC Swinhoe – Bernice – leaning forward with her usual attentive expression. A good detective, that one, reliable, got on with the job – just don't call her Bernice. Charlie cleared her throat. 'So, our medical report states that the passenger was, in fact, dead before the accident. Suffocated by persons unknown, at a location also unknown. We don't have a definite ID yet, but we do have an address for Marley. Bola, George, you're off to the salubrious Oxford road, to number eleven Lorne Street. Does Marley have a partner? Did he live alone? Whoever you find, they won't be aware that he's no longer with us, so if you'd like to break the news when appropriate?'

Nods.

'DC Collingworth, see what you can do with this photograph. Someone must know him. I want a name and address by lunchtime. Think you'll be able to oblige?'

'You'll have it by morning coffee break, boss.' Collingworth's reply slid easily from his mouth. 'Mind if I start now?'

'Yes, I do mind. You'll wait till Briefing's over like everybody else.'

From the corner of her eye she caught Moran's imperceptible nod of approval. Collingworth was good –

very good – at what he did, and had recently impressed a tough promotion board to gain his Sergeant's rank, much to the rest of his team's consternation. But he still needed to apply for the post, and that hadn't happened yet. If Charlie had her way, she'd get him to apply to a different constabulary altogether. She'd lose a good detective, but she'd have a much happier team.

'You're the boss.' Collingworth almost winked, but under the withering laser of Charlie's glare, he settled for a cocky smile of compliance.

'I am indeed. I note that your power of recall is, happily, fully intact, DC Collingworth.' Charlie placed a subtle emphasis on 'DC'.

In the corner of the room, to the right of the pinboard's easel, Moran coughed into his hand.

George McConnell had his hand up.

'Yes, George?' Charlie tilted her chin.

'Want me to check the mispers list while DC Collingworth is playing with his wee pictures?'

This drew a shake of the head from Collingworth, who opened his mouth to reply but Charlie cut him off. 'No, George. You concentrate on Marley for the time being.' George was good at stats and lists, but she wanted Collingworth on the tracing.

'CCTV?' Collingworth suggested. 'Find out where the car was coming from, find the old boy's roost.'

'Yep, go ahead and cover that.' Charlie paused. 'This looks to be a one-off situation, but you never know. I want a thorough job done, OK? Someone's taken a life. It's not just an RTC. Any questions?' She scanned the room. Bernice Swinhoe's arm went up. 'DC Swinhoe?'

'How about a DNA test, boss?'

'Yep, already arranged, DC Swinhoe. Be a couple of days, though. The PM might turn something up in the meantime. And in that regard, I expect DCI Moran will be taking an interest?' She looked pointedly at Moran.

'I will, indeed, DI Pepper. How well you know me.'

A ripple of laughter rose and fell. They all knew that Moran couldn't resist *some* investigative work, especially post mortems.

Bola Odunsi's hand went up. 'How about the iPhone, boss? Might be some data on there to link Marley to the passenger?'

'Be my guest, DC Odunsi. You can collect it from my office.'

Bola nodded.

'Good.' Charlie clapped her hands. 'That's all for now. Let's get to it.'

The team dispersed to their appointed tasks. The guv looked as though he might want a word, the way he was sidling over.

'Nicely handled,' Moran said, *sotto voce*. They weaved their way between the banks of desks towards their respective offices.

'Collingworth?' Charlie arched her eyebrows.

Moran nodded, smiled.

'An explosion waiting to happen, those two,' Charlie sighed. 'Did you see the look George gave him?'

'I did. It's Tess, isn't it?'

'Yes.' Charlie was silent for a second. 'George blames himself – and Collingworth, mainly.'

'I'm the one to blame,' Moran countered, 'if anyone is.'

'That's just not true, guv. You know it's not.' Charlie chewed her bottom lip. 'How is she?'

Moran shrugged. 'Pretty much the same. I've been meaning to pop in, but…'

Charlie frowned. 'You've been flat out, guv. And that business at your house last month, I can't imagine how—'

Moran's hand signalled caution. 'Ah. Less said about that, the better.'

Charlie fell silent. 'Sure. Sorry.'

Moran waved Charlie's discomfort aside. 'Come in for a sec.' He held his door open. 'Give it a shove,' he advised. 'It's still not right.'

The door opened reluctantly on misaligned hinges. They exchanged knowing looks. Moran had been offered an alternative room following the recent attempt on his life by a man posing as a maintenance worker, but he'd declined. He liked to be where he could keep an eye on things. And, to be fair, that's where Charlie liked him, too. She had confidence in herself, but all the same, it was good to know the guv was around.

'Have a seat,' Moran offered.

He looked at her thoughtfully over his desk, toying with a set of keys. He seemed distracted, as if he didn't know where to start. 'It's only fair I should tell you what's going on in my mind, just now, Charlie.'

That didn't sound good.

'You mentioned the problem I had at home. Well now, the thing is, regarding that, I've a mind to sort a few things out. I'd hate to think I'd lived out my life with…well, with any loose ends trailing, if you get my meaning.'

'Not entirely, guv.' Honesty was always the best policy with the guv'nor.

'No. Of course. I don't mean to be deliberately obscure.' He paused, rattled the keyring again. 'I've been thinking – for a while now – that maybe it's time to bring this to an end.' He waved his arm to encompass his office, the open-plan beyond. The whole building.

'But–'

'Wait.' Moran held up his hand. 'Hear me out.'

Charlie felt her mouth soundlessly open and close.

'It has to happen sometime, Charlie. I'm not getting any younger. And the problems I need to address – well, let's just say that it wouldn't be entirely appropriate to address them as a serving police officer.'

Charlie felt a lead weight in her stomach. She had an inkling what this might be about. The incident at Moran's home had involved an old friend, who'd turned out to be some kind of terrorist sympathiser or facilitator, and there'd been some kind of spook involvement too. His friend, or a neighbour? It all sounded well dodgy.

'Why not take a sabbatical, guv?'

'Not burn my boats, you mean?' Moran smiled sadly. 'I suspect my sailing days will be over if things turn out the way I think they might.'

'Guv, you're worrying me.'

Moran stood up. 'Nothing's going to happen for a while, Charlie. I'll keep you posted. And don't look so stricken. Things will work out…well, the way they'll work out.'

He held the door open for her. 'Best not mention any of this to the troops, eh?'

'Sure. Of course.'

Full of foreboding, Charlie went to catch George before he left the office. He'd spoken to the guv that particular weekend, the weekend of Moran's 'problem'. The guv had asked about some car registration, but it couldn't be traced to a specific owner. Just an organisation – if that was the right word for an Embassy.

The Russian Embassy.

CHAPTER THREE

George McConnell eased the car into Lorne Street, a minor side road off the Oxford Road, found a space, parked, turned to his colleague. 'Ready?'

'Are *you*, George? That's what I want to know.' DC Bola Odunsi didn't look like he was going anywhere until he had a satisfactory answer.

'Meaning?' George snapped.

Bola sighed. 'Come on, George, you're wound up like a spring.'

'I'm fine.'

'Don't let him get to you.' Bola shook his head. 'He ain't worth it.'

George leaned back in his seat, rested his head. Bola meant well, he knew that.

'Besides, he's got his promotion. He could be gone soon.'

'You think?'

'Sure.' Bola nodded. 'Collingworth's got no sense of loyalty. Except to himself. He'll apply for the first post that comes up, you watch.'

'I can handle him,' George said.

'You just got to let it wash over you, that's all.'

'Easier said.'

'I know, man. I know. Listen,' Bola's face radiated concern. 'How is she? Any change?'

Change. George had been waiting for the smallest sign. But, as yet, Tess Martin hadn't given the slightest inkling that she even knew who he was. He shook his head. 'Not yet.'

'There will be, man. She'll come out of it, you'll see.'

'Sure. Thanks.'

'You want to talk about it, anytime, OK?'

'Yeah. Thanks. Anyway,' George masked his discomfort in bluster, 'shall we?'

'Lead on, Macduff.'

'That's a rival clan. Careful, now.' George allowed himself the briefest flicker of a smile.

'*Woah.*' Bola's hands went up. '*McConnell.* Sorry, no offence.'

'None taken.' The smile was still playing around George's mouth as he double-checked the house number. 'Numero eleven. Here we go.'

The house was one of twenty or so conjoined terraces. There was no front garden. A set of mossy stone steps led down to what appeared to be a basement flat, while three rather more worn steps led up to the front door. A series of buzzers confirmed what George had already anticipated. He gave Bola a look. 'Bedsits.'

Bola nodded. He knew what George meant, especially in this area. Bedsit land. Itinerant residents. Drugs, probably. He ran his finger down the labels. 'Here you go. *Marley.*' He pressed the buzzer.

'Nothing,' Bola said after thirty seconds.

'Lived on his own.' George was scanning the other names. 'First on the list, let's give it a whirl.' He pressed the button next to the label which read *Turner*.

Twenty seconds passed before the sound of footsteps on bare boards caused the policemen to exchange glances. The door opened to reveal a young guy in blue overalls, his hair flecked with white paint, roller in one hand and cigarette in the other. 'Yes?'

George showed his warrant card. 'DC McConnell, and this is my colleague, DC Odunsi. Thames Valley Police. This your place?'

'I'm the owner – landlord, yes. What's up?'

'Bedsits are they?' Bola cast his eyes to the upper storeys.

'Yeah.'

'Could I have your name, please, sir?' George asked politely.

'Turner. Nick Turner. What's up? I've done nothing wrong.' He inhaled smoke and let it out in a thin stream.

Bola coughed. 'We'd like some information regarding one of your tenants, a Mr Isaiah Marley.'

'Oh yeah? What's he done?'

'Mind if we take a look around his flat?'

'Sure.' Turner sniffed, stepped aside to let them into the narrow hallway. 'First on the right. Dunno if he's in or not.'

'He's out.' George said. 'But you'll have a key.'

'Sure. Hang on.'

He went to the stairwell, called down. 'Win? Bring up the keys, love, would you?'

A petite blonde woman put her head around the

stairwell, ducked back, and then a bunch of keys came flying up towards them. Turner snagged them from the air.

'My missus.' Turner told them, as he led them into the building and worked his way through the jangling bunch of keys. 'Doesn't like the police much.'

'We're used to it,' George said.

'I bet. Here you go.' Turner selected a key and opened the door to their right. 'All yours.'

'How long has Mr Marley lived here?' Bola asked.

Turner tapped ash onto the bare boards. 'Couple of months.'

'And did he seem … all right to you?'

'Meaning?'

'Was he agitated, nervous, would you say?'

'Didn't see a lot of him, to be honest. We're busy doing the rest of the place up. Not much time for chit-chat.'

'As long as the rent gets paid, right?'

'Yeah. Exactly. What the tenants get up to is their business. And he's a good payer, anyway.'

'Oh yes?' George pricked up his ears.

'Six months up front. I'm not complaining.'

Bola and George exchanged looks. 'OK, thanks, Mr Turner,' George said. 'We'll give you a shout when we're finished.'

Turner shrugged. 'Sure.'

The room was tiny. A sofa bed, a small table, a Belling two-ring grill, bare walls. The sash window looked out on an unkempt garden. Bola rubbed grime from the glass. 'Nice.'

'Bloody depressing.' George poked around in the only cupboard, a second-hand cabinet that had seen better days. 'Leastways, he doesn't have to come back to this.'

'So better off dead, is what you're saying?' Bola pulled up a chair cushion, looked underneath. Nothing but dust.

'Well, maybe. I mean, just *look* at this room,' George waved his hand in the air. 'I mean, you'd top yourself after a couple of weeks, let alone months.'

'Maybe he didn't spend much time here.'

'Maybe not.' George was down on his hands and knees, checking under the sofa-bed. 'Hello. What's this?' He fished around in the dust, withdrew a slip of card. 'Train ticket. Edinburgh to Reading. January.'

'Couple of months old.'

'Right. So, our friend has recently moved south.'

'Could've been visiting friends?' Bola said.

'Naw. If you were visiting, you'd have a Return, wouldn't you? Not a Single.'

'The man has a point.'

George bagged the ticket. 'Anything else?'

'Guy travelled light,' Bola said. '*Lived* light.'

George nodded. Couldn't deny that; there was next to nothing in the room. No spare clothing, not even underwear. Nothing of a personal nature at all.

'Worth getting forensics over?'

'I suppose,' George replied. 'Not much to check over, though, is there?'

'Mr Anonymous.'

'Isn't he just? What about his iPhone?'

'I had a quick flick. His FB friends list falls well into the 'sad' category.'

'Like, under ten?'

'Yep – even less than you.'

'Ha ha.'

Bola grinned, ran his finger along the mantelpiece, inspected the resulting grime and made a face. 'So, I don't think that level of social media engagement will tell us much, but that won't stop me pulling it apart anyway. One thing I did notice, though.'

They went into the hall, George closing the door behind them. 'Oh yes?'

'He's got a VPN app set up on the iPhone.'

'So?'

'His IP address'll be masked. Which means he doesn't want his online activity tracked.'

'So, he's just paranoid, or–'

'He's scared someone might trace him.'

George worried at a hangnail. 'Uh huh. So ... he's scared. Very little in the way of personal effects. Zero social media activity – bare minimum. Anonymous bedsit. VPN. What's that sound like to you?' He went to the stairwell. 'We're going, Mr Turner,' he called into the void, but the only response was the blaring of a radio, the sound waves wafting on a heady aroma of paint and turpentine. George shrugged, called over his shoulder, 'We'll let ourselves out.'

A group of teenagers watched them suspiciously from further up the street. One made an inaudible comment and pointed. The two detectives heard their laughter rise and fall until it was drowned out by a passing motorbike.

'It sounds,' Bola said, as George pulled out onto the Oxford Road, 'like Mr Marley was someone who didn't want to be found.'

A sabbatical. Well now, Moran admitted to himself, there was an idea he hadn't fully considered. He'd surprised himself, the way he'd confided in Charlie, the way his thoughts had shaped themselves, unbidden, into words. Truth was, his mind, overactive at the best of times, had been working overtime on his ... *problem* since the strange night of Liam Doherty's arrival – and unpredictable departure.

A sabbatical. He turned the word over, playing with its syllables. Trendy, these days, to take time out. Often to travel, or work with – or for – some charitable cause. But was he not a little long in the tooth to be taking time out? Higginson would find it odd – and he didn't intend to appraise his boss of the details. Trouble was, he'd still be formally attached to the Thames Valley Constabulary. Anything that happened during a period of time out would automatically affect his job, career, life, whichever way he looked at it. But if he made a clean break – well then, whatever happened would fall firmly into the 'post-career' silo, and therefore wouldn't reflect badly on what had gone before – for his team, or for himself.

But where to start? Moran went to his internal window, lifted the corner of the blind. A hive of activity, earnest conversations, eyes glued to screens. All searching for the keys to unlock the secrets of a dead man's killer. They'd succeed, Moran had no doubt; Charlie was back on top form, her recent illness behind her. She was sharp, respected by the team, keen to get the job done. A possible successor. There was a thought: to be succeeded. Replaced.

He watched the team at work, and an unexpected stirring of emotion washed through him.

Pride.

Yes, he was *proud* of them. And why shouldn't he be?

The team's results spoke for themselves. So many complementary skills under one roof, a strong sense of camaraderie, a cohesion of like-minded detectives, all focused on one goal: to get the job done. They'd manage without him, no problem.

No one is indispensable, Brendan...

But could he *really* imagine life outside the Force? He'd faced this beast before, had always been the first to blink. But that was understandably, surely, with such unfocussed prospects? A lonely retirement, another house move, perhaps. But where? Why? Life would still be repetitive, meaningless, wherever he lived. A pint down the local of an evening. A walk along the river. Everything behind him, very little ahead, except illness, decline. Death.

Furthermore – increasingly so, these days – Moran felt as though his role had settled into a predictable routine, that he was merely biding his time. He'd reached that part of a song where the chorus simply repeats till fade, until eventually the needle skates off the last groove into an eternal loop of crackling silence.

His case involvement these days was mostly consultative, the paperwork endless. Reports, statistics. Meetings. Sure, he still allowed himself a little involvement when an opportunity presented, but only when and where he felt he wouldn't be cramping Charlie's style. Infrequent chances to get out and about, get his hands dirty; the occasionally autopsy – but, these days the opportunities were fewer and farther between. Or so it seemed.

He let the blind down with a snap. Retirement. No. Not for him. Not yet. There must always be something ahead. As, in fact, there was now. He had a 'situation' on his hands. A mystery – an adversary too, in all but name. An old friend who had forfeited the right to that title.

Joe Gallagher. Politician, terrorist sympathiser and facilitator. Was it Moran's job to stop him? *Must* it fall to him to embark upon what amounted to a personal crusade?

Moran returned to his desk, sat down and rested his head on his swanky new chair's comfortable headrest – one tangible benefit of his recent (and still much talked-about) brush with an onsite assassin. The office had been refitted and refurbished – after a fashion – but, from this angle, he could see that the light shade was nevertheless well past its sell-by, and the cobweb he'd noticed a few weeks ago was still casting delicate tendrils as far as the top of the bookcase, a precarious bridge for any spiders with ambitions above their station.

Moran sat quietly, gave his thoughts some space.

No, it wasn't inappropriate ambition that was driving him, but rather a sense of fair play. What had happened was wrong, and he wanted to…what?

Fix it.

Which was, he knew, quite impossible. What was done, was done, but then…but then…

…but then, he had the recording.

And he didn't know what to do with it.

He'd considered taking it to MI5, but to whom? Could they be trusted? What would they do with it? He couldn't be sure. Maybe his hesitation, procrastination, whatever, was merely the product of loyalty to an old friend, whatever that friend had now become. In his mind's eye he could still see Joe Gallagher's irate expression, the fanaticism in his eyes as the politician held court in

Moran's own lounge and nailed his Republican colours to the mast. Moran knew every word. Could repeat it back *verbatim*, he'd played it so many times. What had prompted him to retrieve his voice recorder from his coat pocket as it hung in the hallway? He only used the machine from time to time, to record his thoughts, case notes, trivia, anything that came to mind.

Something had prompted him to turn it on, though.

Now, he almost wished he hadn't.

And then there was Samantha Grant's abrupt disappearance to consider. Last seen in a riverside car park, being bundled into a car. A vigilant neighbour had taken photos and Moran had studied the prints, so he had the registration, clear shots of the two guys. ANPR had found a match which had led to the Russian Embassy, but from that point onwards he had met with a wall of impenetrable silence.

So there it was: four parts of a problematic puzzle. Joe Gallagher, recently elevated to the post of Ireland's Minister for Foreign Affairs and Trade; a missing MI5 operative; the Russian Embassy; and a voice recording of Gallagher's own admission of support for Republican terrorism.

And the fifth part? A senior detective on the cusp of retirement, who didn't take kindly to being threatened in his own home, who wanted to help someone he'd considered – and still did consider – a friend. But how could he help Samantha Grant? She could be anywhere.

You have no idea, Brendan. None.

Moran tapped his fingers on the desk in a repetitive pattern that swiftly escalated in volume until his left hand brought the ostinato to a crescendo with a thump that

toppled the teetering top layer of his in- tray.
   But you have to try…

CHAPTER FOUR

Chris Collingworth was in an upbeat mood. The year had started well. He'd passed his promotion board, which meant, as he'd always known, that he was a cut above his colleagues. Nice to have it officially confirmed. Now it was just a case of securing a role. Here, or elsewhere – he didn't care too much. Although... yes, there was DC Stiles to consider, to be factored in to his calculations. She'd been gradually warming to his subtle advances for several weeks now; the moment was almost upon him. She'd say *yes*, he was confident of that. He just had to choose his moment, simples. After a couple of drinks down the local – the tried and tested method.

Julie Stiles shared a house in Calcot with two housemates, both female. Perfect. It wouldn't be hard to persuade her to invite him back for a coffee, and then...

'Any progress?'

Collingworth started, but quickly collected himself. Charlie Pepper had his number, was always on his case, but that didn't faze him. He liked a challenge. He swivelled in his chair to face her.

'Sure. Got a trace on the Inner Distribution Road, our own roundabout, thirty-five minutes before the accident. Turned onto the Tilehurst Road at Castle Hill. Twenty minutes later, camera at the petrol station near IKEA picked him up, heading for the M4. Driving was a bit erratic.'

Charlie nodded. 'Good work. But what he was doing before he hit the M4? What goes on in the Tilehurst Road area?'

Collingworth shrugged. 'Not a lot. Few pubs. There's a park, a church.'

'OK, keep on it. I want that name.'

'You got it, boss.'

'But I *don't* have it. Not yet.' Charlie kept eye contact briefly, before turning and walking away.

Collingworth gripped the mouse tightly, glared at the screen. *Snotty cow. You wait. I'm catching you up. Just wait till I'm the DCI and you're still where you are. That's all. Just wait.*

He clicked onto Google Maps. Tilehurst Road. The road to nowhere.

Wait. The stiff was an old boy, right? And there was an old peoples' home around there, somewhere. Collingworth racked his brains. Maybe...

His fingers danced on the keyboard.

Got it.

Chapelfields Home for the Elderly. Matlin Road.

He tapped the screen with his biro. Not a definite, but worth a shot.

He sat back in his chair, phone tucked under his chin. Julie Stiles was chatting to a colleague by the water cooler.

Come on, babe. Just a little look ... come on, feel the force...

She glanced in his direction, the smallest of glances, but

it was long enough for him to turn on his well-rehearsed, five-star smile.

She coloured, turned back to her colleague.

'Hello. Chapelfields. Can I help?'

Collingworth dragged his attention away from Stiles' shapely legs. 'Yep. This is DC Chris Collingworth, Thames Valley. I was wondering – are you missing any residents?'

Bola's face was a picture of concentration. George, at the adjacent workstation, watched the big man flicking through the iPhone's apps, searching for something, anything, to give them something to go on. Collingworth had just left in a hurry. As he'd shrugged his jacket on he'd given George a look. A look that said: *What you got, George? Nothing, I'm betting...* And with a smirk, he was gone.

That wouldn't do. He'd wipe that smug smile off Collingworth's face. He swivelled his chair to face Bola's workstation.

'Well?'

Bola looked up from his search. 'Nothing yet. Nada.'

'No phone numbers? Recent calls?'

'Come on, man. Give me some credit.' Bola shot him a hurt look.

'How about we give it to our boffin buddies? If there's anything on there, they'll find it.'

'I'm *on* it, OK?'

Bola was a calm guy, but even he had his limits. George knew when to stop. He turned back to his own PC. But a moment later, a sudden thought struck him. He swivelled again. 'Where would you keep phone numbers, if not in Contacts?'

'Notes. Reminders. Tried them. All blank.'

'I mean, if you needed to remember them, but didn't want to write them down.'

'George, man, what are you on about?'

'Voice memos. In the Utilities folder.'

Bola sighed. 'OK, just for you.'

George waited as Bola tapped the screen. His expression said it all. George sprang to his feet. 'What? What's it say?'

'Hold on, hold on.' Another tap. Then, from the iPhone speaker:

Oh perfect number twice lawn – eight zero plus mid-nineties dob

'What? Play it again.'

Bola obliged.

'Great. He's not stupid. It's a code of some sort.'

Bola shrugged his large shoulders. 'Phone number? Could be anything. Bank account number, maybe?'

'I'm betting phone. Why take the trouble to code a bank account number? You still need PINS and passwords to get into an account. No, this is a phone number.'

'Want to hear it again?'

'Write it down this time.'

Bola scribbled on a Post-it note. Both men looked at the result.

'What the hell?' Bola sighed. 'How we going to figure this one?'

'We're detectives,' George said. 'It's what we do, right?'

'Right.'

George wheeled his chair over. 'OK, so let's start at the beginning. *Oh perfect number*.'

Bola frowned. 'Numerology ain't one of my strong points, but–'

George gnawed the soft part of his hand, at the base of his thumb. 'What?'

Bola sat back, folded his arms. 'In the Bible, the number seven is significant. It's used to indicate completeness.'

'Or perfection?'

'Maybe.'

'OK.' George seized the pencil. 'So let's say we have zero – for the *oh*, and seven.'

'07. Sure.' Bola nodded. 'But *twice lawn*. What the hell? Whose lawn?'

George inspected the red bite mark he'd left on his flesh. He turned his attention to the pencil, tapped it on his knuckles. The tea trolley clanked past, causing a collective shuffling for purses and wallets from nearby workstations. A queue formed, along with a buzz of conversation.

George focused on the Post-it note. It couldn't be that hard – Isaiah Marley would never have remembered it. He frowned, twiddled the pencil. The lightbulb flared, lit up.

'Not *lawn*, you knob. *Lorne*. The street. His bedsit.'

'Ah, right. Nice one.' Bola's face lit up.

'We're not done. Come on. Focus. What have we got so far?'

'Let's see. 0711. Wait, it said *twice* Lorne.'

'No, it's the seven that's twice. *Perfect number twice–*'

Bola looked doubtful. 'Could be twice 11.'

'So we try them both. We try all combinations till we get someone picking up. 07711. Sounds like a mobile number already. Then we've got eight zero. He must have got bored trying to figure out a clue for that one. 07711

80–'

'Then *mid-nineties*.' Bola scratched his head. 'So let's go for the obvious. 95.'

'Agreed.' George scribbled on the pad. 'Dob. Date of birth. You've got his FB account there, right? He put down his birthday?'

'He did.' Bola grinned. 'Hey, this is easier than I thought.'

'I'll post your MENSA application on the way home. Let's have it.'

'1984. So it says.'

'We'll try it. 07711 809584. Definitely the right format.'

'I'll do a Ripper application. Shouldn't take long – as it's a murder enquiry.'

George grunted. 'The guv'll still have to sign it off. May as well make the call while we're waiting. Who knows? – They might even volunteer their address.'

The tea trolley queue had shortened to one. 'A co-operative POI, you mean? I doubt it ve-ry much.' Bola raised his hand. 'Hang on, though. I need to fix me a coffee and a bun before the big call.'

'Make that two.' George said. 'Large, if you're buying.'

CHAPTER FIVE

Higginson's reaction had been one of curiosity, which, given the possible alternatives, was a relief. Moran had kept things vague, open-ended. A spot of leave, from next week, for a month or so. As far as the team were concerned, no need to elaborate; he was just taking time off, that was all. Charlie was more than capable, Higginson had agreed. As he had shut the door on the superintendent's ordered domain, Moran's response to Higginson's green light had been relief, rather than any great sense of expectation.

So now you have the time. But where to start, Brendan?

Thames House, maybe. But somehow he couldn't see those doors swinging open at his approach. And who to contact? He didn't have a name – unless he asked for Aine's daughter. But what could she do? MI5s 1970s Irish operations were covert for sure, some more than others. The setup Joe Gallagher had been involved in had to be right at the top of that particular list – its existence only known to a select few. They'd sanctioned murder, albeit, as Samantha Grant had admitted, for the greater good, but still…

Moran reached down, unclipped Archie's lead, and watched the little dog dash off to the canoe ramp, his favourite spot for a dip in the Thames. The water meadows were still partially flooded from the recent rain but there was a freshness in the air that promised change. Moran strode on, deep in thought.

He'd called his old guv'nor the morning after Liam Doherty had burst in upon him. It'd been good to talk to the old man after all this time, not just for the evident pleasure his call had conferred, but also because Moran needed to hear a friendly voice after the trauma of the twelve preceding hours.

'Brendan Moran. Well, well, well. Not a name I was expecting to hear when I picked up the phone this wet and windy evening. Not at all. Tell me, how are things in the sunny Thames Valley? All ship-shape, decks sparkling and a brisk wind in your sails, am I right?'

Moran had smiled at the memory. Same old Dermot Flynn. Should have been a naval officer like his old man, instead of a high-ranking Garda officer.

'And to what do I owe this pleasure, DCI Moran? How can a retiree like myself, scuttled in the depths long, long ago, be of assistance? Or is this just a social call?'

'Both, sir, to be truthful.'

'I think we can dispense with the *sir*, don't you?'

Moran smiled. The voice crackling down the line was clearly weakened by the weight of years, yet Flynn's sharpness of mind appeared to be very much intact. 'Old habits, sir.'

'Very well, Brendan. You'll at least allow me to be informal?'

'Of course. Absolutely.'

They exchanged news, reminisced, discussed the state of the Republic, Brexit, the weather, until Flynn steered the conversation back to Moran's reason for calling.

'That's all by the by,' he said. 'And you've something more important to tell me, I'll be bound.'

And Moran told him. After he'd finished the line was quiet. All Moran could hear was Flynn's deep, regular breathing as he digested the information. Presently, Flynn cleared his throat.

'Well, I'm sorry you had to endure all that, Brendan. Deeply unsettling, I'm sure, even for a man of your experience. And Joe Gallagher! Extraordinary. The man's an absolute pillar these days. Or appears to be. And you have a recording, you say–?'

'Yes, sir. One of those old-school mini-cassette machines. Something made me turn it on. Now I just don't know what to do with it.'

'I see. I see. Well, let me play devil's advocate for a moment. Should the burden be all yours? It sounds as though MI5 are already on the case.'

'Maybe they are, but they're not making a particularly good job of it. Besides, there's a personal aspect to this.'

'Ah, yes, so you say. But this … foreign influence you detected,' Flynn spoke quietly now, so that Moran had to strain to hear his old mentor's words clearly, 'it doesn't bode well for our future, you don't think?'

'I don't believe so, sir.'

'Well, you know, the Eastern warlords are no strangers to our shores, Brendan. Wherever discord can be sown, they'll be there.'

'Is there anything I should know about Gallagher?'

Moran wanted to focus Flynn's thoughts on the specifics; the ex-police chief was advanced in years, plenty of time on his hands, accustomed perhaps to viewing the world through a wider-angled lens than Moran. 'Anything you've heard, maybe, which could be … helpful, in any way?'

Another long silence. 'I have no idea if this is any help at all, but I do happen to know that Gallagher is a keen sailor.'

Moran frowned. 'Oh yes?'

'Quite involved in the sailing club at Ringaskiddy. Chairman, or some such. You know the place?'

Moran did. It was a village fifteen kilometres along the N28 from Cork. 'Yes. There's a port – and I believe there's a ferry service?'

'There is – and was,' Flynn confirmed. 'The Swansea connection is shut now, but you can still get a ferry directly to France.' The old man paused for so long that Moran wondered whether he was going to continue. Eventually he said, 'And that's all I know, really.' Another long pause, then: 'You know, Brendan, I wouldn't worry too much about this business. You've had a good career. I should leave it to those who walk the corridors of power, hm? They're best placed to steer this particular ship – and who knows, they've probably got it all under control by now? I'd advise against stirring up a hornet's nest. I don't believe it'll do you any favours.'

'You're probably right, sir. Listen, I mustn't keep you any longer. It's been good to catch up.'

'Lovely surprise to hear from you. Don't leave it so long next time, Brendan,' Flynn said. 'And be sure to drop in next time you're over.'

'I will. That's a promise.'

Moran whistled to distract Archie from the moorhens and swans congregating by the canoe ramp. The spaniel came bounding over, shaking the river from his fur in a halo of spray. Moran stepped back to avoid the deluge.

His clipped Archie to his lead, much to the little dog's frustration, and made for the exit turnstile. Archie planted his feet and pulled in the opposite direction until Moran at last resorted to bribery and produced a paper bag of treats.

On his way to the station an hour later, he reflected again on the conversation he'd had with his old boss. Joe Gallagher had never shown much interest in sailing when Moran had known him back in the day. Could be something, could be nothing. The thought stayed with him for the remainder of the morning until a fresh discovery regarding Cleiren's wrecked transporter was brought to his attention.

'Semtex? One hundred percent sure?' Moran raised his eyebrows.

Charlie Pepper nodded. 'Yep. Small traces, but traces nevertheless.'

'Could be legit? Demolition and so on.'

'Ah, yes, it could be. But maybe not if you also take Forensics' other discovery into consideration.'

'Go on.'

Charlie ran a hand through her hair. 'Under the driver's seat. A Baikal pistol. Adapted.'

Moran frowned. 'CS gas weapon, right?'

'Usually. This one, as I said, adapted – to fire 9mm bullets.'

Moran sat quietly for a few moments. Someone thought

Cleiren might need a weapon – which implied that persons unknown were taking an interest in the Dutch driver's cargo and itinerary.

'Do we have the route traced?'

'We do. And this *is* interesting. Big artic, bound for Ireland, via Fishguard, naturally, cause they all go that way, don't they?'

'They do,' Moran said cautiously.

'Well, so did Cleiren. Except he made a small detour before he hit Fishguard.'

'Let me guess. Another harbour…' Moran frowned. 'Tenby is down the road, isn't it? Twenty miles or so?'

Charlie's face fell. 'How the heck did you know that?'

'It's a lovely spot. Been there a few times in my youth. Nice harbour. Boat trips and so on.'

Moran's mind was racing ahead. *Surely not…*

Charlie was looking at him. 'What? What is it?'

'Nothing. Maybe. I don't know.' Moran went to the coat stand, grabbed his jacket. 'Let's go.'

'Go? Where?'

'I want to see it. Cleiren's artic.'

'Er, guv. You're forgetting something…' Charlie looked pointedly at Moran's stick, propped up against the wall.

Moran gave her a withering look, retrieved it with a flourish, and shook it at her mock-threateningly.

'For your own good, guv.' Charlie stood her ground.

'Thank you, DI Pepper. And since you insist on treating me like an invalid, we'll take your car.'

CHAPTER SIX

Chapelfields nursing home was a small but well-run establishment. Chris Collingworth picked that up immediately; well-tended flower beds, freshly painted car park tramlines, sparkling windows. He buzzed. The door was opened by a smart, middle-aged woman in an immaculately pressed dark blue uniform. Her name badge proclaimed her to be Mrs Judith Miller, manager.

'Detective Constable? Do come in.'

Collingworth followed Mrs Miller into the warm interior. He braced himself for the usual assault on his senses – the smell of age, micturation, institutionalised food – but, surprisingly, it felt more as though he'd stepped into a modest but friendly four-star hotel. He was shown into a small office, offered a chair.

'Thank you.' He smiled warmly. Always charm the older woman – that way, you get what you want, more smoothly and usually a lot quicker. Collingworth was a man in a hurry, so quick ticked the boxes. 'So, you said you were about to call us this morning?'

'Yes.' Mrs Miller frowned. 'One of our residents was

collected yesterday evening for a minor operation – at the Dunedin Hospital. Only–'

'Only they weren't booked in?'

'Exactly. We called this morning to find out what was going on, and they said no, the operation wasn't due till next week.'

'No sign of your resident?'

Mrs Miller looked down at her hands and clasped them in a swift, anguished gesture. 'None. I can't understand how–'

'Can I get the resident's name?' Collingworth said.

'Yes, of course. It's Mr Daintree. Such a nice man – teacher by profession, very knowledgeable. And pretty *compos mentis* most of the time,' she added quickly.

'But not all the time?'

'Well, he's in his nineties, so there's usually a little confusion creeping in by that stage.'

Collingworth jotted in his notepad. 'Can you describe him?'

'Yes. He's tall – rather imposing in the classroom, I imagine, in his day. Grey hair, still thick, brushed back from his forehead. A pencil moustache. Well-groomed. He likes to keep himself looking respectable.'

'Uh huh.' Collingworth looked up. 'And who let him out?'

Mrs Miller moistened her lips. 'I was off duty last night. It was one of the temp carers – she hasn't been here long. And the fellow who collected Mr Daintree seemed very genuine, so I can't blame the girl–'

'I see. Can you describe him? Is the carer here now?'

'Yes, as a matter of fact she is. She's rather upset, as you can imagine. We can't think where Mr Daintree has got to.'

'Ah, I'm afraid I have some bad news in that regard,' Collingworth said.

As he delivered the news, he noted Mrs Miller's reaction. It was understated but profound. Her skin grew pale beneath the heavy layer of foundation, and her eyelids fluttered. 'Murdered? Suffocated? But why?' He hands unclasped, gripped the edge of the desk as though it might support her.

'That's what we're trying to establish, Mrs Miller. Now, the carer?'

'I'll fetch her straight away. One moment.'

Collingworth stretched his legs, belched surreptitiously, and allowed his mind to wander to more pleasant pastures: Julie Stiles. Great legs, and that smile...

'Detective Constable? This is Connie Chan. Do you want me to stay, or–'

'No, that's all right,' Collingworth told her, sitting up straighter. 'This will only take a minute.' His attention was only half on Mrs Miller as he spoke, because Connie Chan was an absolute stunner. Petite, with a face that looked to have been sculpted in porcelain by a master craftsman. She was, quite simply, off-the-scale beautiful.

Mrs Miller nodded briskly. 'I'll leave you to it.' She closed the office door with a firm *click*.

'Now then, Miss Chan, there's nothing to worry about,' Collingworth flashed his best reassuring smile. 'You're not in any trouble at all. Please,' he indicated Mrs Miller's vacant chair. 'Have a seat.'

He watched Chan slip reluctantly into her manager's chair. She wore her long, glossy hair over one shoulder, tied loosely in a gold band.

'There we are. Comfortable? Good. Now then, just tell me exactly what happened.'

Moran sniffed the air. The remains of the transporter had been arranged into manageable sections. This was the section immediately behind the driver's cab. Forensics were moving around the shell like ants, dusting, checking, peering into cracks and corners.

'Here you go, guv.' Charlie proffered a thick plastic evidence bag containing the Baikal.

He held it up, hefted it, handed it back. 'So what was he worried about, our Mr Cleiren, that he might have felt the need to wave this around at any given stage of his journey?'

'Ben Ruiter might have some insights – the senior CSI. D'you know him?'

'Nope.'

'Seems all right. Let's have a word.'

Charlie led them around the side of the vehicle towards what sounded like an animated conversation between a disgruntled-looking sergeant and one of the Forensics officers. As they approached, Moran caught the tail-end of the conversation.

'I've got six more vehicles booked in here,' Ruiter said peevishly. 'You said you'd be done by two at the latest.'

'I said two-ish,' the Forensics officer replied. 'And that covers us till at least two-fifty-nine. We're going as fast as we can, all right?'

'No later. I mean it.' Ruiter pitched his final words towards the Forensics officer's retreating back. 'Bloody Forensics,' he muttered. 'Think they have all the time in the world.' He caught sight of Moran and Charlie approaching and stiffened. 'Ah, DI Pepper. I was just–'

'It's all right, Sergeant,' Charlie reassured him. 'DCI Moran and I were just wondering if anything else of interest has turned up.'

'Oh, right.' Ruiter looked relieved. 'Let me take a look.' He took out a pair of flexible glasses, hooked them around his ears and riffled through a sheaf of papers on his clipboard. 'Let's see now. This morning. Last three entries of interest. The pistol–'

'Yep, we know about that.'

Ruiter glanced up. 'Yes, of course. We've had the dogs go over the vehicle since we last spoke. They had a good sniff around, so we now have traces of human cargo – the forensics reports have all the detail. And–' he peered through his lenses. 'Gunpowder. From magazine cartridges, apparently. Again, the details–'

'Sure, Charlie smiled. 'All in the reports.' She glanced at Moran, raised her eyebrows. 'Thanks, Sergeant. We'll let you get on.'

'No ordinary haulage company, then.' Moran replied to the unspoken question. 'Explosives, people trafficking and firearms. Not necessarily in that order.'

Charlie nodded. 'Cleiren wouldn't have wanted to hang around once he'd made those kinds of deliveries. He was caning it back to Dover as fast as his wheels could carry him. So, double-unlikely that he deliberately caused the accident.'

'Agreed. Another Smart statistic.'

'*Ergo*, no connection with Isaiah Marley either. Just a random shunt?'

'It does look that way. But let's see what George and Bola pull out of the hat before we dismiss it altogether.'

He frowned as his mobile buzzed. 'Moran?'

'Hello guv, it's DC Swinhoe.'

'Yes? How can I help you…' Moran checked himself; he'd almost said Bernice. 'Detective Constable?'

He listened to DC Swinhoe's precise briefing. 'Right. Thanks for letting me know. This could be very useful.'

'Good news?' Charlie asked.

'We've been contacted by Police Scotland. Our Mr Daintree came up on a search this morning. Apparently they have two similar – and as yet unexplained – deaths in the Highlands, of all places. Same MO – care home resident goes missing, turns up dead.'

'Suffocated?'

'Exactly.'

'And they want us to help?'

'Sounds like a two-way thing,' Moran smiled. 'They've already despatched one of theirs to Heathrow. Fancy popping up the M4 and collecting him?' Moran glanced at his watch. 'He'll be landing round about now.'

'Finally. It's ringing.' George cupped a hand over the phone and mouthed the news to Bola, who was draped over his chair, apparently deep in thought. This was the tenth try, at least, and George had begun to think that the perma-engaged status meant that the mobile was out of commission. Another dead end, like the bedsit, but at least Bola had nailed the provider and the address – super-quick. George was surprised at the speed, not to mention the location.

'Hello? Is that you, Isaiah?'

Female. Middle-aged. Wife, partner? 'It's about Isaiah,' George said.

'Who is this?'

Deep suspicion in the tone, unsurprisingly. George went for urgency. 'Don't hang up, please. This is DC George McConnell, Thames Valley Police.'

'Thames Valley? What's wrong? Where's Isaiah? Has something happened to him?'

'Who am I speaking to, please?'

A pause. *'His sister.'*

This was always the hardest part of the job. Never an easy way. Always best to keep it simple. 'I'm afraid I have bad news. Is there someone with you?'

Hesitantly. *'No. I live on my own.'*

'I see. I'm sorry to say that Isaiah was killed in a road traffic collision yesterday evening.'

Silence.

'Hello?'

'I heard you.'

'We'd like to have a wee chat – about Isaiah.'

'No.'

The line went dead. George held the phone up, exasperated. 'Great.'

Bola stepped forward, 'Here, let me try.'

'No point. She'll be on the alert. She'll either ditch the mobile or refuse to answer.'

'So now what? The address is out of our jurisdiction – by a country mile.'

George scratched his cheek. Beard needed a trim. That wouldn't do; he planned to see Tess later on. 'Aye, it is that.'

'But your neck of the woods, eh?' Bola grinned. 'Hey – d'they still wear that blue face paint like in *Braveheart* up there?'

'If you weren't bigger than me, I'd knock you down for that.' George's face reddened.

Bola went into rapid reverse, spread his hands. 'Come on, man. I'm only kidding. Where the heck is Aviemore, anyway?'

'I might be able to help you with that.' A voice spoke behind them – a Scottish voice.

Bola did a double take. 'George, you said that without moving your lips.'

The next voice was Charlie Pepper's. 'All right guys. Take a break. I'd like you to meet DS Ian Luscombe, Police Scotland, Major Investigations Team–'

'Don't tell me,' Bola interrupted. 'Aviemore.'

'See?' Charlie appealed to the newcomer. 'I told you they were a bright lot, didn't I?'

'You did indeed, DI Pepper.' DS Luscombe's expression wasn't giving much away, but George discerned the hint of an appraising glint in his eye.

'Briefing in ten,' Charlie told them. 'I'll leave DS Luscombe in your capable hands until then. Perhaps you can show him the delights of the canteen?'

CHAPTER SEVEN

'We have two victims, same MO. Both elderly. Both suffocated by a person or persons unknown.' DS Luscombe paused to allow the impact of his words to register. 'Whoever is responsible leaves little or no trace. Our killings are three months apart. So far, our investigation has drawn a blank. We have two sets of very unhappy relatives, national press interest and a high percentage of public investment in the outcome. In short, the media is buzzing like a swarm of flies around a dead dog, and our boss is in the frame for being eaten alive. I'm here to assist you with your investigation in the optimistic hope that it will help us with our own enquiries.'

Charlie watched Luscombe's delivery with admiration. He was a tall, confident Scot in his mid-thirties with a thick head of hair that he wore longer than fashion currently prescribed, but stylishly all the same. He exuded health, fitness, and efficiency. From what she'd seen so far in his short time with George and Bola, he also sported a good sense of humour and the knack of getting along with his peers, while at the same time commanding respect. In short, Luscombe was someone who kept your attention. As Charlie watched for the teams' reactions she noted the female officers' rapt expressions, hanging on his every word and, Charlie suspected, mentally assessing his gym-toned physique.

'These are our deceased.' Luscombe pinned two photographs to the board. 'James McMillan, aged eighty-four. Anthony Lewis, aged seventy-nine. The first was killed at his own home in Grantown-On-Spey, the other was removed from his residential care home in Nethy Bridge and suffocated, we believe, in the car in which he was found. The car was stolen, and the vehicle abandoned in a Waitrose car park. Forensics found nothing in the car to incriminate the perpetrator. Literally nothing. Whoever did this was extremely careful. All surfaces were cleaned down with some kind of antiseptic, no prints. DNA analysis of the car interior only revealed traces of the vehicle owner and the deceased. We are assuming that the killer was suited-up, masked, gloved, the lot.'

'A professional?' Bola's hand was up.

'An assassin? We don't think so, but well-prepared nevertheless.'

George: 'Anything in common between the two victims?'

Luscombe shook his head. 'Apart from the fact that they're both retired, no. Mr McMillan had a less stable employment record – in the sense that he moved jobs a few times during his career – he was latterly a small business owner – whereas the other gentleman, Mr Lewis, had a long career in education. Aside from that, they're both unmarried.'

The double doors at the rear of the room swung open

and Chris Collingworth came in, coffee in hand, and sat down on a vacant chair at the back next to DC Stiles. He whispered something and Stiles giggled, coloured. Collingworth looked pleased with himself.

'DC Collingworth. Thanks for joining us.' Charlie broke in before George could ask a follow-up. 'Next time, leave the coffee for after the briefing.'

Collingworth raised his cup, gave a rueful shake of his head. 'Sure, boss.'

'Care to give us an update, now you're here?'

'My pleasure.' Collingworth swaggered to the front. 'I'm sorry, we haven't been formally introduced.' This to DS Luscombe.

Luscombe extended his hand, which Collingworth shook warmly before facing the assembled officers.

'So, I tracked the victim to a residential care home in Matlin Street. Manageress was off last night, but there was a new temp staff member on duty who let Marley in. She took him at his word, let Marley take the old feller away.' He took a swig of coffee. 'Is all.'

'We have a name?'

'Frank Daintree. Been at Chapelfields for eight months.'

'And you'll have checked his room?'

'Of course, boss. Clean as the proverbial. No photos, diaries, letters, nothing.'

'Eight months. So he came from where exactly?'

Collingworth placed his coffee cup carefully on the table by the whiteboard. He took out a notebook, flicked to the latest page. 'Don't trust myself to pronounce it properly,' he grinned. 'Should ask DC McConnell really, he'd do it justice. Like a foreign language, eh?' He shot Luscombe a challenging, tight-lipped smile.

'Spare us the linguistics, please, DC Collingworth.' Charlie felt her hackles rising. Cocky little so-and-so. She glanced at Luscombe but his expression gave nothing away.

'Sure, boss.' Collingworth cocked his head. 'He moved from his own place of residence, a small place called Kingussie. Connie Chan told me he used to live down south a long time ago, and, being an old boy, the winters north of the border were starting to get to him.'

'And who exactly is Connie Chan?'

'The temp carer who let him out, boss. Very pleasant young lady, too.'

'I'll bet,' Charlie muttered. 'Relatives? Must be a local connection, surely? Was Ms Chan able to appraise you of any detail in that regard, Detective Constable?'

'Nope, but the manageress stepped in with a name. A daughter – currently away on business. Runs some kind of marketing operation.'

'Great. So, she won't know what's happened yet.' Charlie tugged at a lock of hair, folded her arms. 'We'll need to get hold of her somehow. Got an address?'

Collingworth tapped his notebook. 'It's all in here.'

'OK, that's your next port of call.'

'Kingussie? That'll be Scotland?' Bola piped up. He was looking at George, but it was DS Luscombe who answered. 'Correct. It's near the A9, Badenoch and Strathspey ward.'

Charlie clucked her tongue. 'Which is just down the road from–'

Everyone looked at Luscombe.

Luscombe nodded. '–Aye, Aviemore.'

Moran shut Higginson's door behind him and made his way along the corridor to his own office, deep in thought. The summons hadn't exactly been unexpected, and the Superintendent's logic was entirely reasonable. They'd found a strong lead for Luscombe to follow up and, although a connection was as yet unproven, it nevertheless seemed likely. It therefore made sense to despatch a senior officer to accompany Luscombe in a show of mutual support and co-operation. Both logical and politically astute. Higginson all over.

But Charlie's absence would mean a leaderless team, unless Moran was willing to postpone his sabbatical for a short period – perhaps only a week, ten days at the outside, Higginson had predicted in his usual optimistic manner.

'We *could* let Police Scotland handle the interview,' Higginson had said. 'But now we're involved I'd like to keep it that way. Charlie can feed back any useful intelligence and be on hand to follow up any further potential leads after this woman's been interviewed.'

'If she's still in situ,' Moran pointed out. 'She sounded rattled – less than co-operative on the phone, so George tells me.'

'How far can she go?' Higginson countered. 'Their uniform can run her to ground, surely? And when they do, who knows what useful information we'll pick up?' The Superintendent straightened his keyboard with a deft movement, steepled his fingers. 'Luscombe tells me the press are all over this. If their elderly folk aren't safe at home or in their chosen places of care, then we have a duty to help them reverse that trend – lickety split. Not to mention the fact that we might be faced with a repeat performance at any time here in Reading. We've got to get this sewn up, Brendan. All I can say is I'm sorry to have to call upon you when you've made a very reasonable representation for time off. After everything you've had on your plate over the last couple of years, I haven't made this decision lightly. I hope you understand.'

'Of course, sir. I'm sure I can hold on for ten days or so.'

'Don't be afraid to get your hands dirty, Brendan,' Higginson said. 'I wouldn't normally say that to a man of your rank and experience, especially in your particular situation – you've earned the right to let the youngsters do the heavy lifting. But–' Higginson shrugged, 'we are where we are. I need a safe pair of hands, and I know I can count on you.'

'Thank you, sir. I'll see what I can dig up.'

'DI Pepper will be leaving first thing tomorrow. Make sure you have a thorough debrief before she flies.'

So that was that. Moran grabbed a hot drink from the canteen trolley, exchanged the usual banter with Alice, the tea-lady, parked in her usual spot outside his office door, shut himself in and pondered the events of the last twenty-four hours. Should be straightforward enough. Charlie knew what she was doing. She could look after herself, and the team were attacking the case with their usual verve and enthusiasm.

He stirred his tea, swirled the hot liquid in its cardboard cup.

Come on, Brendan. When was anything ever straightforward?

CHAPTER EIGHT

Mrs Perkins, his neighbour, had left a note. Not unusual in itself; they often communicated in this fashion, the subject matter primarily relating to Moran's Cocker Spaniel, Archie, and his regular routine of walks. Mrs Perkins was a mixed blessing – always up for a chat, always on the lookout for unusual or newsworthy local events. Her observations of late had fluctuated wildly from the banal to the disquieting. And then there had been the photographs…

He slipped the note from the letterbox as he turned the key.

'Hello Brendan. Thought you'd like to know – a young man called for you earlier. Smartly dressed. Dark hair. Drove a Mercedes A Class, grey. He had a good look at your house, too. I popped my head around the door, asked if I could be of any assistance. Not a word. He gave me a look, got into his car and drove off. Archie and I had a lovely walk today. We saw the squirrels again. I fed him at five. Mrs P.'

Moran slipped his stick into the brolly holder, left his keys and wallet on the hall table. In the kitchen he poured himself a half glass of Sangiovese, went into the lounge and drew the curtains. There was the spot on the skirting board where a strand of Samantha Grant's hair had been stuck to a congealed blood stain. There was the couch where Joe Gallagher had sat, one leg crossed casually over the other, calm and composed. Where he had warned Moran off, refused to disclose Samantha's fate – even her whereabouts. And safely stashed in the bureau, there were Mrs P's photographs, taken in the car park by the water meadow. Two men, one woman. In distress, or maybe just disoriented. Two drakes and a duck.

Moran sank into the armchair, took a deep draught of the red wine. This wasn't over. Not by a long chalk. On impulse he got up, went into the hall, lifted the heavy Bakelite telephone receiver, unscrewed the earpiece, made a quick inspection. He lifted the base unit. Nothing untoward.

In the lounge he went to the window, moved the curtain a fraction. The street was clear.

Paranoia. But, under the circumstances, justifiable.

He returned to the armchair, and with a conscious effort turned his mind to the current issue, the care home abduction. There were gaps in the timeline. Where had Marley taken the elderly Mr Daintree to kill him? Had he just driven around the corner and smothered his victim in the car? Or had he driven to some pre-arranged address? If indeed Marley himself was responsible.

And the big question: why? Marley seemed to have very little by way of what Moran called *life detritus*. Everyone left footprints in their day-to-day lives, especially in the age of social media, but Marley's footprint was skeletal, if not invisible. A cryptic voice memo, a phone number. A template Facebook account. A bare bedsit. That was all. That suggested a couple of possibilities: one, Marley was on the run, using fake ids. Or two – and this seemed more likely – he was an illegal.

Moran absently stroked Archie's head as he considered possible motives. Robbery? No. Daintree wouldn't have been carrying money, or indeed anything of value. And why go to all the trouble of abducting a care home resident, just to rob them? If, as Moran suspected, Marley was in the UK illegally, he was highly unlikely to have made the acquaintance of an elderly, retired man in care. Unless, of course, Marley was a care assistant, and had previously been employed at the Matlin Road care home. But he hadn't. The manager had never heard of him, and neither had the description furnished by Connie Chan rung any bells.

Moran took another sip of Sangiovese. The wine was warming his stomach, relaxing his mind. Had Marley known Daintree in some other capacity, before Daintree had been admitted to Chapelfields? Moran made a mental note to find out if DC Collingworth had managed to contact Daintree's daughter. She would be able to fill in some blanks. Perhaps she could shed light on her father's past, his hobbies, interests.

Archie dropped his tennis ball in Moran's lap.

'All right, boy. I get the hint. Five minutes.' Moran smiled at the spaniel's earnest expression.

He swirled the last inch of wine in the glass, sniffed the aroma. This was from a good cellar, no doubt about it. Mrs P had recommended it, and Moran had to admit that, for all her eccentricities, his neighbour knew a good red when she tasted one.

Moran reluctantly drained his glass and went to find Archie's lead. There was another possibility that shouldn't be discounted, and this seemed to him the more likely scenario: Marley hadn't been acting independently, for motives of his own.

Marley had been working for someone else.

Charlie followed DC Luscombe down the steps of the BA Airbus onto the concrete apron. It had been an early start and Charlie's eyes were prickling with fatigue. Her mind had been racing all night, going over the briefings, the teams' updates, trying to piece the puzzle together. It was a weird one, that was for sure. An old man, killed for what purpose? And two here in Scotland? Was it the work of some crazed euthanasia group? Was Marley responsible for the Scottish deaths as well? Try as she might, her mind would not allow her rest, and her dawn alarm had found her wide awake, still working the case over.

The flight had proved uneventful, and DS Luscombe a reticent travelling companion. Not, Charlie concluded, an early-morning person.

She followed the tall detective through the airport and into the car park, wheeling her case behind her. She'd packed for the few days she anticipated would be the length of her stay. If it proved to be a longer secondment, she'd just have to find time to pop into the local M&S to replenish her underwear supply.

Luscombe beeped his keyring and the tail lights of a dark blue BMW lit up. He opened the boot, threw in his overnight bag and gestured for her to do the same.

'What's the first stop?' Charlie asked as they left the airport environs and joined the A9.

'Check in at the station for updates, ma'am. Then straight to the address. I don't want to lose any more time.' He said it in such a way as to imply that his journey south had been an unwanted distraction, that he had somehow lost the advantage by his absence.

'OK by me,' Charlie said, trying to keep the irritation out of her voice. 'And please, skip the 'ma'am'. Informal is fine while I'm on your patch.'

She stared fixedly out of the window, annoyed. *Look, buster, if it wasn't for us lot you'd still be going round in circles...*

What she'd really wanted to do was to drop her bag off at the Premier Inn she'd booked, freshen up, then start the day's work. But Luscombe hadn't offered, and she didn't want him to think he'd been saddled with some weak southern female who needed mollycoddling. She clamped her jaw shut and watched the fields and houses flit by. The names were unfamiliar, some sounding like outtakes from *Lord of the Rings*. Findhorn, Moy...

'Been up this way before?' Luscombe broke the silence.

'No. Always wanted to. Never got round to it.'

'It's fine country,' Luscombe said. 'I'm from a wee bit further up. Hopeman. Bet you've never heard of it.'

'Can't say that I have,' Charlie replied, pleased that Luscombe had made an effort to communicate. 'Sounds nice, though.'

'Aye, it is. Started out as a wee fishing village. Bit bigger these days, but still has that local feel about it. Gets a little rough during the winter – I've seen some storms in my time, I can tell you.'

'And your family. They all come from Hopeman?'

'Aye. Right back to my grandfather – he was headmaster of the local school. Moved to Grantown eventually, became the rector at the local grammar. Made quite a name for himself – he was one of the educationalists involved in the founding of Gordonstoun.'

'Prince Charles' school? Wow. You must be very proud of your roots.'

Luscombe shot her a sideways glance, the hint of a dour smile. 'I'm a Scotsman. Of course I'm proud.'

Charlie grinned, and the silence that followed for the next mile and a half was more comfortable. She brought her mind back to the murders. Something Luscombe had said…Then she remembered. 'You mentioned Grantown? That's where–'

'Uh huh. Where James McMillan was murdered.'

'So you know the area pretty well?'

'I do.' Luscombe indicated, overtook a dawdling Fiat. 'McMillan lived opposite the bowling green. Lived a quiet life, on his own – wife died a few years back.'

Charlie was quiet for a moment. 'It's got to be a grudge killing. Did you make contact with any of McMillan's friends, surviving family?'

Luscombe shook his head. 'When you get to a certain age…'

'Right. Yes, I see. But he was fit and well? Able to care for himself?'

'He was. And still a bowls club member, too.'

'What about the club? Did–'

'We interviewed them *all*. And the wives. Till we were blue in the face. No motives. No ideas why someone would want to kill old Mac.'

Charlie picked up the tone. 'I wasn't implying any criticism – just trying to get a little background.'

'Aye,' Luscombe said. 'I know. Nearly there.'

Charlie turned her attention once more to the local scenery, which was breathtaking. 'Loch Alvie,' she murmured. 'It's beautiful.'

'Good fishing,' Luscombe told her. 'Trout, perch and pike.'

'You must love living here.'

'I can think of worse places, for sure.' Luscombe grinned again.

With a frisson of self-awareness, she realised she enjoyed seeing him smile. There was something about the way it transformed his face. 'I'll bet,' she said, not trusting herself to look at him.

They turned through a narrow iron gate into a small car park. 'Here we are.' Luscombe killed the engine and withdrew the keys. 'Not quite as grand as your place, but I like to think it has a certain charm.'

Charlie fished her bag from the boot and followed Luscombe into the police station, trying to work out whether she'd discerned a twinkle in his eye or if her imagination was just working overtime.

CHAPTER NINE

George McConnell pressed the doorbell and stood back. He felt the familiar, conflicting, emotions of peace and disquiet he always experienced when visiting. The grounds were picturesque, spacious. A well-tended lawn stretched back to a line of birches and oaks that half-concealed a small lake, itself delimited by a profusion of pickerelweed and blue flag iris, sedge and arrowhead. George had taken to walking the lake's perimeter after his visit. Time spent in reflection in the lakeside's restful environment helped to alleviate the feelings of helplessness that always threatened to overwhelm him as, after each visit, he would reluctantly concede that Tess had made little progress. But at least, the nursing officer habitually offered by way of reassurance, she seemed 'comfortable' and not in distress.

The door was answered by a new staff member whom he didn't recognise. He explained the reason for his visit, showed his ID. And then he was alone in the hall, the empty staircase beckoning him forward. This was the hardest part. He knew what to expect, and yet a small spark of hope still smouldered. Today she would recognise him. Today would bring the first signs of returning life, maybe a gesture, a look – even better, a word.

Tess was sitting by the window, in her usual chair, looking out over the lawn towards the dark ribbon of partially-obscured water. The sun was shining, and there was a hint of spring in the air. One of the small bedroom windows was open in acknowledgment, and the room felt airy, laced with the faint scent of cut flowers.

'Hi,' George said. This was the second hardest part. Once he got used to the rhythm of the one-way conversation, he knew he would be more at ease, able to rabbit on about all sorts of trivia: what was going on at the station, the new case they were working on, the guv taking time off, how Collingworth was getting on his nerves, big time. Once he started it would all start to flow. He summoned his reserves of courage and approached her. She was dressed in a long skirt and plain top, her hair loose, longer now than she used to wear it. Her face was pale, though, and George thought that she'd lost weight. Last week he'd queried this with the nursing officer, but had been reassured that Tess was eating 'plenty enough'.

'Lovely day out there. I might take a wee walk by the lake, a bit later.'

Tess stayed in the same position, but her head tilted to one side a little, as though she'd heard some faraway, familiar sound to which she would have liked to respond, but, for whatever reason, found herself unable.

George took this as encouragement. He pulled up a chair, drew it in close. He fell short of touching her, although he very much wanted to, because he worried that physical contact might alarm her. The drug she'd been given was, according to the boffins at the hospital, *uncategorised*, a compound mix of various chemicals the like of which hadn't been seen before in the West. Its long-term effects were therefore, according to the chemists, almost impossible to predict. 'The human brain is an extraordinary and largely unknown organism,' the experts had reported. 'Great advances have been made over the last fifty years, but we are still very much in the dark as to exactly *how* the brain functions.'

George was well aware that, in the light of this vague prognosis, there were two possible paths open to him. One led to despair, anger and frustration, the other to a cautiously optimistic hope that Tess would make, if not a full, then, given time and, most importantly, encouragement, at least a partial recovery.

'Charlie's off up north today,' he told her. 'Aviemore. I know it. Used to be a lovely spot. Bit too touristy for me nowadays. Skiing and the like. Nice time to go, though, in the early spring.'

Tess made a soft moaning noise in her throat. What was she thinking? Could she understand him? He pressed on. 'She's gone up with a fella from Police Scotland. Nice guy. Only met him briefly. Luscombe, he's called.'

George chatted away for twenty minutes or so until he felt that he, or maybe Tess, had had enough. He hated leaving her. He knew she was cared for here, but...

He left her with a promise to pop in again in a day or so. His descent of the grand staircase was accompanied, as usual, by a lump in his throat, a fierce stinging in his eyes. He stood in the drive for a few minutes, taking in draughts of pure, clear air, then headed purposefully across the lawn, making for the lake.

Moran had developed a sure instinct over the years. He knew when he wasn't alone. He knew when he was being tailed. And this morning, as he joined the traffic on the Oxford Road, he knew that someone was interested in him, in what he was doing. He glanced in his rearview. There it was, a grey Mercedes A Class, just nosing out a few cars behind him.

Moran wasn't too bothered. This guy wasn't about physical contact. He was just keeping an eye out. But for what? He'd called round, but Moran had been out. So, why not call again, when he was in? He'd been in the whole evening, since he'd taken Archie out for a stroll at eight-ish, and he'd been in all night.

A better question: who was he? Moran turned left at the Inner Distribution Road roundabout, headed towards the station. The A Class mirrored his actions, just two cars behind. When they reached the police station roundabout, and Moran turned into the service road that led to the underground car park, the A Class cruised on past the turning, the driver staring fixedly ahead.

See you later, no doubt...

Moran guided the car into a space, clearing the treacherous concrete posts with an inch or two to spare, and spied the tall silhouette of DC Collingworth walking towards him. Before Moran's feet touched the asphalt, Collingworth called a greeting.

'Guv. I was hoping to catch you early – before we got going, so to speak.'

'Oh yes?' Moran thumbed his key fob and turned to face the detective.

'I understand you're stepping in as SIO on the Chapelfields case, while DI Pepper is away?'

'For the short term, yes. Probably a couple of weeks maximum.'

They crossed the car park and Collingworth punched in the door entry code. They went inside, called the lift.

'You'll be aware, guv, that I passed my sergeant's board recently.'

'Yes. Well done.'

The lift arrived, and the two men stepped inside.

'I was wondering if you might put in a word, if I applied for the internal vacancy – it was posted a couple of days back.'

'Well, by all means go ahead and apply, DC Collingworth. I'm sure DI Pepper will take everything into consideration.'

The lift stopped, the doors slid open and they exited to the reception area.

'That's what I mean, guv.' Collingworth hovered by the internal door to the open plan. 'I'm not sure that DI Pepper and myself … see eye to eye, exactly. We seem to have got off to a bad start.'

Moran squared up to the younger man, looked him in the eye. 'From what I've seen and heard, DC Collingworth, you have the potential to do well. However, I've also heard that there have been occasions where your interactions with colleagues have been less than helpful. If you take steps to improve your peer-to-peer relationships, I have every reason to believe that DI Pepper will look more favourably on the possibility of endorsing you for a suitable role in your new grade.'

Collingworth was silent for a moment. 'I see. It's just that, I thought... well, as DI Pepper is unavailable at present–'

'—you'd slip your application in without reference to said officer?'

'Well, if you put it like that, I suppose so, yes. But I don't see anything wrong with—'

'—No, and that, perhaps, is part of the problem. Now, if you'll excuse me, DC Collingworth I have one or two pressing matters to attend to before briefing, and I'm sure you have plenty to be getting on with in the meantime. I'll see you at ten.'

Moran felt Collingworth's eyes boring into his back as he walked away. A rough diamond. Potential, for sure, but the lad had some way to go. He'd done well at his board; his ability wasn't in question, just his attitude. Moran had seen many a promising career wrecked by a lack of self-awareness in that respect. Would Collingworth see the light? Difficult to tell. His ambition was commendable, but there was rather too much of a self-serving bias to Collingworth's *modus operandi* for Moran's liking – and clearly for Charlie's, too.

Moran sat at his desk and tried to focus on next steps for the Chapelfields murder. His mind kept wandering back to the Mercedes, to Cleiren's artic, to the pistol beneath the dead driver's seat. It all needed following up. But how, logistically, to cover all the bases? He ran through a mental list of available officers. He'd have to split them down the middle. Half to Chapelfields leads, half to the truck. Or should he instead, perhaps, just alert the customs and port authorities regarding the latter? Let them take up the investigation? The artic had been passing though the Thames Valley, but that didn't necessarily mean he had to take it on.

Moran drummed his fingers. No, it didn't feel right. His

instincts told him this was something he needed to tackle head on, especially given the truck's minor diversion to Tenby. Flynn had mentioned Joe Gallagher's connection to the port at Ringaskiddy.

He stood, went to the wall map and traced a line from Tenby to Ringaskiddy. A straight line, pretty much.

A straight line, perhaps, for a crooked operation.

CHAPTER TEN

The house was small, one of a group of terraces. Bleak, was how Charlie would have described it. Colourless. The town and its environs were a place of contrasts – beauty in the surrounding natural landscape, and cheap, ugly housing tucked away in dowdy corners.

Luscombe parked the BMW in an empty space opposite a run down house with a 'for sale' notice leaning at a forty-five degree angle, and switched off the engine. 'Happy for you to take the lead,' he said. 'I'll chip in if anything gets lost in translation.' Again came the grin, the sudden brightening of the eyes. Then he was out of the car and walking towards number eleven.

Charlie followed the tall detective through the rusted wrought-iron gate, and along the short path which led to Isaiah Marley's sister's front door. The rain, which had begun as they'd left Aviemore police station, was teeming down, and looked as though it was likely to stay that way.

'Reckon she'll be in?' Charlie shivered as they waited for a response.

Luscombe shrugged. 'Where else is she going to go?

People who live in this area don't tend to move around much.'

'Unless she was spooked by the phone call.'

'Maybe,' Luscombe said. 'But she must be expecting someone to call about her brother, sometime.'

'George said she sounded scared.'

'Aye, well we'll soon find out.' Luscombe cocked his head at the sound of a chain being slid aside, or perhaps fastened. The door opened a fraction, and a face peered through the gap. 'Who is it?'

'Police,' Charlie said. 'Can we have a moment of your time?'

'This is about Isaiah?'

'Yes.'

The chain rattled again and the door opened. 'Thank you,' Charlie said, and followed the woman inside.

They were shown into a small lounge, where the woman indicated a two-seater settee. The only other chair was an armchair, where, judging by the glass and book resting on the table next to it, she'd been sitting when the doorbell rang. There was a moment of awkwardness as Charlie and Luscombe assessed the available seating. They squeezed onto the two-seater, and Charlie crossed one leg over the other in an attempt to create a little personal space. The woman resumed her place in the armchair.

She was small in stature, of Caribbean descent, dressed simply in a white top, blue cardigan, and jeans. She looked resigned, as if she'd been expecting bad news for a long time. Charlie recognised the signs; the downturned mouth, blank expression, automatic movements. She folded her hands in her lap and looked at them both without a trace of curiosity.

Charlie took a mental deep breath and began. For some reason she was more nervous than usual. 'I'm DI Pepper from the Thames Valley Constabulary in Berkshire. This is Detective Sergeant Ian Luscombe, of Police Scotland. You spoke briefly to my sergeant, George McConnell, yesterday.'

'I knew Isaiah was dead. I dreamed it.'

'Perhaps if we can confirm your full name to begin with?' Charlie gave her an encouraging smile.

'Grace Elizabeth Baxter, nee Marley. Born 1969.'

'Thank you. Tell us about Isaiah, Grace. Did he live with you? What was he doing in Berkshire?'

'Looking for work. An' he told me he might have found a job, workin' at the hospital. I said, I could have got you a job at my hospital, but he wouldn't listen. Stubborn. Always stubborn.'

'You work at the local hospital?' Luscombe prompted.

'I'm a cleaner. They always need cleaners, but Isaiah liked to do things his own way.'

'So,' Charlie pressed on, 'he had his own place here, in Aviemore? Or did he stay with you?'

'He worked around a bit, used to live in sometimes with his jobs. When he had no job he'd come to me.'

'Grace, was Isaiah in this country illegally?' Luscombe pitched in bluntly.

Charlie flinched. That was a potentially interview-terminating question, if Grace took it the wrong way.

'Sure. Of course. He only came here when our parents died. Otherwise he'd still be livin' there.'

'And where is that, exactly, Grace?'

'Where d'you think, girl? Do I sound like a Spanish woman to you, or what?'

Charlie sensed Luscombe suppressing a guffaw. She smiled. 'All right, Jamaica would be my guess.'

'There y'are. So I can see you're a good detective.'

'Did Isaiah confide in you? Did you talk?'

'Only small things. Never any heart-to-heart. That wasn't his way.' She leaned forward suddenly. 'What happened to my brother? Was it his fault?'

A flicker of emotion clouded Grace's features. Charlie would have guessed her age wrongly; she looked older than her fifty-one years.

'No,' Charlie said gently. 'It wasn't his fault. His car was hit by an articulated lorry.'

Grace looked into her lap. 'What was he doing? Was he up to no good?'

'Did he usually get up to no good, Grace?' Luscombe asked.

Grace hesitated. 'He never meant to, but he always needed money. He spent too much – what he didn't have. My parents, they coddled him, y'know? When they passed away he just expected to carry on, like he always had. He couldn't get a permit to work here, but some friend of his say he could come anyway, they'd fix it all for him. So he came.' She shrugged.

'And yourself?' Charlie asked.

'I ain't illegal, dearie. I can show you my passport. I came here in eighty-nine. I wanted a future, I wanted to see this country. I got married. It was all fine, until my husband died. Since then, I just done the best I could.'

'I'm sorry,' Charlie said. 'That must have been hard.'

Another shrug. 'Life's hard, ain't it? No one ever promised you an easy one, eh?'

'When did you last see Isaiah, Grace?'

She paused, knitted her brow. 'I see him in January. He come in to tell me he's goin' south. He didn't stay long.'

'Did he have friends in this area, or contacts? He only had your number in his mobile phone. No one else. Was he hiding something, or hiding *from* something?'

'–Or someone?' Luscombe added.

Grace was silent for a moment, then she answered with her own question. 'Why you so interested in him? He's dead, in an accident. What else is there?'

Charlie exchanged a look with Luscombe. He nodded. 'Grace, there was a dead body in the car with him at the time of the accident. An elderly man. He wasn't killed by the accident, he was dead already.'

Grace put a hand to her mouth, then made the sign of the cross. 'Oh, Lord.'

'We don't know who killed him, Grace,' Charlie quickly added. 'It may not have been Isaiah. We're trying to build up a picture, to establish where Isaiah had been, where he went and why. Can you help us in any way? Is there anything he might have said to you–'

'–Like I said, dearie, he never told me *nothing*.' This was declared emphatically. Grace folded her arms, looked at them both. 'My, but you two make a fine couple.'

Charlie felt herself colouring, her cheeks heating up like two beacons. She rummaged in her bag to hide her discomfiture, trying not to catch Luscombe's eye. 'Mrs Baxter, if you do remember anything – anything at all – please call me. It's very important that we find out who did this.' She handed Grace her card.

'Sure. But like I said, my brother never told me much about nothin'.'

'Do you have other relatives in the UK, Mrs Baxter?'

Luscombe had stood up, was smoothing his jacket, straightening his tie.

'It's just me. Everyone else is either back home, or dead.' She paused. 'Who ... who do I talk to about...' Grace Baxter trailed off, pursed her lips. Her eyes fell to the threadbare carpet.

Charlie reached over and touched the older woman's shoulder. 'The funeral? I'll let you have the necessary contact details. Don't worry. There'll be arrangements in place for this kind of eventuality.' Charlie gave her a tight-lipped smile. 'I'm sorry we had to trouble you today, Grace. But please – call me, even if it seems like something trivial. Nothing is too small, or silly, OK?'

'OK.'

She showed them out, watched them from the doorstep.

As they drove away, Luscombe voiced Charlie's thoughts in two simple words.

'She's lying.'

'Yes. She knows something.'

'Too scared to let it out,' Luscombe said. 'Can I make a suggestion?'

'Of course.'

'She works at the hospital, right?'

'Right.'

'And what do cleaners do, apart from clean?'

Charlie considered the question. 'They chat. And gossip. And keep their ears open.'

'The hospital, then?' He turned his head towards her and the eyes did their unsettling thing.

Charlie kept her voice brusque and businesslike. 'Yep, OK. Let's do it.'

Chris Collingworth was angry. He'd been assessed – no, not just assessed, the board had put him through the mill, big time – and deemed capable of working in the higher grade of Detective Sergeant. In fact, he'd been highly commended by the board for his performance at the interview. But, for whatever reason, the powers-that-be clearly took the opposite view. What was all that about? Sure, Charlie Pepper was always going to be a tough nut to crack and, he had to admit, he'd failed in that respect. His well-honed charm offensives seemed to bounce right off her, as though she was wearing some kind of bloke-resistant armour plating. But he was getting tired of her constant needling. It was like she went out of her way to trip him up whenever she got the chance. Never took him at his word, nothing was ever good enough.

The internal vacancy had been posted just a couple of days back – Julie Stiles had come over especially to tell him she'd just seen it. That was a good sign. So he waited for Charlie Pepper to put two and two together, call him into her office, acknowledge that, despite the fact they didn't get on too well, he was clearly the guy for the role. She'd give him one of her tight smiles, congratulate him, make some comment about starting over, clean sheet and all that. Wish him the best in the new job, hope we can work well together, et cetera, et cetera.

Except it never happened.

She obviously knew about it. She got the HR notices too. She was on the email list. So. Two plus two, he wasn't going to be put up for it.

And then she'd been seconded with that Scottish geezer. Which meant she'd be out of the way for a bit, and when Moran moved into the frame for SIO, that had been one big green light for soliciting the Irishman's recommendation. If he could get that, put it in front of Higginson, make the promotion a *fait accompli* before Pepper got back, wouldn't that be a coup? He'd just love to see her face.

Collingworth ground his teeth and smouldered. He deserved better than this. He was better than the lot of them. He let his eyes wander around the office. George and Bola. Laurel and Hardy, as he privately called them, rabbiting away together like a couple of old women. Bernice Swinhoe – she was another cold fish. Pretty, though, in a forbidding kind of way. She was clicking away on her keyboard, beavering away on some Pepper-related task, no doubt. And there was Delaney, the runner, laughing at some joke with Julie – that wasn't a good sign.

And here was Moran, heading for his office, limping along as usual. Collingworth's lip curled as he watched Moran's awkward progress. There was one guy who should be put out to grass. That was the whole problem, right there: the old never wanted to make way for the young, the more capable. Moran had had his day. He was done. Why couldn't he see it? Life moves on. The world belongs to the strong.

Tomorrow belongs to me, old man…

Moran was heading in a direction that would take him past this bank of desks. Better look busy. Collingworth tapped a few keystrokes, chewed his pencil until Moran had passed by.

Gutted. Thats how he felt. He'd thought more highly of Moran's judgement, but after this morning's car crash of a conversation, it was clear that Moran was just like all the rest.

Collingworth looked at his watch. Midday. Too early for a drink? No. That's what he needed right now. Sod the investigation. It could wait.

He grabbed his jacket from the back of the chair, shrugged it over his shoulders, and headed for the lift.

CHAPTER ELEVEN

The pub was pretty quiet. Too early for most; there were a few folk dotted around the tables, just one guy at the end of the bar, nursing a half pint. Brian Carroll, the long-serving landlord of the *Falcon*, gave him a welcoming smile.

At least someone's pleased to see me ...

'Yes, young man. What can I get you?'

'Can I get a small Scotch.' Collingworth couldn't find a smile in reply. 'And a half of Tennent's.'

'Sure.'

He sat and sipped, lost in thought, until the pub began to fill up and food orders began. Collingworth wasn't hungry. He looked at his watch and grimaced. He should be getting back.

'Bad day?'

Collingworth looked up. The guy at the end of the bar had moved along, was looking at him with a mixture of amusement and ... what?

Oh, great. A gay pickup. Just what I need...

'Get you a drink?'

'No way. Look mate, you've got the wrong idea, I–'
'Chill. I'm a married man.'
'Well, that's reassuring. I have to get back to work.' Collingworth downed the last centimetre of Scotch.
'At the station, yep.' The guy cocked his head towards Thames Valley Police Station, just visible through the pub's far window. 'Busy time right now.'
Collingworth squared up to the stranger. He was a smart looking dude in an expensive dark suit. He was around thirty, clean-shaven. Looked like an insurance salesman. 'You following me, or what? Collingworth stuck his chin out.
'A minute of your time, if you will. It could be, how can I put this… beneficial for you.'
'Scuse me,' Brian Carroll stretched between them to dump a fistful of empties onto the bar.
Collingworth moved back to allow the landlord space. He contemplated just turning his back and leaving. But his curiosity was aroused, and there was something about the guy's manner that didn't fit with insurance salesmen.
'A quiet corner, perhaps?' Collingworth's new friend indicated a recently vacated corner table.
'Five minutes,' Collingworth said.
'That's plenty.'
Collingworth sat down tentatively, and the smart-suited guy took the chair opposite. 'I'll get to the point. You've been investigating an RTC, the one last night on the M4.'
'You're press, aren't you? Which paper?' Collingworth started to get up, but the man waved his suggestion away.
'No. I'm not with a newspaper.'
'Then what?' Collingworth eased himself back down onto the chair.

'Let's just say that I represent a ... government interest.'

Collingworth was paying full attention now. The murmur and hubbub of lunchtime conversation receded as he homed in on what the guy was saying.

'There are certain related matters where, if you were willing, you might be able to assist us.'

'How? In what way?' Collingworth moistened his lips, which had suddenly become very dry.

The guy talked, and Collingworth listened.

Ten minutes later he was on his way back to work, and for the first time since his earlier encounter with Moran, there was a spring in his step.

'So, no change, then?' Bola's eyes were all concern, and George appreciated the sentiment. Bola was a caring guy. Annoying at times, sure, but basically he had George's back, and that was what counted.

'Nope. Well, at one point I thought she might be trying to say something, but it's hard to tell.'

Bola nodded. 'Still losing weight, d'you think?'

'Not according to the head honcho, but she looks damn thin to me.'

'Does she know you? I mean, does she recognise you?' Bola took a gulp of coffee. The canteen was clearing out after the lunchtime rush and staff were buzzing about cleaning tables, working their way closer to where George and Bola were sitting.

'I think she knows my voice. It's hard to tell.'

'Man, it's awful.' Bola shook his head slowly. 'Why? I mean, she let this thing happen to her.'

'We can't be certain of that,' George shot back. 'She was alone with Erjon at the time.'

'Sure, sure.' Bola spoke gently. 'I know, man, I know.'

'Sorry. Don't mean to snap.' George peered into the dregs of his coffee. 'We'd best be getting on.'

'Yep.' Bola finished his coffee and stretched. 'Man, I'm bushed already. Is it just me, or is today going on forever?'

'Briefing with the guv shortly,' George reminded him. 'Your forever is about to be extended.'

'Ha. Ain't that the truth.'

As they passed the lift, the doors slid open and Chris Collingworth almost cannoned into them on his way out.

'Hey, hey,' Bola warned. 'Take it slow, man.'

'Slow is for losers,' Collingworth called back over his shoulder. 'And that's not my category.'

George felt his hackles rising.

'Down boy,' Bola said, in a mock-serious tone, 'that dog ain't worth it.'

'I'm going to kill him one day.'

'Uh uh,' Bola shook his head. 'Save your energy. Guys like Collingworth are like shooting stars, man. They start off pretty strong, but they burn themselves out a lot faster.'

Moran had already taken his place at the front by the whiteboards. George was pleased to see him. There was something reassuring about Moran's presence. You had the feeling that everything was going to be all right when the guv'nor was around. Charlie was great, but the guv – well, he was the guv. George found a chair and Bola plonked himself down next to him.

'Good afternoon ladies and gents.' Moran had hold of his stick – unusually; it was an unpopular accessory, and usually resided in the guv's office. Today, however, he was flourishing it like a weapon. 'What do we have so far? A suspected illegal, a murder that went wrong – at least at the disposal stage – and no idea of motive. Unless…?'

Moran looked out over the room, eyebrows arched. 'Collingworth? You went to Chapelfields. Anything else strike you, apart from the care worker?'

A ripple of amusement broke the ice in the room. Collingworth, as ever, seemed unfazed. George watched him bathing in the warm waters of his Lothario reputation. There was a pencil behind Collingworth's left ear, a habit that George found highly irritating.

'I'm planning on a return visit, guv,' Collingworth spoke up above the noise. 'Chat to a few of the residents, see if they can give me an angle. I'm not hopeful, though. The manager told me Daintree kept himself to himself, pretty much. Didn't like to socialise.'

'He moved down from Kingussie, correct?'

'That's right.' Collingworth nodded.

'So, that's a loose connection to DS Luscombe's victims. And, as Isaiah Marley's sister also lives in the area, I think we can safely conclude that Isaiah, for homicidal reasons among maybe other, as yet unknown, motives, followed him down here.'

'Eight months later, though,' Julie Stiles piped up. 'Why such a gap?'

'Good question.' Moran tapped the whiteboard where a recent photograph of Frank Daintree was pinned next to a sketch of Isaiah Marley's face. 'Why wait? If he intended to kill Daintree, why wait eight months? Or why even wait for him to move south?'

DC Tomlinson's hand went up. 'Maybe he couldn't get to him before? I mean, when he lived in his own house?'

'Good,' Moran nodded. 'Was he living alone at the time? Can someone make a note to ask DI Pepper? She's best placed to answer that. Come on, this is better. Keep it coming.' Moran gestured with his free hand.

'Any clues from the PM, guv?' DC Swinhoe asked.

'Nothing useful, I'm afraid. Frank Daintree wasn't a well man. Prostate cancer. Would have killed him within a year or so, Dr Bagri tells me.'

'That's even stranger then, guv.' Swinhoe frowned. 'Why go to the trouble of killing someone who was so obviously unwell?'

Tomlinson again: 'Beneficiary in Daintree's will? Maybe he couldn't wait to collect?'

'I doubt whether someone from Isaiah Marley's background would be a named beneficiary. Unlikely, but worth following up, just in case. Would you check that out please, DC Tomlinson?'

'Sure, guv.'

'Anyone else?' Moran scanned the room, the tense faces. 'All right, how about this. Marley was here illegally, he needed money, a way to survive. He kept poor company. Maybe someone offered him a job.'

'A contract killing?' George spoke up. 'But even if that were the case, we still need a motive. And to do that, we have to find the contract instigator.'

'Correct.' Moran rubbed his jaw. 'So, as you are no doubt about to suggest, DC McConnell, that takes us back to square one. We'll just have to hope that Daintree's daughter gets in touch soon. She might be the only person who can open the box of Daintree's life a little wider.'

'DS Luscombe didn't think their murders were the work of a contract killer,' DC Swinhoe said.

'There must be something,' George muttered. 'Some angle we haven't considered. It's usually one of four possibilities.' He ticked them off on his finger. 'Greed, revenge, blackmail, jealousy.'

Next to him, Bola said. 'Or hate. Hate crime is popular these days.'

'Targeting a particular demographic?' Moran mused. 'So, an ageist crime? Someone who doesn't like old people?'

DC Swinhoe nodded vigorously. 'Right. An undercover euthanasia group?'

Bola shrugged. 'Sounds crazy.'

'Most murderers are a little crazy,' George said.

'Ain't that the truth,' Bola shook his head sadly.

'Are we a hundred percent sure Cleiren didn't ram Marley's car deliberately, guv?' Bernice Swinhoe suggested. 'There still could be some connection.'

'Sure as we can be,' Moran told her. 'The footage we've seen doesn't tally with a deliberate act. Cleiren wasn't paying attention, but to be fair, he didn't have much time to react.'

'Smart motorway,' someone muttered.

'Don't mention that word,' Moran warned. 'All right. Let's go through everything again, in case we've missed something obvious. CCTV, worth another look. We need to establish where the murder took place. That's what's holding us up. We know it wasn't in the car. Once we have the location nailed, Forensics can turn the place upside down. Come on, you know how this works. We have a killer to catch. That's what we do, isn't it?' He clapped his hands to conclude the meeting, prompting a general shuffling of chairs and chorus of 'yes, guvs'.

Moran watched them disperse, hoping he'd sounded more confident than he felt. This was a strange one, and no mistake. The reality was that they had nothing, and time was slipping away.

He hoped Charlie was making better progress.

CHAPTER TWELVE

Ivy had all but obscured the once imposing gatehouse, but he knew the path so well it was second nature. The old stonework with its elaborate carvings was visible only in patches, and these were crusted with the dirt and moss of decades. No one came here any more. No one had reason to. But he liked to come anyway, to sit for a while in the stillness and contemplate the past, the present and his intentions for the future.

The old huts were still there, old even in his youth, built originally – and hastily – as billets for Canadian troops before their ill-fated journey to Dieppe, and latterly converted into classrooms within whose prefabricated walls he had been made to suffer on an almost daily basis during his time at Eagle Court.

The door to 1A was unlocked, as they all were now. Two trestle tables, four benches. The blackboard, the shelves, the window that overlooked the static water tank, turned into a makeshift swimming pool in the summer. He went to his designated place and sat down, folded his arms, closed his eyes.

It was almost spring. There were only six of them in the classroom. Five he knew from previous terms, one new boy. Only six because of the size of the school. It was what they called a crammer. They crammed you with enough knowledge to pass the exam. It was an exam-passing machine, the whole setup. He'd arrived one sunny June day, the only new boy. Extracted from his old school mid-term, separated from his friends and his usual routine, plunged into this new world of dormitories, houses, matrons and crusty, middle-aged, tweed jacket-attired overseers. Mr Millman, Mr Turner, Mr Harris, Mr Penmore. He quickly learned who to avoid, who to be wary of, and who to shun.

But in the classroom, there was no hiding place, no escape. The torture was relentless. It wasn't hard to understand why he'd been singled out. Mildly dyslexic, he'd struggled with English comprehension, languages, history, geography. These disciplines all involved skills he sadly lacked. He could not express himself clearly on paper; the words would blur, the letters crossfade into one another. Nothing made sense when he tried to write.

And the bamboo cane would be there, always, at the ready.

Now, in modern, more enlightened times, if the school had still been a going concern – and because there was now a name for his condition – things would no doubt be better. But in those dark days, there was little understanding and his condition went unrecognised. He was lazy, stupid, backward. A dummy.

An imbecile.

And, after a few months of such treatment, he began to believe them.

He opened his eyes. There was a wide cobweb in the top left-hand corner of the prefab, and a spider with long, web-spanning legs sat motionless in its centre. The paint had begun to peel from the walls, the roof was leaking and a small puddle had formed beneath the crack, rotting the wooden boards. Three damp shards of chalk still rested on the long runner beneath the blackboard.

His shoulders began to heave, and an awful noise came from the back of his throat, spewing from his mouth in a howl of anguish that shook the building. The windows rattled and the floorboards moved with the sound; the vibrations were familiar to the molecules of wood and metal that held the classroom together. A small boy's abject terror had been imprinted into its architecture as surely as the maintenance man had applied layers of paint year after year, term after interminable term, to the window frames, doors and fittings of Hut 1A, Eagle Court.

When he had regained control of himself, he rose, left the classroom. The old house still towered over the drive, its dark, empty windows staring vacantly, some with glass intact, others cracked, many just open to the elements. He could picture the corridors within, the changing room, the showers, the library, the staircases, the dormitories. The headmaster's room at the top, the eyrie that overlooked the grounds. He walked past the once-imposing front door, and into the expansive gardens. They were overgrown now, untended. He'd put that right. Once forbidden to all but the masters and prefects, in the very near future they'd be a welcoming space for all.

He found a garden seat, brushed away some stray leaves, sat down. The classrooms would have to go, of course. New buildings for the staff would replace them – smart, modern apartments. This, he realised, would probably be his last visit before the bulldozers came, at his behest, to destroy the physical conduits of his suffering. Of course, the memories would never be completely erased. Bleak, sad, friendless memories, since even his peers had taken the masters' side, mocking his shortcomings.

Only one person had buoyed his spirits in those terrible times, had seen the abuse first hand – not in the classroom maybe, but on the rugby fields. Afternoon after freezing afternoon, hands blue and brain fogged with cold, he was made to exercise his clumsy limbs up and down the field until he felt as though his mind were entirely separate from his body. A defence mechanism, of course, as he now understood.

Dropped it again, have you? Five lengths of the field. Go! …

He remembered the friendly face watching anxiously from the touchline. During a circuit of the field when he felt as though he must sink to his knees in sheer exhaustion, their eyes had met in a meaningful, lingering gaze, and he had known he had an ally at last.

They met, illegally, whenever they were able. Behind classrooms, the bike shed. In the shelter of the entrance gate in pouring rain, when everyone else was sheltering inside. They talked.

And he endured.

It was hard to imagine how things would have turned out, had they never met.

And yet, the past was still haunting him.

Maybe it always would.

The view across the downs was breathtaking. He drank it in, enjoying the movement of the trees as they were stirred by the cool currents of air. The sun emerged from behind a cloud, turned the slopes into a golden carpet. He could see sheep grazing on a distant hillside.

He was putting things to rights. That's what he was about, these days.

Perhaps, in time, he would even manage to lay his own ghosts to rest.

'Where to start?' Charlie hesitated in the hospital's entrance foyer. The area was buzzing with people coming in and out, doctors hurrying past with bundles of case notes under their arms, a few nurses chatting in groups by the coffee bar. She felt a shiver of anxiety run down her spine – it wasn't long since she'd been an in-patient herself. Not an experience she was in a hurry to repeat.

'With a pick-me-up, I suggest.' Luscombe pointed to the coffee stall.

'Great suggestion.' Charlie felt a stab of gratitude. Mrs Baxter hadn't offered them refreshments and her head was woolly with fatigue.

Luscombe bought the drinks and set them down on one of the tiny two-seater tables clustered round the coffee bar. 'Five minutes won't hurt.'

'Thanks.' Charlie stirred the cappuccino with the wooden stirrer, took a long sip.

Luscombe was watching her, as though sharing her enjoyment. 'Coffee aficionado?'

'Couldn't live without it,' she told him truthfully. 'I suppose that makes me an addict.'

He laughed. 'We're all addicted to something, whether we admit it or not.' He held her gaze and raised his cup in a toast. 'Cheers.'

'Cheers to you.' She nudged her cup against his. It felt curiously intimate.

'Me, I'm addicted to results.' He took a sip.

'Do you get them?'

He set his cup down. Two cleaners went by, side by side, chatting to each other as they went. Luscombe's eyes followed their progress until they disappeared through a set of double doors signed *Hunter Ward*. 'Oh yes. One way or another.' His eyes bored into hers until she had to look away.

When she looked at him again, he was warming his hands on the coffee cup. 'I should tell you that Isaiah Marley's name was known to us – not as a person of interest, we never got that far. We weren't sure of his full name, or even if it was his real name. But we knew of him. In fact we wanted to talk to him along with a few others in connection with Mr Lewis' death.'

Charlie was shocked. 'You didn't mention any of this at the briefing.'

'Our jurisdiction.' He shrugged. 'Your team won't get an opportunity to conduct interviews here.'

'Well, I might just decide otherwise.' Charlie bristled. 'Now I'm *in situ*. Is there anything else you elected not to mention?'

Luscombe was unruffled. 'We haven't just been sitting around, waiting for an,' he described quotation marks in the air, '*Isaiah* incident to happen somewhere else. We *have* actually done some work on the case.'

'So maybe now would be a good time to share where you've got to? So we're both on the same page?'

Luscombe took a leisurely swig of coffee. 'Of course. But first of all, I think we should catch those lovely ladies before they go off shift.' He indicated the nearby ward. 'Ready to go hunting?'

'When we're done here, I want a full debrief.' Charlie got to her feet, grabbed her bag, began to walk away.

Luscombe called after her. 'Wait. You haven't finished your coffee.'

She didn't turn around. 'No,' she flung back. 'It left a bad taste in my mouth.'

Charlie shouldered her way into the ward. The two cleaning ladies were half-way along the short corridor to the nurses' station, dipping mops into buckets and talking animatedly to each other. The space was filled with the sound of their laughter. Charlie approached them, took out her warrant card. 'Morning ladies. Can I ask you one or two questions?'

She felt Luscombe's presence behind her.

'Oh my. What have you done now, Etta?' They exchanged glances. The nearest giggled, put a hand over her mouth.

'You haven't done anything,' Charlie assured them. 'Do you know Grace Baxter?'

'Gracie? Sure, hen, Gracie's one of us.'

Charlie read her name badge. 'Thanks, Rosie. We wanted to ask if she ever mentioned her brother, Isaiah.'

Again, the swiftly exchanged look.

'Oh my Lord,' the other woman, Etta, answered. 'We didn't go a day *without* hearing about Isaiah.'

'In what regard?' Luscombe broke in.

The two woman looked Luscombe up and down. 'She worried about him all the time,' Etta said.

'Him and his fancy girl,' Rosie added.

'Fancy girl?' Charlie raised her eyebrows? 'A girlfriend?'

Grace Baxter hadn't mentioned any girlfriend.

'Sure, she worried she was leadin' him astray, right, Etta?'

'That's right,' Etta confirmed. 'She sounded like – what I call – a grabbin' woman.'

'In what way?' Luscombe had moved to Charlie's side.

Etta folded her arms. 'The kind of a woman who leads a man astray, that's what. All kinds of fancy ideas, Gracie was sayin'. Wanted it all, she did. Gracie said she don't love Isaiah, she just usin' him.'

'Do you recall a name?' Charlie prompted.

Etta frowned. 'Why don't you ask Gracie herself? She's on shift at five.'

'We'll talk to Grace,' Luscombe said. 'When we're ready.'

'Oh. All right, then.' Etta looked doubtful, exchanged a worried look with her colleague.

'You're being very helpful,' Charlie smiled. 'If you can remember a name, that would help us even more.'

Etta scratched her head. 'You remember it, Rosie?'

'I got an idea it might have been Carrie?'

'No, no.' Etta waggled her finger. 'Not Carrie. *Connie.*'

CHAPTER THIRTEEN

'Thank you for seeing me.'

'Please. Have a seat.' Moran indicated the empty visitor's chair.

Mrs Fowler sat down, placed her handbag on Moran's desk. She was a serious looking woman in her forties. Carefully styled shoulder-length auburn hair, tasteful makeup. Bright, grey-green eyes. A businesswoman through and through. Used to high-level meetings, driving home her point of view. Moran suspected he was going to experience the full force of that right now.

'So. Let me summarise. My elderly father is escorted from a safe residential care home by an unknown person, driven to an unspecified location, and smothered to death. Does that cover it?'

Moran took a deep breath. 'Yes, That's about the length and breadth of it. I'm so sorry for your loss.'

'Thank you. My father and I didn't get on particularly well. In many ways he was easier these last couple of years – the dementia. It's known to cause distress, make people hard to deal with, but in my father's case it seemed to soften him. He wasn't as obstreperous as before.'

'I see.' Moran relaxed. Maybe this wasn't going to be the ear-bending he'd anticipated. 'I assume it was at your behest that he moved here from Scotland?'

'Yes. I needed him closer, to keep an eye. I'm away a lot, but at least I didn't have to make any extra trips up north to see him every time I came home. I could just scoot over in the car, say hello, make sure he was all right.'

'I understand.'

'Fat lot of good it did, as things have turned out. Have you found the culprit? Some lunatic, I assume?'

'We're in the early stages of our investigation,' Moran told her. 'We're keeping our options open at present. Of course, when I have something concrete—'

'Yes, yes, I understand.'

Moran leaned forward, joined his hands together. 'Mrs Fowler, I have to ask; did your father have any enemies that you know of? Is there anyone he's been associated with – friends, family – who might wish him harm?'

'God. I don't know. Hundreds, probably. He always called a spade a spade. He was a teacher, you know. Not a particularly popular one, either. He was quite the disciplinarian. Old school.'

'I see. And which schools did he work at? It would be helpful if you have any documents, correspondence.'

Mrs Fowler pursed her lips. 'I have his old trunk. You're welcome to delve in there if you like. He spent many years at a prep school in Sussex. I forget the name. Then he moved to a comprehensive. Hated that. Eventually he moved to Scotland, did a little supply teaching, I think, before retiring.'

'I see. That's very helpful, thank you.'

'Tell you the truth, Chief Inspector, although it's not the way I'd have wanted him to go, I'm glad it's over. I'm sorry if that sounds callous, and of course I want the criminals brought to justice, but I can't find it in myself to be very sorry. He was an awkward old so-and-so.'

'I understand, Mrs Fowler. Did your husband get on with your father, by the way?'

Mrs Fowler hesitated before answering, straightened her back. 'My husband died ten years ago, Chief Inspector. Cancer.'

Ah. Nicely done, Moran...

'I'm so sorry. I wasn't aware.'

'Of course you weren't. It's all right. I have my business, it keeps me occupied. What's past is past, and I can't change it.'

'Indeed not.'

'Well, is that all, Chief Inspector?'

'Yes, for the time being – I'll send someone round for the trunk, if that's all right. Please don't be afraid to contact me if you remember anything you think might be relevant.'

'I'm not afraid of anything, Chief Inspector. Not anymore.'

Moran lingered in his office after Mrs Fowler had left. He recognised a fellow sufferer, someone who had loved and lost. Someone who was making the best job she could of the rest of her life, knowing it could never be the same, never be as fulfilling. Someone vital was missing, creating a void that could never be filled. He understood.

What's past is past, and it can't be changed...

The hands of Moran's wall clock made a close right

angle at three pm. Still he sat, deep in thought, his mind's compass dial inexorably fixed in the direction of Rotterdam, Fabrice Cleiren's starting point and his return destination. Something was happening in Rotterdam, which was somehow connected to Ringaskiddy, and highly probably to Joe Gallagher.

Semtex, weapons...

He had the name of Cleiren's company, the haulage firm. *Guust Vervoer*. He had an address. Interesting that no one had made contact, so far as Moran knew, to establish the fate of their driver. Which meant what? Which meant that the company didn't want to raise its head above the parapet. Its representatives surely must have found out what had happened to Cleiren? It had been reported in the media. Were they preparing themselves for an imminent investigation? Were they, even now, ensuring that their dark corners were properly hidden, that there would be no trace of impropriety when the authorities came knocking? What would they be expecting? A full-scale joint raid by customs, the Dutch police, officers from Moran's patch?

Well, for now at least, they had nothing to worry about, because Higginson was procrastinating. Yes, there was evidence of explosives, but that could be legitimate; building companies regularly used explosives. Cleiren's inventory, if it had ever existed, had been lost in the fire. Gunpowder? Could be residual from any legal shipment of munitions. No need, therefore, for counter-terrorism to get involved. People trafficking? Not enough evidence. It was a haulage accident. What about the gun? Cleiren could have been paranoid, Higginson had suggested. Just a precaution. He may even have owned a license.

ROCU involvement, then? No, Higginson had maintained, there was zero evidence – nor any sign of – organised crime in the area related to the truck, no hint of Cleiren belonging to such a gang. Taking all these factors into consideration, the matter was something to be fed back to the Dutch authorities, not for Thames Valley to deal with. When Forensics completed their investigation, as soon as they confirmed there was nothing further to be found that might relate to Isaiah Marley and his unfortunate passenger, the results – including the vehicle carcass – would be handed over to the Dutch – should they wish to conduct an investigation of their own.

Moran understood Higginson's caution, his reasoning. His priority – and therefore Moran's – was the murder investigation. But the thought of what might be happening in Rotterdam wouldn't leave Moran alone. He flicked his smartphone to *calendar*. Friday tomorrow. He could be in Rotterdam on Saturday, Friday evening even, and be back on Sunday evening. Just to satisfy his … what? Curiosity?

No, it was more than that. Much more. There was something of huge significance in this RTC, he knew it. He could feel it. And he wasn't comfortable allowing it to fall between the cracks, whatever Higginson had decided. Fate, or providence, or just blind luck had decreed that the incident should occur on Moran's patch. He might have to let it go, officially, but what he did in his own time was his own business…

Moran went to his window, looked out over the busy roundabout towards the tall, turn-of-the-century Bath Stone terraces of Castle Hill. One weekend, that was all. Two days to investigate Cleiren's destination, Rotterdam.

What did Moran know about the Dutch city? That it was Europe's largest seaport, boasted a well-respected university, enjoyed a vibrant and a lively culture, was proud of its long maritime heritage. There it was again: that connection to the water. Europe's largest port...

Moran wiped a smear of condensation from the glass, returned to his desk.

The Chapelfields murder was shocking, absolutely, and needed to be addressed as a priority. But Cleiren's ill-fated journey represented something of a different order, something much bigger than a parochial homicide, of that Moran was convinced.

George McConnell put his head around the door. 'Guv?'

'Yes, George?'

George waved his smartphone. 'I've got Charlie on the blower. She wants a word.'

'Sure.'

George handed the phone to Moran and half-retreated, hovering in the doorway.

Moran listened as Charlie brought him up to date. 'Good work,' he said. 'I'll get someone round to Chapelfields pronto.'

He finished the call and gestured to George. 'Come in, George, for goodness' sake.' He returned the phone. 'You and Bola – get over to the nursing home as soon as. That care worker Collingworth interviewed? Looks like there's a good chance she's Isaiah Marley's girlfriend.'

'Right you are.' George's eyes lit up at the prospect of action. 'So, you don't want Collingworth to do the deed?'

'Not this time. In fact, if you could ask him to pop in, I'd like a word.'

George beamed. 'With pleasure, guv.'

CHAPTER FOURTEEN

Collingworth left Moran's office with a face like thunder. Sidelined again. Well that was the last straw. How fortuitous, then, that he knew exactly what to do about it.

The guy in the pub had supplied him with some very interesting information. He'd heard rumours about Moran's recent weekend 'problem' – some kind of hostage situation where some weirdo had held him at gunpoint. It had all been swept under the carpet, and for good reason too, it seemed. He understood from a long-serving sergeant downstairs that it had something to do with Moran's early days as a *Garda* in Ireland. Which fitted with what the pub guy had told him. Dodgy past, dodgy goings-on in the present. Had to be true, if the security services were onto it.

So, all in all, Collingworth mused, he was in a *very* strong position. Information is power, especially when there was a plan afoot to topple the dodgy goings-on once and for all. Who knows? His involvement might accelerate his career way more than a mere sergeant's board could ever hope to. He'd done what he'd been asked to. Now, all he had to do was watch and wait. That was the name of this game.

Watch and wait...

'Temp staff?' Bola pressed the question. 'So, what's Chan's background? Where might she have gone?'

Judith Miller folded her arms over her ample bosom. 'I have no idea, Detective Constable Odunsi. Where the casual staff go after they've worked here is not something we monitor very closely.'

'OK,' George butted in, 'let's start again. Connie Chan came to you three weeks ago. Through an agency.'

'Yes, we get most of our care workers though the agency.'

'And you were satisfied with her conduct, her work ethic while she was here?'

'Yes. She worked hard, got on fine with the residents.' Judith Miller shrugged. 'There was nothing remarkable about her. Apart from her looks, of course. Very pretty. Malaysian, I believe.'

'Did she talk a lot?' Bola asked. 'With the other staff? You know, chat? Gossip?'

'Well, you'll have to ask around. I'm always rather busy in the office, or attending to new admissions, or any particular crisis on any given day – they happen a lot, you understand, the residents being the age they are.'

'Did she have any special interaction with Mr Daintree?' George was tapping his forefinger on the desk.

'Special? Well, she would have taken him his meals. Wheeled him into the lounge to socialise – not that he was a very social sort of gentleman. Brought him a cup of tea when appropriate, that sort of thing. All very normal.'

'And what shifts did she tend to work?' Bola could feel George's impatience, feel the explosion brewing.

'Oh, that's easy. Hang on.' Mrs Miller tapped her computer keyboard. 'Here we are.' She swivelled the screen so the two detectives could see. 'All evening shifts. I remember she said she had some cleaning job during the day. They often do – have more than one job on the go, I mean.'

'What was the agency's name again?' Bola's pen was at the ready.

'Blue Javelin. There's a girl called Sara we usually speak to about vacancies.'

'Thank you.' Bola tucked his notebook away. 'Is there anything else you think might be of help, Mrs Miller? Anything unusual you remember about Connie Chan, or maybe something one of the other staff members may have spotted?'

'I really can't think,' Judith Miller frowned. 'You'll have to speak to the rest of the staff to see if they can remember anything. I can make a room available for you.'

'Great – let's get on with it.' George stood up.

'I can't believe that little Connie Chan could have been involved in anything.' Mrs Miller shook her head. 'She was so sweet. Graceful, too. You know, like the Malaysians are. Very respectful.'

'That could be exactly what she wanted you to think.' Bola had also got to his feet. 'Thanks for your time, Mrs Miller.'

'My pleasure. I do hope you find out what happened. I feel so terrible. That poor man.'

'We will,' George assured her. 'We always do.'

'We're not getting anywhere,' George said. 'No one knows anything. Damned agency weren't much help, either. Worth calling them again?'

'Nope, I don't reckon,' Bola replied. 'Her references all looked good, according to Sara Catton. All written up on company-headed paper. They all looked legit.'

'But did they actually try to contact the referees?'

'Not as such. Chan talked a good story, as they say. And a written testimonial carries more weight than a phone call. Like I said, it looked legit.'

'Yeah, right. Counterfeit money looks legit too, until you take a really close look at it.'

'They didn't try to place her in another contract?'

'Nope. She signed off, and went off.'

'OK, so what now?' Bola was feeling George's frustration. Chan was a ghost. Here one minute, vanished the next.

'Let's get back. Maybe someone's come up with something.'

They left the bedroom which Judith Miller had provided for them. 'It's empty,' she'd told them. 'Resident died last week. Help yourselves.'

George lingered in the hall. 'Better sign out.' He picked up the supplied biro, scanned down the visitors' sheet. One of the residents was making slow, painful progress along the corridor; her Zimmer clunked on the carpet, she shuffled to meet it and then it clunked forward again. Bola caught the woman's eye as she inched slowly towards them, her mouth set in a determined line, gnarled hands gripping the frame for all she was worth. Bola beamed her a smile of encouragement.

'That's it,' George said. 'Lets be off.'

'Wait.' The voice was weak, tremulous, but both George and Bola picked up the note of urgency.

'Hello,' Bola reprised his smile. 'Do you need any help?' Perhaps she needed assistance to manoeuvre herself into the lift.

'No, but you might.' She came to a halt, puffing for breath. Thirty seconds passed as the old woman recovered from her exertion. George and Bola waited politely.

'Is there something you'd like to tell us?' Bola asked her.

A bell rang. The woman shook her head. 'Tea time. Luke-warm and weak as cats' pee.'

George glanced at Bola. *Let's move on.* He began to punch in the exit code.

'Elizabeth Hurleigh. Not the movie star. With an 'eigh'.' She raised her hand, waved it briefly in the air. 'I can't shake. I might topple over.'

'That's fine, no problem,' Bola told her. George was wrong. Mrs Hurleigh was totally *compos mentis.*

'The girl, isn't it? The one who came and went? You want to know about her? Well, I'll tell you a few things.' Another pause for breath. 'Emphysema,' she explained. 'It'll see me off in the end. But I'm all right if I take it slowly.'

'In your own time.' George was giving her his full attention now.

'All smiles, that one, until she was alone with you. Sadistic streak. Used to taunt me. Keep my food and drink out of reach. Make me think I'd forgotten to take my medicine. Made me question my sanity.' Another breath. 'But I worked her out.'

Bola was shocked. He'd heard about this kind of thing, but never experienced it. 'She abused you? Did you tell anyone?'

'No point.' The hand waved again. 'In any case, 'abused' is a strong word. She had a cruel streak in her, that's how I'd put it. She enjoyed being in a position of power. And that Miller, she's useless. Never around when you need her. Place is run by the carers. Some are all right, others not. Miller keeps herself away from the nitty-gritty. And besides, she liked Ms Chan.' Hurleigh raised an eyebrow. 'If you understand my meaning? Any complaints would have fallen on deaf ears.'

'Ah. I see.' George tapped the side of his nose.

'Look, would you like to sit down?' Bola pointed to the lounge door. He could see one or two residents dozing in their chairs.

'You're joking. Took me ten minutes to get up. Let's savour the achievement.' More deep, painful breaths followed.

'So, about this Ms Chan, you wanted to tell us something specific?' George encouraged her. Elizabeth Hurleigh reminded him of his late mother. She had endured a similar condition, and eventually, after months of suffering, her end had indeed come.

'That night. When Mr Daintree left. I saw her in the car park.'

'Mr Daintree was collected by a young man,' Bola said. 'Did you see him leave?'

Hurleigh shook her head. Her hair was thin and grey, clinging to her scalp, but her eyes were bright and sharp. 'Not then, but later. She went out the back. I saw her, from the kitchen – she left the building.'

'So,' George frowned. 'She left the premises after Mr Daintree. Did she come back? What happened then?'

'It was at least an hour later. I saw her from my bedroom window. I always sit by the window. Gives me something to look at. She came around the back, didn't use the front door.'

'So, she bunked off her shift, for reasons unknown, returned later that same evening.'

'That is correct. And she didn't want anyone to know.' Elizabeth Hurleigh broke into a fit of coughing. Bola felt a mixture of compassion and helplessness as he waited for her to recover. 'I'm sorry,' she said eventually.

'Take your time. You said she didn't want anyone to know?' George prompted. 'How do you know that?'

'She lied. I heard her.' Hurleigh was emphatic. 'Told the Miller woman she'd attended to her duties all evening. Nothing to report. Of course, they quizzed her about Mr Daintree. She mentioned nothing about her absence, just said he was collected as scheduled.'

'I see.' Bola said. 'This is very helpful, Mrs Hurleigh.'

'Well, I hope so,' she replied. 'Daintree was a miserable old sod, but he didn't deserve that. Oh, by the way, she spun the other policeman a whole lot of nonsense, too. I made it a priority to park outside Miller's office when she was in there.'

'You're very astute, Mrs Hurleigh.' George said. 'Thank you for your observations.'

'No one pays any attention when you're this age,' she said. 'They think you're doolally. But I keep my ear to the ground. Keeps me on an even keel.'

'Well, thank you again for the information,' George said. Hurleigh was clearly struggling to keep hold of the Zimmer. She needed to sit down.

'I'm not finished.' She looked George up and down.

'This'll be familiar to you, young man, judging by your accent.' With a huge effort she kept one hand on the frame, delved into her handbag – which was hanging by its strap from the Zimmer's handlebar – and produced a piece of paper. 'Here. I found this.'

'Thank you.' Bola accepted the paper. 'What is it?'

'I found it. In her housecoat. Call me nosy, but I knew she was up to no good.'

Bola examined the paper, and George peered over his shoulder. 'A complement slip. Chapelfields, Aviemore.' Bola's eyebrows went up. 'There's another residential care home with the same name in Scotland? Chapelfields?'

'Yes, yes. There are ten homes altogether, I believe – and there are plans for more. All run by the same person, the entrepreneur Duncan Brodie. You must have heard of him, surely? One of the richest men in Scotland.'

'Now you mention it, yes,' George confessed. 'He's been on TV. Mousy little chap. Glasses.'

'That's the man.' Hurleigh nodded. 'Very shy, so they say. Hardly looks the part, but there we are. Looks can be deceiving. Anyway, does that help at all?'

On the paper was written in scrawled biro: *meet King's X. 09.45. I x*

'King's Cross. That's the station for all points north, right?' Bola flicked the corner of the complements slip.

George rubbed his hands together. 'Yep. Train to Edinburgh. Connections to Aviemore, among others. We'd better let Charlie know that a little bird is on her way home.'

He turned to thank Mrs Hurleigh, but the old lady had already shuffled off on her way.

'Much obliged,' he called after her frail figure.

A gnarled hand was raised briefly in acknowledgment. They watched as their unlikely informant turned the corner and was gone.

CHAPTER FIFTEEN

The hotel room was exactly as Charlie had anticipated – characterless, but clean and tidy. She plonked herself on the bed, flopped onto her back. Her eyes were gritty and her mouth felt dry and dehydrated. It had been a long day.

Luscombe had dropped her off at the Premier Inn with a promise to collect her at eight sharp tomorrow. She'd wanted to ask him what his plans were for the evening, but couldn't formulate the question in a way that didn't sound as though she was angling for an offer. She hadn't quizzed him about his private life, though she'd been sorely tempted. He didn't wear a ring – not that that necessarily meant anything. If he'd offered her hospitality of any kind, though, she'd have jumped at it.

What are you thinking, Charlie?

She groaned, covered her eyes. It had been a long time since there'd been anyone special in her life. The job wasn't conducive to relationships, a lesson she'd learned from two previously shipwrecked liaisons. She wasn't looking for anyone, was reluctant to even consider the possibility of finding a partner.

A lover…

And again, Luscombe's easy manner, the way he carried himself, the way his eyes bored into hers, rose to the forefront of her mind, chipping away at her emotions like an archaeologist seeking to uncover the true state of something long-buried.

Oh dear, Charlie, oh dear…

She let her arms fall to her sides. She could hear the background noise of traffic, the murmur of conversation, snatches of dialogue as guests hurried by in the corridor. She allowed her mind to wander and a parade of images drifted across her subconscious: the distant Cairngorm mountains, the glassy surface of the lake they had passed *en route*, the tall pines, the bleak open spaces that somehow filled her heart with longing.

She drifted into unconsciousness and the images skewed towards the surreal. She was climbing a sheer rock face. Luscombe was above, encouraging her. Her limbs were leaden. She looked down and vertigo hit her hard. Her head spun. She heard Luscombe calling, cajoling, bullying her to carry on. She grabbed a handhold, a slim outcrop of rock, but it gave way in her hand. She twisted on the rope, tried to maintain her footing but that was crumbling too. Her feet scrabbled for purchase and found nothing but empty air.

An eagle flew overhead, its beady eyes regarding her disdainfully as if to say: this is *my* domain. She felt the breath of its wings. She clung to the rope, spinning round and round. Luscombe's voice was receding. He'd given up on her, left her to her fate. The rope was catching, she could feel the rock cutting into the hemp as she hung helplessly, dangling from the mountainside. It wouldn't hold. She had to grab something, *anything…*

Her hands reached out, but the rock had become smooth, glassy. There was nothing to hold onto.

This is it, Charlie…

The rope above her was a thread, down to a single strand.

It separated with a jerk and she was free-falling, turning over and over and over…

The phone on her bedside table jangled and her eyes jerked open. Her fingers were clinging to the bedclothes like claws, her heart racing.

A dream. Just a dream…

The relief made her giddy. She sat up, reached over and picked up the phone.

'Charlie Pepper.'

'Finally,' Luscombe's voice said. 'I thought for a moment you'd run out on me.'

Her sleepy brain struggled to make sense of the statement. 'What? Sorry. I fell asleep.'

'Two things.' Luscombe sounded amused. 'First, your guv is trying to get hold of you. Second, I'm at a loose end this evening. Wondered if you fancied tackling a steak and a bottle of red. There's a nice wee place just down the road from where you are. I could pick you up in, say, forty-five minutes?'

Charlie's head reeled. 'Right, er, sorry, I'm not really with it. Yes, that sounds great. No shop talk, maybe?'

'No shop talk,' Luscombe agreed. 'See you shortly.'

Charlie replaced the receiver, went to check her mobile. Dead battery. That explained it. She mussed her hair, fumbled in her handbag for the charger, plugged it in. She sat at the cheap dressing table, looked at her drawn face in the mirror. *God, I can't go out looking like this…*

Her mobile sprang to life, the screen filling with missed call messages. She found Moran's number, waited for him to pick up.

'Moran?'

'Hello, guv. Sorry, battery was dead. You were trying to get me?'

'I was. Interesting development.'

She listened as Moran's mild Irish tones filled her ear. By the time he'd finished, she was wide awake. 'Right,' she summarised, 'so Chapelfields is a chain of homes run by this Brodie guy. And Isaiah Marley has a clear connection to the one here in Aviemore?'

'That's about it, yes. He wrote a note to his girlfriend on the home's notepaper.'

'We'll pay them a visit first thing tomorrow. And the girlfriend, she might be headed our way?'

'Well, we thought so.' Moran sounded a little distracted. He paused for a few seconds until she felt she had to check to see if he was still there.

'Sorry, Charlie. A lot going on here.'

'Sure. The girlfriend?'

'Yes. They had a rendezvous arranged – Chan and Marley – at King's Cross. But as far as we can tell, she was a no-show. George and Bola's eyes have changed shape staring at the CCTV footage; no sign of her yet, but we're still keeping an eye out. Their plans were sabotaged by the RTC, is my gut feeling, so her next move is anyone's guess. She may have other contacts, friends, relatives.'

'So, she could have gone to ground with anyone, anywhere?' Charlie replied. The guv sounded uncharacteristically vague. This wasn't like him, not at all.

'See what you can dig up at Chapelfields in Aviemore,' Moran said. 'Isaiah Marley was employed there in some capacity, despite what his sister might have told you about his employability.'

'Righto, guv. Will do.'

'I'll keep you in touch with developments,' Moran promised. 'Keep your phone handy.'

'Sure. Sorry, I'll make sure it's charged.'

After the call, Charlie sat for a minute, thinking hard. Marley and Chan. What was the motive? Why would they kill a helpless old man? Daintree had had nothing stolen from his room in Reading – he had no worldly goods to steal. Unless, as the guv had surmised, they were acting on behalf of somebody else.

She glanced at the clock and her heart jumped. Luscombe would be here in fifteen minutes and she still looked a state. Charlie abandoned the conundrum, stripped off her clothes and headed for the shower.

CHAPTER SIXTEEN

The following morning, Charlie heard Luscombe's *beep* bang on eight-thirty. She grabbed her bag and closed the bedroom door. The faint odour of fried eggs and bacon wafted along the hotel corridor from the restaurant but she wasn't hungry; she'd eaten enough for two the night before – and drunk too much wine to boot. Luscombe had proved to be engaging company, regaling her with Highland tales past and present. He was a natural raconteur, so she'd been able to sit back, relax and enjoy the meal.

Luscombe hadn't strayed into his personal life at all, which was curious and yet, in a way, also something of a relief. He'd dropped her back at the hotel around ten-thirty and she'd fallen into a dreamless sleep twenty minutes later.

Beep beep!

She hurried past the checkout desk and into the car park. Luscombe opened the passenger door and muttered a cursory 'morning' before joining the traffic and eventually merging onto the Grampian Road. He preempted her first question with a gruff statement: 'Not far.' From this she concluded that he wasn't in a talkative mood and the rest of the short journey passed in silence until they turned into a wide driveway signed *Chapelfields Residential Care Home*.

Mrs Fiona Brodie was a handsome woman in her late fifties. If she was surprised to find two detectives on her doorstep she was hiding it well. Her manner exuded calm professionalism. She ushered Charlie and Luscombe into a spacious lounge where one or two residents were dozing in a corner with the TV flickering silently above them on a hinged wall bracket. It was very warm. Mrs Brodie invited them to sit down and Luscombe opened the proceedings.

'Does the name Isaiah Marley mean anything to you?'

Charlie noted her reaction. There was no attempt at evasion. Instead, Mrs Brodie nodded and said, 'Yes, Isaiah worked with us for a short time. A little admin, some driving on occasion.'

'Were you aware that he was in the country illegally?' Charlie asked.

'Illegally? Goodness me. No, not at all.'

Luscombe probed further. 'There must have been paperwork, references, prior to you taking him on?'

Mrs Brodie frowned. 'Well, my husband usually takes care of that side of things; his secretary would have run the standard checks.'

'Can we speak to his secretary?'

'Ah, well, she works remotely. It's a company we use – a virtual PA and secretarial service. I can give you the details, if you like.'

'That would be helpful,' Charlie said. 'Where is your husband at the moment, Mrs Brodie?'

'Away on business.'

Charlie nodded. 'And when are you expecting him back?'

Mrs Brodie made a non-committal gesture. 'Who knows?' She gave a short laugh. 'He comes back when he's concluded whatever deal he's currently working on.'

'I see.' Luscombe frowned. 'Are we able to contact him?'

'What exactly is the problem, Detective Sergeant?'

Luscombe looked at Charlie, held her gaze. Was he asking her permission? Or were those eyes telling her something else? She gave an imperceptible nod, looked away.

'Isaiah Marley was killed in a road traffic collision a few days ago,' Luscombe's tone was conversational. 'But we believe that he may have been involved in the murder of his passenger. An elderly gentleman.'

'Murder?'

'So anything you can tell us about Mr Marley would be enormously helpful,' Charlie suggested.

Mrs Brodie looked genuinely shocked. 'Murder? Isaiah? No, no. That's not right. He's such a gentle soul. Was. Oh dear, how awful.' Her hand went to her mouth. 'Always kind, nothing was too much trouble.'

Luscombe rolled out his next question. 'How long was he in your service, Mrs Brodie?'

'Oh, I don't know. A few months, on and off.'

Charlie leaned forward. The temperature was beginning to get to her. Her eyelids felt heavy. 'Mrs Brodie, did Isaiah ever mention a girlfriend? Or did you ever see him with a woman?'

Mrs Brodie toyed with her necklace. 'No, I don't recall. But then, you see, we're always on the go here. We have people coming in and out, visiting you understand, all the time. And on top of that we have nurses, the occasional doctor, deliveries. Oh, the list goes on. But I don't remember ever seeing Isaiah with a woman, no.'

'He wasn't … friendly, with any staff member in particular, I mean?'

'It's hard work here, Detective Inspector. I simply don't have time to notice any romantic dalliances that may be blossoming under our roof, and neither would I expect any staff member to behave in such an unprofessional manner during working hours.'

'You've built up quite a business,' Luscombe observed. 'Ten care homes, is it?'

'There's a need, Detective Sergeant. We are in the privileged position of being able to fulfil that need.'

'Quite a success story, your husband.' Luscombe said. 'He's becoming something of a celebrity.'

'The television appearances? Oh, I suppose so. But look, he doesn't enjoy the limelight. He's not like that. He just has a knack, I suppose you could call it. A good head for business.'

'You'll have heard about the two local murders?' Luscombe changed tack. 'Both elderly gentlemen.'

'Yes, of course. Have you not found the perpetrator yet?'

'We're working on it,' Luscombe said. 'It's only a matter of time.'

'Tell me, are these events connected in some way?' Mrs Brodie frowned. 'How do you imagine we can help?'

'Just routine enquiries for the moment,' Luscombe said.

Charlie took over. 'We'll leave it there for the time being, Mrs Brodie. I'm sure you have a lot to be getting on with. Thank you for your time.' She stood up, extended her hand. Mrs Brodie's grip was dry and firm.

'My pleasure.'

Luscombe nodded. 'You're not from around these parts, Mrs Brodie?' He pitched the question at her retreating back as they followed her through the lounge double-doors and into the hall.

She paused by the front entrance. 'No. I was brought up in England. They tell me I'm sounding more Scottish every day, though.'

'You've a way to go yet,' Luscombe shot her a dour smile. 'I can always tell a local from an outsider.'

'Well, I don't feel like an outsider any more, Detective Sergeant. I feel very at home here.'

Luscombe buttoned his jacket. 'We'll be in touch. And I'd appreciate it if you could let us know when your husband intends to return.'

'I'll be sure to ask. Good day to you.'

'About time you met the team,' Luscombe said over his shoulder as they waited for the lift. 'They're a good lot.'

'I don't doubt it.' When she was sure Luscombe wasn't looking, Charlie surreptitiously checked her appearance in the lift mirror. She hooked a stray lock of hair behind her ear as the doors slid open onto a short corridor. Luscombe banged through a set of double doors and Charlie followed before they closed on her.

Heads turned.

'Morning all.' Luscombe led Charlie towards a corner

desk and waved vaguely in her direction. 'DI Charlie Pepper, Thames Valley.'

There was a chorus of hellos. Charlie counted five in the team altogether.

'Just had a call from James McMillan's son, Sarge.'

'Oh, aye?' Luscombe hung his jacket over his chair and indicated a spare for Charlie. 'Have a seat, by the way.' He turned to the officer who had spoken, a girl in her late twenties with strikingly pale skin, Scandinavian for sure, Charlie thought. Luscombe encouraged her with a jut of his chin. 'What'd he have to say for himself, Jenny?'

'He said he'd remembered something that might be something, might be nothing.'

'Namely?'

'Just that his father was due to give up his house next month. Mr McMillan junior said he wasn't sure if he'd mentioned it before.'

'I don't recall that he did. So that's it? He was giving up his house? To move in with his son?'

'No, Sarge, he was due to move to a care home, the big place on the Grampian? One of Duncan Brodie's homes.'

'Was he indeed?' Luscombe sat on the edge of his desk, hands in pockets. 'Thank you Jenny, that's very interesting, because DI Pepper and myself have just come from said establishment. Are you thinking what I'm thinking, DI Pepper?'

'Why would Mrs Brodie not have mentioned it?' Charlie pursed her lips. 'She's bound to be up to speed with upcoming vacancies, new applications and the like.'

'Quite. And we did mention the two murders specifically.' Luscombe nodded. 'There are two sins a person of interest can commit. Sins of commission, and–?' He looked at each officer in turn.

It was Jenny who finished his sentence. 'Sins of *omission*.'

CHAPTER SEVENTEEN

Jenny drove in silence, despite Charlie's attempts to encourage conversation. All she got back was one *yes* and two *nos*. The silence was uncomfortable and Charlie was glad when they pulled up at the nursing home.

'Oh, hello again.' Mrs Brodie looked surprised. The clank and clink of food preparation spilled out into the car park. Lunch was underway.

'Sorry to trouble you,' Charlie said. She glanced over her shoulder at Jenny, standing a pace behind her. 'This is DC Armitage, by the way.' Charlie could feel Jenny's hostility sweeping up and down her spine like a laser. *I've touched a nerve here, somewhere...*

Mrs Brodie was looking at her quizzically, so she hurried on. 'There's one other thing we need to clarify. Sorry if it's an inconvenient time.'

'Not at all. We're fully staffed today. Come in, come in.' Mrs Brodie stood to one side.

Charlie braced herself for the wave of warmth, this time laced with the smell of cabbage and boiled meat. Her stomach contracted involuntarily. They followed Mrs

Brodie into the lounge once more, and this time the manageress offered them a seat by a table piled high with well-thumbed magazines.

'Thanks. May I have a look at your waiting list?' Charlie asked brightly.

'Our waiting list? Well–'

'If it's not too much trouble. You do keep a record? Nice home like this, you're bound to have folk queuing up to get in, I'll bet.'

Mrs Brodie gathered herself. 'Of course. One moment.'

'I'll go with her.' Without waiting for Charlie's response, Jenny followed Mrs Brodie.

Charlie watched, a little nonplussed. The Detective Constable had been all smiles at the station, but as soon as Luscombe had departed, the shutters had come down. Charlie sighed. *Maybe I'm stepping on toes here...*

Whatever. It would have to wait. *Mind on the job, Charlie.*

The manageress was rattled, that much was clear. *Catch 'em on the back foot*, Moran always said. If the Brodies were hiding something, Charlie was set on winkling it out. She wondered how Luscombe was getting on with Mrs Baxter. He'd charm the information out of her, she had no doubt. The Scot's easy manner would charm any member of the opposite sex – a disquieting thought. Charlie felt a frisson of jealousy prickle the hairs on her arm.

'Here we are.' Mrs Brodie reappeared with Jenny. The DC was carrying an A4-sized ledger which she set down on the table next to Charlie with a testy flourish.

'You'll both excuse me for a wee minute?' Mrs Brodie said. 'I like to be on hand during lunch service.'

'Of course. Don't let us hold you up,' Charlie replied.

The ledger began in 2015. They went through it page

by page. 2016. 2017. The names and addresses were inscribed in the same meticulous handwriting. Charlie scanned down the list until her attention was caught by one entry. Her heart gave a little lurch.

McMillan, James, dob 12/10/32, G-on-Spey

There. 'Jenny, could you take a photo?'
'Sure.' Jenny took out her smartphone, snapped the entry. Charlie took a place mat from the table, inserted it in the ledger. Her finger travelled down the page, turned to the next, and the next. The din of clinking cutlery was escalating, the tinny chatter peppered with the entreaties and encouragements of staff members. The strains of *Happy Birthday* drifted in with the kitchen smells, followed by a smattering of half-hearted applause.
God, don't let me end up in a place like this…
Charlie's fingers moved down the ledger, and half way down 2018, she found it. 'Here we go.'

Daintree, Francis dob 05/05/35, Inverness

Unprompted, Jenny took a second snap, slipped the phone into her bag.
There it was in black and white. Two pensioners, both with their names down for Chapelfields.
Both murdered.
Charlie felt a thrill of exhilaration.
Right, Mrs Brodie, let's pose a few more questions, shall we?

'That's weird. They sang *Happy Birthday* at Chapelfields.' Charlie wrinkled her nose. 'I won't ask what the damage is.'

'No secret,' Luscombe grinned. 'Thirty-nine and still breathing.'

'Well, congratulations. I'd have got you a card if you'd told me earlier.'

The station had cleared; just Charlie and Luscombe were left. Outside, rain pattered on the tarmac, sprayed against the windows in wind-driven flurries.

'Och, it's a working day. And I don't like a fuss.'

'Typical bloke.'

Luscombe laughed. 'Well, thank you, ma'am.'

'No *ma'am*, remember?' Charlie furrowed her brow. 'So, are you celebrating tonight?'

'Maybe. But business first. Tell me about Mrs Brodie.'

'Brodie was all right. It was Jenny I had a problem with. Or rather, vice versa.'

Luscombe snorted. 'Pay no heed. Jenny's all right. Can be a wee bit moody.'

'You don't say.' Charlie laughed. 'Anyway, Brodie. Evasive, I'd call her. Thing is, 'Daintree' had been circled in the ledger, *and* underlined. That implies significance, but when I put that to her she just shrugged and explained it away with some comment about a telephone reminder or some such.'

'Bullshit.'

'Agreed. But how do we play it?'

'Husband due back soon?'

'She wouldn't be drawn. He has a new project – another Chapelfields home down south. Sussex, apparently. Could be away for weeks, overseeing the builders et cetera, et cetera.'

'So, no further. I–'

Charlie shook her head. 'Wait. I also spoke to one of the care workers while Mrs Brodie was busy in the dining room. She knew Isaiah.'

Luscombe was paying full attention now.

'She remembers a woman – a very pretty lady, as she called her. Used to pop in when Isaiah was working. Clearly a love interest.'

'Description?'

'Oriental. Beautiful.'

Luscombe whistled. 'Hello, Connie Chan.'

'Mrs Brodie still denied anyone of that description was ever around the home.'

Luscombe wagged his finger. 'The lying wee madam.'

'And Mrs Baxter?'

'Ah. We talked about life for a while. She brought the subject up herself – Isaiah's woman. Only met her the once, she said, but once was enough. She says she doesn't like to think about her. That the first time she set eyes on her, she knew it was going to end badly for Isaiah.'

'Oh?'

'She said the first thing she did after Connie Chan left her house was double-lock the doors.'

CHAPTER EIGHTEEN

Moran was impressed. The railway station was located thoughtfully just a few steps from the Schiphol Airport concourse. Moreover, the noticeboard proclaimed the Rotterdam train to be due at 10:07, and at 10.07 precisely the train swished silently into view, an achievement that spoke volumes about the Dutch way of getting things done.

Just under an hour later he emerged from Rotterdam Centraal station, slightly bewildered and very conscious of being alone in a strange city. A large route map, situated conveniently just outside the station frontage drew his attention, and he quickly plotted a theoretical route to the hotel, which, if he elected to walk, Moran reckoned he should reach in twenty minutes or so.

As he walked, he felt again the buzz of nervous anticipation, the same buzz he'd felt as Collingworth had handed him the latest forensic find from Cleiren's burned-out truck. The contents of the plastic bag were charred, but still readily identifiable: a credit card. And not just any credit card. The name had been partially erased, the corner of the card destroyed by the heat, but the remaining letters had been easy to read:

... *mantha Grant.*

It had shaken him, he had to admit. But here at last was a clear connection. He knew at that point that a visit to Rotterdam was no longer optional, it was mandatory. Ireland, the Netherlands, Russia – and Samantha the link in the chain of events which joined them all together. Was she here? Or was he too late? It didn't take much imagination to figure out what Russian Intelligence might do with an MI5 agent unfortunate enough to fall into their hands.

Barring the number of bicycles and ever-present tram lines, the streets of Rotterdam were not unlike those of any other European city. He passed a McDonald's which was doing a lively trade, cafés, clothes shops, restaurants, bars. A tall building loomed on the opposite side of the road, the headquarters of Robeco, and Moran's first landmark. He crossed two main roads, a wide, open space which he surmised was reserved for some kind of regular market, and eventually found his hotel wedged between a bar and a mini supermarket.

Moran's mobile buzzed just as he was scanning his keycard. He pushed into the hotel room and threw his bag on the bed.

'Guv?'

'Hello, DC Swinhoe. What can I do for you?'

'Just had an update from Charlie, guv. They've got another connection to Chapelfields. One of Luscombe's victims was due to move in there, but the manageress forgot to mention this fact when Charlie and Luscombe interviewed her.'

'So they'll be speaking to the good lady again, I trust?'
'Yes, I believe so.'
'Any sign of the girlfriend?'
'Not yet. Kings Cross is a definite no-show – we'd have spotted her by now.'
'So she may not be heading for Aviemore.' Moran thought for a second. 'Has anyone checked back at Isaiah Marley's bedsit?'

A brief silence. 'Um, no, I don't think so.'

'There you go. Worth a look. She could have backtracked, decided to hole up there for a few days. She's probably sussed out that the police have inspected the room – i.e. been and gone.'

'Good point, guv.'

'And I'd ask Charlie to pose a few more questions regarding Chapelfields' waiting list. What's the process, how do they admit new residents, and so on. It might tell us something.'

Another brief silence, a little longer this time.

Moran figured the reason. 'You can tell DI Pepper that you've spoken to me – my suggestion.'

'Right. Thanks, guv. Will do.'

Moran signed off, smiling at Bernice Swinhoe's well-tuned sensibilities. Teaching granny to suck eggs was probably not the best way to endear yourself to a senior officer, even one as reasonable and well-balanced as Charlie Pepper.

Moran sat on the bed and inspected Cleiren's company address. It was in the dockside area – by his calculations, a ten minute walk, maximum. He'd decided on a direct approach for two reasons: first, to test the waters for a possible later, more clandestine, visit; and second, to witness the company's reaction to what he had to say firsthand. A risky strategy, especially if his suspicions proved to be correct, but time was short. He had the remainder of the day and the best part of tomorrow before his evening flight. And one other possible timeframe.

The wee, small hours.

George held Tess' hand in his. It was limp and lifeless, but she was looking at him intently, as though some faint flicker of recognition was fighting to get through. Encouraged, George prattled on.

'We've made *some* progress, but it's a bizarre case, to say the least. Two dead in Scotland. Same MO as our Mr Daintree in Reading. Marley's girlfriend's vanished. Literally. And she's the key to all this.' George let Tess' hand drop gently into her lap. 'So, where we go from here, I have no idea. Charlie's running with a lead in Aviemore, but there's no guarantee she'll turn up anything much.' He smiled, shook his head. 'I don't know where to look next, that's the truth of it. We've got an empty bedsit, nothing in the record books, and a dead pensioner who surely didn't deserve to die the way he did.'

A sunbeam chased across the faded carpet, lit up Tess' face. She blinked, moved her hand to shade her eyes. This was a good sign, surely? Her reactions were more finely tuned than he'd noticed before.

'Here, I'll draw the curtains a little.' George made as if to get up, but her arm reached out and rested gently on his. Shocked, he sank back onto the hard surface of the chair, his heart thumping. She'd never responded like that before. 'I'll leave them open, shall I?' He swallowed.

There was a sharp knock on the door and one of the

carers breezed in, retrieved a tray from Tess' bedside table, cleared the crockery and cutlery into a plastic container, stacked the empty tray on top of the others. George caught her eye. 'She moved – I mean, she made a deliberate physical action.'

'That's good,' the young woman replied. 'You're obviously helping.'

'Yes, yes. I hope so.' George turned back to Tess who had reverted to her customary blank expression. 'Anyway, what was I saying? Oh yes, this girlfriend, Connie Chan, we just don't know where to start.'

If George had been startled by Tess' earlier reaction, he was gobsmacked by what she did next. Her eyes widened and her mouth opened as if to speak. Her lips moved soundlessly, but nothing came out.

'What? What is it, Tess?' He leaned closer. 'What are you trying to tell me?'

'Co–'

George's eyes widened. She was trying to speak. This was the first sound he'd heard from her in all these months. 'Connie Chan,' he said, 'that's right.'

Tess moved her head one way, then the other.

'No?' George held her hand. 'It's OK, this is great, take your time.'

Tess' face screwed up in an agony of effort. 'Col–'

George put his face closer. 'Cold? You're cold? Let me shut the window.' He made as if to get up but again came the slow movement of her head, left to right, right to left. It was taking a huge effort. A thin crown of sweat had appeared on her forehead. George reached over to the occasional table and grabbed a tissue, wiped it away. 'It's all right. Take it steady.'

Tess wasn't finished. 'Col-l-d.'

George was at a loss. What did she mean? Perhaps she was just reacting irrationally, without logical thought. Maybe she imagined she was cold, but…

'*Casss…*' The word came out as a painful exhalation.

'Listen, Tess. Don't worry. Just relax. It's OK.' He didn't know how to help her. The effort it was taking scared him. But the more he tried to calm her, the more insistent she became.

'Cold-d-d…'

He sat helplessly, gripped her hand. '

'Cas-s-s…'

Understanding exploded in his head. 'Cold *case*? That's it, right? You're telling me about a cold case?' His heart was banging like a drum solo. 'To do with Connie Chan? You've heard the name, you remember something about her? You worked on the case?'

A flicker of a smile raised the corners of Tess' mouth.

'You're *there*. My God,' George marvelled, scarcely able to believe it. 'You're *in* there, Tess, aren't you? You understand?'

This time her chin tilted up, then down.

'Listen,' he told her, 'I'm going to fetch the manageress, get her to send the doctor in to see you, OK?'

But Tess' eyes had closed, exhausted by the effort. George gave her hand a final squeeze, and left her to doze quietly. He made himself walk normally along the corridor, though his instincts were telling him to sprint. His head buzzed with renewed hope and electric excitement. *She can think. She's still in there… she gave me a* **lead** *…*

He took the stairs two at a time.

CHAPTER NINETEEN

Moran peered through the tall steel gates. The sign told him he was in the right place; *Guust Vervoer* was emblazoned atop the gates in electric red and blue, matching the livery of Cleiren's ill-fated artic. He could see a security box a few metres beyond the gates. A fleet of transporters of various sizes were parked diagonally in their allotted spaces. Beyond the forecourt a tall green and grey warehouse dominated the skyline. In the absence of the usually ubiquitous Portakabins, Moran assumed that the company's onsite offices would lie inside.

This isn't much of a plan, Brendan...

He was beginning to draw attention; a small group of men in overalls had noticed him. One pointed, and a moment later, a uniformed guard emerged from the security box and made his way purposefully towards him.

'*Kan ik u helpen?*'

'Sorry, I don't speak Dutch, I'm afraid.' Moran constructed a friendly smile and showed the man his warrant card. 'I'd like to speak to your transport manager, if he's available?'

'*Beheerder? Nee.*'

The body language told Moran that his request hadn't met with the success he'd hoped for. He tried again. 'Police. English. I need to speak to the manager. *Beheerder.*' He added, for emphasis.

Moran became aware that the group of men had disbanded, one towards the warehouse, and the other two headed in his direction. The first, a tall shaven-headed thirty-something, spat a phrase to the guard which Moran didn't catch, but it was evidently some kind of command. The guard retreated to his box, and Moran waited to see what the bald guy had to say.

'*Engels?*'

'Yes, English. Police.'

'*Politie? Engels?*' Overall man shook his head. '*Nee.*' He waved a meaty hand dismissively, as though shooing away a stray dog.

Moran stood his ground. The man's arms were huge, biceps protruding through the thick material of his overall. An amateurish tattoo stained his neck, an inky, smudge of blue.

'I have some information of interest,' Moran persisted.

The guy squared up to Moran, invading his personal space even with the metal gates between them. '*Informatie? Inlichting?*' The last word was delivered with a dry laugh.

This wasn't going well. Moran played his last card. 'Fabrice Cleiren.'

The name had an immediate effect. '*Fabrice? Wat is er met hem?*' He reached through the bars of the gate and snatched Moran's warrant card from his hand. '*Wacht!*' He turned on his heels and made off towards the warehouses.

Moran watched to see where he was headed. He went

into the smaller warehouse on the left, entering through a side door with a dirty, sticker-covered, plate of glass in its upper quadrant. The security guard was loitering at the entrance of his box, keeping an eye on him. Moran gave him a nod and a smile.

Minutes passed. The sky darkened and heavy droplets of rain soon began to fall, driven into the old port by the gusting, onshore wind. The gusts drove the downpour horizontally, ensuring that, by the time the bald guy reappeared, Moran was wet through and freezing cold.

Overall man made a signal and the electric gates opened slowly, allowing Moran access to the compound. He gave the security man a brief wave in passing, and followed overall man through the grubby side door into a small reception area. A glazed window to the left revealed an office and a short, middle-aged man in a cheap suit working at a paper-strewn desk. Overall man opened a door beside the counter and signalled that Moran should go through into the office beyond.

The door closed behind him.

For a few seconds, the man at the desk continued to tap away at his keyboard, referring occasionally to some kind of list or inventory, until, apparently satisfied with his final entry, he removed his thick glasses, pushed his chair back and regarded Moran with weary suspicion.

'You don't speak Dutch, so you must put up with my English.' He said it in a resigned, bored sort of way, which implied that he was often called upon to speak English, but didn't care for it much.

'Of course. That's perfectly all right. I wish I could speak a European language, but I've never had the time to learn.'

'Ah, the time, the time.' The man sighed deeply. 'If only we had more of this.'

Moran couldn't think of a suitable response, so he just nodded noncommittally and waited for the man to continue.

'Here we have to speak English. It is something we need for business.' A shrug. 'So,' he peered at Moran's warrant card on the desk beside him. An oily smudge indicated where the bald guy had held it. 'My name is Andries van Leer. Manager of the transport *Operatie*.'

'The *Beheerder*?'

'Ah, you see? You are learning already. And so, what can I help you with, Inspector ... Moran?'

'I've been investigating an RTC – a road traffic collision – on the M4 motorway, near Reading. One of your drivers, a Fabrice Cleiren, was unfortunately killed.'

'Yes. We are aware. It is unfortunate.'

'You knew? I don't believe you've been in touch with the police in England?'

'We have been informed,' Van Leer confirmed. 'And we will be ... making ... *afspraken.*' He waved his hand, searching for the word.

'Arrangements?'

'Indeed. To recover the vehicle in due course.'

'There's not a great deal left to recover.'

There was a second door and a large window behind van Leer, through which Moran could see a bustle of activity in the main body of the warehouse. The air was heavy with diesel, even in the enclosed space of van Leer's office, the noise of revving engines making it difficult to converse.

'Ah, of course, this is to be expected. A most

unfortunate, yet not uncommon, scenario, Inspector Moran. It is not the first time we have lost a driver.'

'No?'

'Of course not.' Van Leer rested his pudgy hands on his lap. 'The organisation delivers across Europe as far as Russia. Casualties are unavoidable.'

'You take a very pragmatic view.'

Another shrug. 'Shit happens. We go on. What can I say?'

'Eloquently put. Did you know Cleiren well?'

'Not particularly,' Van Leer shook his head. 'We have so many drivers.'

'Were you aware that he carried a firearm?'

Van Leer hesitated for a fraction of a second. 'That is not official company policy, but some roads are... more dangerous than others, Inspector.'

The slight narrowing of the eyes as van Leer delivered this statement made Moran wonder if the manager was issuing some kind of veiled threat. 'So, you turn a blind eye?'

'If you like to put it this way, yes.' Van Leer smiled. 'It is a good expression. I must remember it.'

'The vehicle was returning from Ireland. Do you have a full inventory of contents prior to delivery?'

Van Leer was silent for a moment. 'Why are you here, Inspector? What is the purpose of your visit?'

Moran was ready for the question. 'It's quite simple. We need to ensure that we have all the facts so that we can provide accurate information to the accident investigation team. There was another car involved, another fatality.'

'That is very unfortunate. But you say *we*. Is this correct, Inspector, or do you mean to say, *I*?'

Van Leer was more astute that he looked. 'I'm the Senior Investigating Officer, so *I* or *we* covers it all, equally.' It sounded weak but it was the best Moran could come up with.

'I see.' Van Leer nodded. 'Well then, let me assure you – and your superiors – that we shall be taking steps to recover whatever remains of our property – very little, it seems – and I will also personally undertake to inform Cleiren's next-of-kin.'

'And the inventory?'

'Will be collated and forwarded to your headquarters in due course.'

'Thank you. I'm very grateful.' Moran hadn't expected van Leer to hand anything over immediately, if at all, especially to an unexpected visitor.

The door behind van Leer opened with a crash and Moran's tattooed overall man came in, rattled off some request far too fast for Moran to deduce its meaning, and retreated into the warehouse as quickly as he had arrived. Van Leer had sprung to his feet at the interruption. 'You will excuse me a moment, Inspector? There is a pressing matter I must attend to.'

'Of course.'

'Please help yourself to a coffee - the *apparaat*, like me, is past its best days, but still it does the job.' Van Leer indicated a battered-looking drinks machine in the corner of the office, wedged in between two filing cabinets.

'Thank you, I will.'

Van Leer left the door to the warehouse swinging shut behind him.

Moran cast his eyes around the grubby office. The noticeboard was studded with yellowed, curling lists, semi-pornographic calendars, and various forgotten reminders. Next to the noticeboard, on a makeshift hook, hung a bunch of keys. Moran went to the coffee machine and experimentally stabbed a few buttons. His eyes were drawn again to the keys. Keys would be missed. But then, there were many keys on this particular keyring, spares possibly, or even little-used.

Really, Brendan?

He was taking a risk, there was no doubt in his mind. If Higginson got wind of this visit, there'd be questions to answer – questions he might well not have satisfactory answers to.

One chance, Brendan. One chance and that's it…

The wheezing machine gave a final cough and Moran gingerly withdrew the plastic cup. It smelled vaguely of coffee. He put it to his lips, took a tentative sip, grimaced, and went to examine the lock on the external door. A simple affair, mortice. He noted the shape, the locksmith's insignia.

Returning to the office, he could see van Leer through the window, in conference with a group of similarly-clad drivers – or warehouse workers, perhaps. Moran estimated that it would take the little man thirty seconds or so to cover the distance back to his office. Keeping half an eye on the window, Moran checked through the bunch of keys. There were twelve altogether, a mixture of Yale-type and mortice. Only one had the same inscribed insignia as the external door's lock. Another glance into the warehouse. Van Leer was on his way back, having dismissed his workers to their allotted tasks.

Now or never…

Still he hesitated. If they found a key missing, the

conclusion was foregone. A stranger alone in the office, a missing key – a no brainer. All sorts of bad stuff would descend on Moran's head, probably following van Leer's official complaint to Thames Valley HQ. He'd be roasted alive. Higginson would have him for breakfast.

Moran was rooted to the spot, in an agony of indecision. He could see van Leer making brisk progress across the warehouse floor. Another twenty seconds and the moment would be gone. He gave the inside of the office one final scan, one final perusal, searching for justification.

That was when he saw it – an object so unmistakeable that his stomach gave a sick lurch of recognition.

A handbag, its tooled leather patterns forming a distinctive, unique design. He remembered remarking on it the first night they'd met at a neighbours' party. Special order, she'd told him. From a master craftsman, a guy who owned his own mini-tanning factory, created works of art in leather and hide. He remembered it in crystal clear detail, resting on the sofa next to its owner the night Liam Doherty had forced his way into Moran's home at gunpoint. And here it was, discarded in a corner, resting at the base of a cheap wooden hatstand. No ordinary handbag. No doubt at all as to its owner.

It was Samantha Grant's handbag.

CHAPTER TWENTY

Moran sat on the edge of the bed. The hotel-supplied bedside clock read eleven forty-five.

Almost the witching hour…

How to assemble his thoughts into some kind of ordered plan? He went over the facts time and time again, spun the key on its dirty length of string, caught it, repeated the action.

*The **stolen** key, Brendan, let's be upfront about this…*

He caught the key again, crushed it into his palm.

OK, so he hadn't known what to expect from this trip, but something had prompted him. A gut feeling? Serendipity? Who could say? But right from the start he'd sensed there was something dirty about Cleiren's mission. Something that connected it to Joe Gallagher, Moran's onetime friend, now a heavyweight Irish politician.

And someone else.

Samantha Grant.

The first time they had met he'd hoped for more than friendship, but as it had turned out she'd played him like a Stradivarius.

She'd set him up – her and some rogue department within MI5.

But Samantha Grant had got more than she bargained for. The tables had turned, all in the space of twenty minutes.

Another agency had stepped in. Fast, efficient. Ruthless.

And she was gone.

Just like that.

Moran had no doubt as to who was responsible for her abrupt disappearance. He'd traced a suspicious car to the Russian Embassy.

A dead end. A no-go zone.

But now…

Moran sprang to his feet, stuffed the illicit key into his pocket, grabbed his coat and his bag, and left the room. There was no one around, either in the corridors or in the hotel lobby. Outside, a thin drizzle distorted the muted street lighting, creating a series of indistinct halogen sunsets against a backdrop of inky sky.

He took a deep breath and began to walk in the direction of the Old Harbour.

The yard at *Guust Vervoer* was empty. No sign of life – but Moran was relieved to discover that, although the concrete apron was lit by two arc lights, there were nevertheless pockets of relative darkness around the skirts of the warehouses where it might be possible to evade detection, give him enough cover to get to van Leer's office door. If he could get past the first hurdle, of course, which was the six metre steel gate with reinforced personnel entry point – and then there was security guard presence to consider, if indeed van Leer considered it necessary to employ nighttime security. Moran had a strong feeling that this was not something the perceptive Dutchman would overlook.

But the first obstacle, at present, seemed insurmountable. To add to Moran's difficulties, a distant clamour of raised voices told him that some very drunk people were headed his way. Probably a bunch of kids trying to navigate home after a night out at the Old Harbour bars and clubs. Moran slunk behind a parked saloon just across the service road from his target and waited.

They came into view presently. Four of them, two intertwined, the other two zigzagging around the couple like unsteady satellites. The tallest, a lad in a pair of skinny jeans and baseball cap, was making all the noise. Moran didn't understand a word, but the others also seemed to be having some difficulty interpreting the gist of his pronouncements. The guy was absolutely slaughtered. Every few metres he would stagger into the couple, drawing shouts of protest with each collision, while the other guy, who was either more sober or just had a better grip on his motor faculties, wandered around nearby.

As they drew closer Moran had a brainwave. A long shot, but he had nothing to lose and no clear alternative. He found a loose piece of concrete that had broken away from the low wall running the length of the various industrial sites dotted along the service road. Judging his moment, he waited until the group of youngsters had just passed the *Guust* gates, cap-boy bringing up the rear, and heaved the concrete missile up and over the gates towards the security box. He heard it strike wood, and retreated to his hiding place to await a response.

Sure enough, Moran heard a sharp *click* as the security guard emerged to check on the unexpected disturbance. Footsteps approached the gates, and the electric *clack* of the personnel door opening told Moran that the guard had taken the bait. He heard a guttural shout as the guard made the connection between the missile and the youngsters' unsteady progress up the road.

Moran waited to see what would happen next. As he prepared to make a hobbling dash for the open personnel gate, he worried about cameras. But, he reasoned, the cameras would be live CCTV, and if he was out of sight by the time the security guard returned to his post, the guy would be none the wiser – unless he played the recordings back, of course, in which case there was nothing Moran could do. But he probably wouldn't unless he found evidence of an intruder.

The security guard had taken several steps away from the compound gate towards the kids. He repeated his angry request. The kids were standing, bemused, wondering what the guy was on about. Cap-boy yelled something which sounded less than complimentary. The guard responded by closing the distance between them in a series of short, angry steps.

Moran broke cover, walked quickly across the road. If the guard turned around now it was over. But the guy was still engaged in a slanging match with cap-boy, who by now was really going for broke. As Moran slipped into the compound he reflected that, if this particular incident was any kind of indicator, Dutch was a language tailor-made for abusive exchanges.

Hugging the shadowed perimeter of the yard, Moran

made an indirect beeline for van Leer's office. As he inserted the key, he considered the possibility of internal alarms.

Too late to worry about that, Brendan...

He turned the key as the sound of the returning guard's footsteps echoed across the concrete. Moran slipped inside, shut the door behind him. He peered through the filthy glass. The personnel gate was closed and the guard was outside his box, muttering imprecations and taking short, irritated puffs on a cigarette.

Moran's first check was the handbag. He found it in the same place. Empty.

But she had been here, at some time, for sure.

Next, van Leer's desk. Moran rummaged carefully. A mobile phone. Purple. He tried to switch it on. Dead. He took out his mobile charger, plugged the phone in, slipped it in his pocket. He wasn't certain, but van Leer didn't look like a man who'd leave his own mobile lying around, nor choose purple as a colour.

There was nothing else in the drawers to indicate malpractice. He went to the rear door, the door through which the tattooed giant had interrupted his meeting with van Leer, and tried the handle. It was unlocked.

The warehouse was a vast open space. The smell of diesel still hung in the air. Two artics were parked off to the right, giant vehicles dwarfed by the scale of the building in which they were housed. Far off, to the extreme rear of the building, another series of doors indicated the presence of additional offices or storerooms. Moran returned to the office, checked the security box outside. All was quiet.

He entered the warehouse cautiously, acutely aware of

the possibility of appearing on one of the security room CCTV monitors. He craned his neck, scanned the high reaches of the warehouse roof. No cameras in evidence. Perhaps *Guust Vervoer* had reasoned that external cameras would suffice. After all, no one would get past gate, and security box and locked door without being picked up, would they?

Moran crept carefully along the length of the warehouse, trying not to imagine lurid headlines along the lines of: *Thames Valley Chief Inspector appears in court – breaking and entering Dutch haulage company premises ...*

He stopped, held his breath. There was movement somewhere – not in the main body of the warehouse, but at the far end, muffled, as though something had been moved, or dropped. He stole a quick glance behind him. Van Leer's office door was still shut, as he had left it. It looked a long way off, like squinting through the wrong end of a telescope. He felt a rush of vulnerability, exposed in the warehouse's yawning emptiness.

Press on, Brendan...

The sound started up again. A scraping, straining sound, as though some material was being forced against another. Moran flattened himself against the warehouse wall, half-expecting a door to burst open somewhere, disgorge a posse of overall-clad heavies armed with crowbars – or worse.

Thirty seconds went by. Now the only sound was the whirring of some hidden aircon unit. Moran unglued himself from the wall, continued his journey. Now he could see two projections, similar to van Leer's office. More offices, or storerooms, perhaps. The room on the left was glazed, not so the other. As he drew closer, Moran saw immediately that the unglazed door wasn't locked in a conventional manner; it was barricaded from the outside. A horizontal bar ran directly across the threshold, secured on one side by a tough, metal cradle. Anyone inside wasn't going to get out simply by picking a lock, or forcing the door. This was belt and braces secure.

Moran approached with caution, checking the glazed room for any sign of life. It was indeed a similar office to van Leer's, if slightly more orderly. A pedestal desk took up most of the room, along with the usual paraphernalia of office management. He moved a few steps to the left, and halted in front of the barred portal. He put his ear to the woodwork. Was it his imagination, or did he detect a faint rustling, a furtive movement?

The crossbar wasn't padlocked. It would simply be a matter of lifting it, and opening the door.

He hesitated. So far, he had only the empty handbag to go on, but this told him nothing he hadn't already suspected. If he got out now, he'd be none the wiser.

He lifted the bar. It slid noiselessly into its vertical bracket. Moran put his ear to the wood a second time.

Silence.

Somewhere in the near distance, a dog barked.

He hadn't considered dogs.

The possibility of being apprehended by some huge, slavering German Shepherd made his mind up.

He turned the handle and pulled the door gently open.

The room was dimly lit by a single bulb which spilled light from an corner cubicle – a toilet, by the look of it. In the opposite corner was a dirty mattress, and a pitcher of water stood atop a wooden packing case. The air in the confined space was fusty and stale and, as far as Moran could tell, the room was quite empty. He took a tentative step forward.

A tiny movement, just the hint of a preparatory expulsion of air close by, made him duck his head. Something passed above him with a *swish*, made clattering contact with the doorframe. He stifled a yell, raised his arm to protect himself. Something hit him hard in the midriff. He fell forward, onto his knees, winded. He struggled to lift his arm again, protect his head against the blow he knew was coming, but seconds passed and … nothing. He rolled onto his side, fighting for breath, vaguely aware of the door closing, someone standing over him.

The voice was an urgent whisper, but easily recognisable nonetheless. 'I won't say you were the last person I was expecting,' Samantha Grant said, panting from her exertion, 'but, by God, Brendan, you come pretty damn close.'

CHAPTER TWENTY-ONE

'An RTC? An *accident* led you here?'

Moran replied in a hoarse whisper. His stomach ached from the punch she'd given him. 'Yes. But now is not the time for discussion.'

'Agreed. The trucks usually roll in around two-thirty.'

'We won't be here.' He took out the purple phone. 'Yours?'

'Yes.'

Moran passed it to her, along with the charger. 'Probably enough charge to use it for a few minutes if need be.'

'You've thought of everything.'

'That'll make a change, right enough. Look, I'm fairly sure they're running firearms.' He watched her gather what few belongings she'd been allowed to retain – a jacket, hairbrush, basic toiletries. 'Explosives too, probably. Through the UK to Ireland.'

'If you say so. I haven't seen much of anything for the last few weeks.'

'They've kept you in here twenty-four seven?'

Samantha spread her hands. 'I had a toilet. I could wash. I'm still alive.'

He looked her up and down. She was wearing a stained blouse, ragged jeans. Her hair was awry and unwashed, her skin sallow and pale. There were deep, dark bags beneath her eyes.

'You look bloody awful.'

'Well, thanks a bunch, Brendan. You sure know how to make a girl feel good.'

'Did they tell you anything? Interrogate you?'

'Who?'

'Our friends from Moscow. The guys who took you. The two drakes.'

'Drakes?'

'Long story.'

'Brendan, I was brought here, dumped. No one told me anything. I got food, grunts. That's it. I figured I was in Holland by listening to the warehouse guys through the door.'

Moran was baffled. 'So, they're waiting for something – or someone. Otherwise…'

'Otherwise by now I'd be at the bottom of the North Sea wearing nothing but concrete boots? Yes, you're probably right. I haven't been idle, though.' She went to the half-concealed window, drew aside the ragged curtain. The pane was barred, but Moran could see that one of the five metal uprights had been sawn through at its base, slotted carefully back into position.

'One down, four to go. Gave me something to do. Steel nail file, if you were wondering. Not the kind you get in Boots.'

Samantha was putting on a brave face, but it was

obvious to Moran that she was far from OK. This wasn't the cool, confident agent he'd last seen in his own sitting room. Perhaps her isolation had been a softening-up exercise, a prelude to interrogation.

'We're leaving,' he said gently. 'But, before we go, I need proof. I want to be sure.'

'Lead on. You're mission control right now.'

Moran closed and barred Sam's cell, and they headed right, towards the rear of the building, where he'd previously noticed a stacked row of wooden crates next to a triad of forklift trucks, huddled close together as though in the middle of some private, mechanical conversation. They had made it almost as far as the crates when the rumbling of a diesel engine and the clank of the perimeter gate announced an end to their solitude.

'Here they come. Regular as clockwork.' Samantha still had hold of the broom handle she had swung at Moran as he entered her cell, and she was hefting it in her right hand like an athlete awaiting the javelin event in a decathlon. 'Can I suggest making ourselves scarce?'

They scurried to the rear of the warehouse and crouched behind the crates, the noise of the engine growing in volume by the second. Presently the massive warehouse doors peeled slowly apart and a truck rolled noisily in from the compound, coming to a halt fifty metres from their hidden position with a hiss of air brakes and a final burst of noise.

'We can't stay here, that's for sure.' Moran raised his head, quickly ducked down.

'I'm not objecting. You're the one who wants to poke around.'

The truck doors were open now; it wouldn't be too long

before the forklifts were assigned to the task of loading or unloading.

Moran rapped his knuckles on one of the crates. 'I need something to prise the lid off.' He cast his eyes about and found what he was looking for; a selection of tools had been left on the floor close by, probably for use in packing and securing the crate contents. Keeping his head down, he shuffled to the end of the line and selected a slim crowbar. He waved it in the direction of the truck. 'Keep your eyes peeled. This won't take long.'

A minute later he had the crate open. The dim overhead lighting revealed the contents: a neat row of what appeared to be automotive parts. Whatever they were, they weren't illegal. Gear machinery, driveshafts? Engine parts? Moran had no idea. He lifted one item out, then another, and another until he had a whole set of parts laid out on the floor beside him. A glance in Samantha's direction was rewarded with an affirmative nod. *Carry on. So far, so good.*

He poked around in the straw, feeling for the next layer. Material. Jackets. No, *Kevlar* jackets, or flak jackets as they used to be known. Getting warmer. He piled the jackets on the floor next to the crate. His fingers touched metal. He began to free the object from its packing, but before the whole thing was uncovered, he knew. He brushed the residue of straw aside, felt in his pocket for his mobile, took three photographs before removing the item. Kalashnikov machine guns. PK series, with and without mounts.

Samantha hadn't moved. There was time. He selected two samples from the disassembled weapons, a receiver and a barrel, placed them in his bag, hurriedly replaced the engine parts he'd removed, secured the crate lid as best he could. No point trying to reseal it, too much noise. He'd just have to hope that no one noticed, or that the loading crew assumed that some distracted employee had forgotten to secure it correctly. In any case, Moran wasn't planning on waiting to find out. He'd used all his reserves of luck for one day.

He became aware of the sound of approaching footsteps in the same instant that he registered Samantha's absence. One second she was crouching at the far end of the row of crates, the next, she was gone.

The footsteps were headed for the opposite end of the row of crates, the end that Samantha had recently vacated. Moran looked desperately for cover. His only recourse was to ease himself around the corner of the crate stack when whoever it was came into view. But that would expose him to the rest of the warehouse. *No choice, Brendan...*

He backed away, trying to judge the optimum moment to round the corner. The footfall behind was soft, but audible. Before he could turn, something cold jabbed into the small of his back.

'Draai je langzaam om.'

A hand grabbed his shoulder, twisted him around. Tattooed overall man, Moran's acquaintance from his earlier visit, curled his mouth into a grimace that Moran guessed was intended as a sardonic smile. 'Ah, *Detective*.'

Now that he was facing the opposite direction, Moran had an unobstructed view. A glance to his left told him that, so far, the workers swarming around the newly arrived truck hadn't spotted what was going on in the distant corner of their warehouse. He could also see what was going on behind his captor, and so he concentrated on holding the man's attention for the few seconds it would take. He spread his hands disarmingly. 'I'm afraid there's been a mistake.' He offered an apologetic smile.

'*Mistake?*' The giant spat the word back at him. In the next moment his expression changed to one of puzzlement as he tried to make sense of Moran's instinctive grimace of anticipation.

Samantha swung the broom handle in a wide arc, like a baseball player with an outsized bat. It was a long, sturdy length of wood and it struck the back of the man's bald head precisely at the base of his skull. His eyes rolled up and he sank to the floor like a collapsed balloon.

'OK, quickly.' Moran got hold of the arms and between them they dragged the body behind the crates.

Samantha's phone gave one short beep, and then another. Moran raised his eyebrows.

'They found me,' she said simply. 'That's all they needed. My phone.'

'The good guys, you mean?' Moran was watching the progress of the truck team. One had broken away from the group and was walking purposefully towards them, hands deep in his overall pockets.

'Yep. There's an encrypted tracker routine built into the circuitry. But the phone needs to be on for it to work, obviously.'

'Obviously,' Moran replied. They backed away from the crate stack and flattened themselves against the wall. The rear warehouse door was a smaller version of the entrance, and would almost certainly be electronically operated. There was, however, a personnel door built into its metallic frame. It was probably locked, but it looked as though it might be forced, given enough weight and impetus.

The truck team guy was almost at the crate stack now. No, wait. He had made a slight alteration to his course; he was heading towards the forklifts.

'Are you thinking what I'm thinking?' Samantha voiced the question in a hoarse whisper.

'Maybe. But what's outside?'

'A smaller yard. Fenced. Tall gate. Topped with wire or glass; I couldn't see it that clearly.'

'And beyond that?'

'A service road. Runs along the sea wall.'

Moran watched as the guy in the overalls started up the forklift. 'And how urgently are your buddies likely to respond, now they know where you are?'

'Within fifteen minutes. Maybe faster.'

Moran nodded. 'OK, so all we have to do is get to the service road.'

'In theory.'

'In *theory*?'

'They're good. Just trust the process.'

'If you say so.'

The forklift was skimming across the floor towards the crates. The operator clearly intended to begin at the side closest to him. Which was logical, and also good news, because tattoo man was lying at the other end. It would take two or maybe three journeys back and forth before the guy clocked that anything was wrong.

Samantha shot him a sideways glance. 'You any good with forklifts?'

'If you'd care to reprise your broom routine, I'll be happy to give you a quick demo.'

'You're on.'

Samantha waited until the forklift had manoeuvred to a fresh stack, the rear of the vehicle towards them. She broke cover, crept forward, cat-like, until she was directly behind the machine. The broom handle swung again and the forklift operator toppled out of the vehicle and onto the floor.

Driverless now, the forklift swung to the left and began an unscheduled detour in the direction of the articulated truck. Samantha was busy pulling the body behind the crates. The forklift was gathering pace – the driver's body must have knocked one of the controls as he fell.

Any moment now and the runaway vehicle would be the centre of attention.

Moran made a dash for it. His leg, never the most helpful asset in situations like these, shot him a bolt of pain from his ankle to his hip. He wasn't going to break any land speed records but he judged that he was moving slightly faster than the forklift. He increased his pace, gritting his teeth, aware that his damaged limb might simply collapse completely, just shut up shop. He hadn't moved this fast since the Blasket mortar attack, and his body was letting him know all about it.

A shout. Someone pointed, heads turned. He was a metre or two shy of the forklift. It seemed to be speeding up; with a final effort, Moran drew alongside, hoisted himself into the seat, jabbed at the pedals, searching for the brake. He guessed right on the second attempt, and the truck slewed to a standstill. Four levers. Which one? Moran spun the wheel, engaged the first lever. The truck span on its axis, pointed to the rear.

Good guess, Brendan...

He stamped on the accelerator. If it was an accelerator...

It was. The truck lurched forward. Moran kept his foot flat on the floor.

Samantha was standing by the personnel door. She was making signals. Two hands, raised, jabbing forward.

The forks. That's what she meant, the forks...

He fumbled with the second lever. Nothing happened. Behind him, the sound of feet slapping on the warehouse floor.

The third lever.

A grinding noise of hydraulics. The twin forks lifted. He waited until they were roughly at the height of the centre of the personnel door, leaned on the lever a second time.

He was, what, ten metres away?

Samantha moved aside as he hurtled towards her. The door loomed. He made a slight correction. Just before impact the thought occurred to him that the door might be reinforced. If that was the case, he was surely headed for Rotterdam's A&E department – if van Leer's employees felt generous enough to call an ambulance.

Which was doubtful.

The twin forks struck the door dead centre. Moran was pitched forward against the wheel and a terrible rending noise preceded a cloud of plaster, brick dust, wood splinters, a sudden sharp pain in his shoulder ... and then fresh air against his cheeks, someone shaking him.

He was lying on his back and someone was shaking him.

Shouting, confusion.

'Get *up*.'

Samantha's voice.

He stumbled to his feet, Samantha's arm supporting him.

A car engine, revving. A second impact, screech of tyres. Someone got hold of both shoulders, hauled him up, shoved him hard. His head bumped glass – a window. He felt leather beneath him. A door slammed. More revving, his stomach left behind as the vehicle reversed, skidded, righted itself, hurtled away. Voices yelling, protesting, fading away.

Moran dragged himself upright. They were in a four-by-four. A driver, himself and Samantha in the back. The vehicle was breaking every traffic regulation in the book, but Moran didn't care. He let his head flop back on the headrest, watched the lights of Rotterdam whizz past, like a blurry trail of multicoloured fireworks.

CHAPTER TWENTY-TWO

'She recognised the name, I'm telling you.' George paced up and down, back and forth, next to Bola's workstation.

'George, keep still, for crying out loud. I can't concentrate.' Bola screwed up his eyes, picking through the onscreen table, one row at a time.

'It'll be in there, somewhere. *Has* to be.'

Bola sat back in his chair, clasped his hands together behind his head. 'George, I've been through the list ten times, at least. I've searched all the permutations of *Chan* I can think of.'

'Let me take a look.' George gestured impatiently. 'I'll find her.'

'Be my guest.' Bola got up. 'Look, man, it's six-thirty. I'm knackered. We can carry on tomor–'

George seized the arm of Bola's chair, spun it round, sat down. 'You want to go home? Fine. I'm staying.' He turned to the screen, made a selection, pressed the *enter* key.

'All right, all right. But let's think about this.'

George gnawed his fist. 'Think *what?* Tess knows the

name. It's a cold case. *Ergo*, it's got to be on file, right?'

Bola nodded, was silent for a moment. 'But not necessarily here.'

'What?'

'When did Tess get posted? Where was she before?'

George furrowed his brow and withdrew his fist from his mouth. Angry indentations studded the flesh of his left hand. He snapped his fingers. 'Southampton.'

'Although technically, it should still be on the generic database,' Bola said.

'Whatever, *yada yada*, as our American friends might say.' George was already flipping through the online directory. 'Here we go. Southampton. General enquiries, Serious Crime, Archives...' He picked up the phone, tucked the receiver under his chin.

'You'll be lucky to get anyone this time of the week,' Bola muttered. His eyes tracked the progress of a pretty admin girl on her way out. 'All right, Jane?' Bola shot her his best smile. She coloured, hurried off in the direction of the lifts.

George cupped the receiver. 'Can't you think about *anything* else?'

'Yeah. Dinner. A pint of lager. I could go on.' Bola sat on the corner of the desk, ruefully watched the double doors click shut behind the departing girl.

'Ah. Hello. This is DC George McConnell, Thames Valley. I was wondering if you could help with an enquiry. A cold case.' George listened intently. 'There is? Great – mind putting me through?'

Bola sighed. It was shaping up to be a long evening.

Chris Collingworth snapped awake. He lay quietly,

trying to work out what had disturbed him. His bedside clock was ticking softly, his wife's breathing regular and easy on the ear. Three o'clock. All quiet.

He swung his legs out of bed and went to the window. A nearby street lamp bathed his front garden in an orange glow. A cluster of parked cars, the dark shape of a cat crossing the road, sleek and elegant in the artificial light. Collingworth went to the bedside table, picked up his phone. One unread text message. No name, a number only. Five words.

Same place. One o'clock sharp.

Collingworth got back into bed. His wife moaned in her sleep, turned over, muttered something unintelligible. What did they want now? He'd done what they'd asked him to do. It had been pretty straightforward, although the CSI guy had given him a penetrating look when he'd produced the burned credit card.

'*Where* did you find it? We've been over that vehicle with the world's finest-toothed comb. Literally.'

Collingworth had shrugged. 'Easily missed. Almost missed it myself. All right if I pass it straight to the guv'nor?'

And if Collingworth's new friend was to be believed, his little plant would stir up the mother of all crises for *DCI* Brendan Moran. The Irish connection. Collingworth allowed himself a quiet chuckle. Who'd have thought it? Brendan Moran, the paragon, with a dodgy background in the Irish troubles. Well, this would sink Moran once and for all, or so the smartly dressed young man had assured him. A poisoned connection to his chequered past. Collingworth was intrigued, eager to cut to the chase, see the thing to its conclusion.

He allowed his mind to fill with pleasant images. Moran's swift and sudden removal. A replacement, someone who would recognise Collingworth's potential. Promotion, and then...

Who knew? The world was his oyster, and with new friends in high, if secretive places, as far as Collingworth was concerned, there were no limits.

One o'clock sharp, then.

'Mate, the sun'll be up soon.'

'When I'm sure we've got what we need, we'll call it a day,' George replied.

The Southampton storage facility was bleak and colourless, and Bola's eyes were twin circles of grit.

'Here we go.' George tapped the file with a grubby stub of pencil. Bola leaned over the desk, poorly lit by a flickering misalignment of spiderweb-crusted strip lighting, and tried to concentrate.

George read aloud. 'Zubaida Binti Ungu, native of Malaysia. Wanted by Malaysian authorities. Suspected of killing her uncle and absconding with worldly goods. Arrived in the UK 1990 or thereabouts. Wanted in connection with the unexplained death of a seventy-four-year-old man in Bursledon. Not enough evidence—' George looked up. 'This is it, the cold case Tess worked on. They never found her – look, *assumed left country*. Last known alias... Connie Chan, or Connie Chandra.'

'Bingo. Game, set and match,' Despite his fatigue, Bola felt a flutter of adrenaline kick in.

George snapped the file closed. Motes of dust puffed upwards and outwards.

Bola sneezed.

'I'm taking this with me.' George tucked the folder under his arm and they headed for the exit, thanking the weary uniform at the door on their way to the car.

The M3 set a new record for roadworks and fifty-mile-an-hour limits. George ground his teeth and feathered the accelerator. 'Zubaida Binti Ungu,' he said. 'In Malaysian, Binti means *daughter-of*.' He turned to his passenger. 'Did you know that?'

Bola's mouth was open, but his eyes and ears were closed.

George swung out of the contraflow and muttered a prayer of thanks at the welcome sight of an empty carriageway ahead. His foot hit the floor.

CHAPTER TWENTY-THREE

Moran touched his card to the lock outside his hotel room and held the door open for Samantha. 'After you.'

'Wait.' She pointed to his card, and into the darkness of the interior.

Moran leaned into the room and slotted the card into its mount. The lights came on.

Samantha went in fast, dropped to a half-crouch, spun on her heels. Straightened up. 'Clear.'

Moran pointed to the bathroom. She nodded.

He opened the door, slowly at first, then smashed it back hard against the wall. It hit the rubber floor stop. 'Ditto.'

Samantha sat on the bed. Her shoulders sagged and she let her head fall onto her chest.

The concierge had paid scant attention to their arrival, despite Samantha's dishevelled state. Probably used to a variety of nocturnal comings and goings.

'Chatty guy, your driver friend.'

She raised her head a fraction and Moran saw the exhaustion etched into her eyes. 'He's not paid to talk.'

'Just to drive.'

'Exactly.'

Moran looked her up and down. 'You can use the shower if you like.'

'Do I smell that bad?'

He laughed. 'I hadn't noticed.'

'Sure.'

Moran consulted his mobile. 'We have an hour and twenty, if your colleague's timetable is correct.'

'It's correct.'

They had to be at the main port by five. Arrangements had been made – a merchant ship bound for the Port of London. Slower than air, but safer.

'Tell me about the Russians.' Moran went to the window, moved the blind aside. Street lights winked but there was no one about.

'Before or after I've sanitised myself?'

'Your choice.'

She shot him a weary smile. 'Give me ten minutes, OK?'

Moran busied himself, examined the photographs he had taken. Russian armaments, no doubt about it. Bound for Ireland, into the hands of the guys who wouldn't let go. Fanaticism endorsed and supported by the likes of Joe Gallagher – hand-pressing politician, Republican, friend of Ireland's new breed of terrorist. *Well, old buddy, we're closing down this trade route, you can bet on it...*

Eight minutes later Samantha emerged from the bathroom in a cloud of steam, face flushed and apparently reenergised. She went to the dressing table, sat on the padded stool, examined herself in the mirror, tutted, and began finger-combing her hair. 'This is personal for you,

Brendan, isn't it?'

He looked up. 'You know it is. Joe Gallagher was my friend.'

'It's never going to stop, Brendan.' Samantha crossed one leg over the other, pursed her lips. 'There'll be other Joe Gallaghers. There's always someone ready and willing to pick up the baton.'

'Maybe. But I prefer to deal with things one at a time.'

'This is *way* out of your jurisdiction, Brendan. It's not your responsibility.'

'What? I should just let it go? No, no no.' He shook his head vehemently. 'If I can do something about it, I'll do it.'

'Persistent. That's what I read about you. They got that right.' Samantha discarded the damp towel.

'I have a file? I'm honoured to be considered important enough to be on record.'

She laughed softly, pulled her damp hair back into a ponytail and tied it. 'Tell me, what happened after the Russians came for me?'

Moran tucked his phone away. He was beginning to feel the strain of his earlier exertions; his leg ached, as did his ribcage, his shoulder – pretty much everywhere. 'What happened? I got back to the house expecting … I don't know what I was expecting, frankly. But Joe Gallagher was sitting on my sofa.'

Samantha froze. 'My *God*. He had the nerve to actually meet you face to face? What did he say?'

'Enough.' Moran bristled again at the memory. 'In a nutshell, he warned me off.'

Samantha looked at her reflection, made a face. 'Hell. I still look like death warmed up.' She swivelled to face him.

167

'Did he tell you anything you didn't already know?'

'Not really. Anyway, I have a recording of the whole conversation.'

'A *recording*? But that's perfect. We can use that.'

'I didn't know what to do with it,' Moran admitted. 'But it's all yours. You can decide.'

'You've made my day. My boss will be over the moon.'

'Be sure to send him my regards.' Moran went back to the window. Paranoia was setting in, but although a faint light had begun to colour the sky the streets were still empty, wrapped in the pre-dawn stillness that preceded the slowly escalating bustle of the city waking up to a new day. He grunted. 'We'd better make a move. Van Leer's mob may yet trace us to the hotel.'

'I doubt that – they'll be too busy repairing the damage – but I'm ready when you are.'

Moran went to the door, checked the corridor. Not a soul. 'All clear. Shall we? I don't want to miss the boat.'

She joined him in the corridor. 'That's something I could never accuse you of, Brendan.'

Moran didn't consider himself a poor sailor, but the crossing turned out to be the roughest he'd experienced. As the container vessel passed the BP refinery, left the *Hoek van Holland* behind, and entered the open waters of the North Sea it began to pitch and roll, driven by the strong westerly wind.

They'd boarded the *Rotterdam Comet* shortly before five in a no-fuss, no-questions-asked manner that Moran found slightly unnerving. When questioned, all Samantha would say was, 'We have an arrangement. Don't stress it, Brendan.' In response to Moran's query, the merchant seaman who'd boarded them estimated their arrival time at London Thamesport, assuming they maintained a steady fifteen knots, at approximately eight-thirty in the evening.

They'd been allocated a basic cabin below deck – two bunks, a connecting low-level table, an adjoining bathroom. It was cramped and spartan, and not only did Moran feel sore and exhausted but also decidedly queasy. The prospect of a whole day at sea held little appeal, but his main concern was that it was another day lost. At least, he consoled himself, he and Samantha were safely on board, and he could communicate with the team via his mobile. He wedged himself between the bottom bunk's headboard and the riveted bulkhead, jabbed the passcode into his mobile. A glance showed him what he didn't want to see.

'Problem?' Samantha emerged from the bathroom, ducking her head to avoid what Moran had already done once, and would probably do again on subsequent visits to the head.

'No damn signal.'

'Yes, it's not unusual out here. Give it an hour or so – we'll come back into range.'

'I've been out of range too long already.'

'Busy back at the ranch?'

'Yes. Several murders, similar MO.' Moran sketched out the details.

Samantha listened and when he'd finished she was silent for a few moments. Then she smiled wryly. 'Well, excuse me for making an observation, Brendan, but what you've achieved this last twenty-four hours is way more important.'

'Than a few oldies who were going to die soon anyway?'

Samantha wrinkled her nose. 'You know what I mean. And what about me? I'd still be locked in that ghastly room if it wasn't for your – forgive me for saying so – rather reckless break-in.'

'I take it that's a 'thank you'?'

'It is. And you know I'm grateful. I was going crazy in there. God, if you hadn't turned up, who knows what would have happened?'

Moran sat up. Somehow lying down made the motion of the ship harder to deal with. 'I expect you'd have received a visit from Moscow in the very near future.'

'You're quite sure the KGB are involved, aren't you?'

'Well, you're not denying it. I know what I saw in Pangbourne, and I traced the car to the Russian embassy.'

'Of course you did.' Samantha went to the porthole and looked out just as the ship pitched forward and water crashed against the thick glass. Moran's stomach rolled with it and he shut his eyes momentarily.

When he opened them again, Samantha was still standing, feet planted apart, and swaying with the motion of the vessel. He took a deep breath, kept his eyes fixed on the doorframe, a solid, unmoving object. Unmoving in the world of the cabin, at any rate. He moistened his dry lips.

'The Russians are in this up to their necks, that's my take on it. They'll take any route they can to destabilise the UK. They've got people in the House of Lords, for heaven's sake. Seriously rich businessmen. And Joe Gallagher's operation fits their bill beautifully. And look at what happened in Salisbury – no pretence about it, their hit squad came in and basically did as they pleased. Never mind that the population of an entire city could have been wiped out if the nerve agent hadn't been isolated and disposed of. No, Moscow has a finger in any number of pies, I'm convinced of that. And right now, the Irish Republic is their flavour of the month.'

'We can put a stop to Gallagher now, Brendan. You have the evidence to bring him down, you have exactly what we need.'

'Well, as I said, it's all yours. I'll be glad to get shot of it.'

'I'd like to get hold of the cassette *asap*, pass it to my senior.'

'Of course. It's easily accessible.' The words came easily, but the wording of Samantha's demand had ripped through his body like an electric current.

'That's good,' she said. 'The sooner we get this out, the better.'

'Absolutely. Listen, I'm going up to the deck for some air. I'm in serious danger of losing my last meal. Quick wash and change first, though.'

He took his bag into the cramped shower room, splashed water on his face, selected a fresh shirt, sat on the loo and tried to figure out his next move.

He emerged a few minutes later. 'See you shortly.'

'Sure. Mind how you step.'

Moran shut the cabin door behind him, swayed along to the staircase which led to the lower deck, clung onto the steel banister as the ship pitched and gravity threatened to throw him back. Once he'd reached the deck level he staggered a few drunken paces to the external door, wrenched it open, reached out for the ship's railing and hung on.

He fixed his eyes on the see-sawing horizon and tried to think. Samantha had said 'cassette'. He had never mentioned the recording format; was this an innocent assumption, or something more sinister by implication? Surely the natural assumption these days would be that he'd recorded his conversation with Joe Gallagher on a smartphone, using the voice recorder.

Surely.

He'd only mentioned the cassette format to one other person – his old boss, Dermot Flynn.

Surely *not*. It was too grotesque to contemplate.

The ship's prow dipped and Moran dipped with it, tried to keep his eyes on the dancing horizon.

He went over the events of the last twelve hours again. Van Leer. The handbag. The purple smartphone, easily located in his desk drawer. Samantha's strangely lengthy incarceration.

The late discovery of the burned credit card. How had Forensics missed it? Unless they hadn't missed it… unless it hadn't been there when they signed off.

And there was the silence of the guy in the four-by-four.

You've just sprung two of your own from a dangerous situation. And not a word. Not a single.

Only one reason Moran could come up with. When you speak, you give away a lot about yourself. You reveal your background, your origin, your country. And if Moran had been a betting man he would have been confidently wagering that the driver's accent would have revealed that he was no product of a British public school, no early recruit into the intelligence service. Not at all. His English would have been perfect, but his accent – that would have been the giveaway. An accent is hard to disguise.

The ship leaned to one side and Moran's legs nearly went from under him. He held on until the *Rotterdam Comet* righted herself and, for a few brief seconds, remained roughly perpendicular to Moran's distant point of reference. His thoughts, however, continued to dip and wheel with the constant movement of the gulls above.

Sure, the guy could have been Dutch, but Moran's money was on a more distant country.

Mother Russia.

CHAPTER TWENTY-FOUR

The pub was filling up, Sunday lunchtime in full swing. Noisy chatter and the tempting smell of roasting meat wafting from the kitchens. Collingworth found his way to the bar, ordered a tonic water. As the barmaid fixed his drink, his eye strayed to the corner table. There he was, dressed as smartly as before. No dress-down Sunday for this guy. Collingworth admired that. Keep up standards, look the part. Nice.

He paid for his drink, excuse-me'd his way across the busy saloon bar.

The guy looked at his wristwatch. Expensive, Collingworth noted. Of course it was expensive.

'Right on time. I like that,' the smartly dressed young man said. He didn't get up or offer a handshake, so Collingworth drew up a stool and set his glass on the table.

'How can I help?' Collingworth sipped his tonic water.

'You've provided a valuable service. I thought you might wish to witness the fruits of your labours.'

'That sounds ... appealing,' Collingworth replied. 'Do I get a name this time, by the way?'

A smile. 'You can call me Alan, if you wish.'

'So, Alan,' Collingworth leaned closer, kept his voice low. 'How about you tell me the whole story? So I have a little context.'

'It's a story from long ago, before your time – and mine, to be fair. It was during the Irish ... ah, let's call them difficulties. They don't like the other word. Your man was young, tempted off the straight and narrow. Got himself involved with undesirables – undesirable to some, I mean. To the powers-that-be, at least. To others, less so, depending on your political persuasion. Long story short, it involved an ambush, several murders.'

Collingworth drank it all in. This was meaty stuff. 'And you have proof, of course?'

Alan sipped his soda water. 'All the proof we need. He's on his way back from Rotterdam as we speak, with a known terrorist in tow.'

'*Rotterdam*? But what–'

'Ah, ah.' Alan wagged his forefinger. 'I can't tell you too much.'

'Right. Of course.' Collingworth nodded.

'I wanted to give you the opportunity to witness the fish being reeled in.'

'I appreciate that. Very much.'

'Not at all,' Alan said smoothly. 'Least we could do.'

'This terrorist. The woman, the name on the card?'

Alan drew his finger across his lips. 'Sorry. But you're on the right lines.'

'Just tell me when and where.'

'Tonight. Port of London, eight-thirty. A container ship – the *Rotterdam Comet*. Dock number 12b.'

Collingworth scribbled the details on his notepad. A

thought occurred to him. 'Anything I can do? I mean, I'm a policeman, and–'

'Won't hear of it,' Alan said, draining his glass. 'Just keep a low profile, and keep your eyes peeled.'

'I will, don't worry. Another drink?'

'Well, if you're offering, why not?' Alan held out his empty glass.

The bar was busy, but Collingworth was in no hurry. Plenty of time to get to London. As he waited for service he allowed himself a little fantasising. DS Chris Collingworth, then *DI* Chris Collingworth, and then … maybe an opening with the security services. Wait – how about sooner rather than later?

'What'll it be, love?'

Collingworth placed his order. Yes, why not? Why not cut through the dead-mens'-shoes promotion prospects altogether? Alan would put in a word, surely? He'd proved himself to be an effective covert operator. He'd completed his mission. Small fry, sure, but that wasn't the point. Why had they approached him in the first instance? Because they'd checked him out, obviously. They'd figured out that he was the right stuff.

'Here we go. Four pounds twenty-five please, love.'

As Collingworth grabbed the drinks, he became aware of some small commotion in the corner. Had someone fainted? Head were turning. He couldn't see. He craned his neck. Where the hell was his change? Here she came.

'Seventy-five pence, love. Thanking you.'

Collingworth pocketed the coins, shouldered his way towards the corner table. The double doors nearby swung shut. The crowd parted and Collingworth did a double take. Someone else was sitting at the corner table. An older man, casual shirt open at the neck, half pint of lager in front of him. Where was Alan?

'Excuse me. My friend and I were sitting–'

'Park your behind on the stool, shut up, and listen,' the man told him.

Collingworth felt his mouth open and close. He sat as instructed, put the drinks down carefully. 'Who are you? What's going on?'

The man leaned forward. 'I said shut up and listen.'

Collingworth felt a cocktail of confusion and anger rise deep in the pit of his stomach, but there was something about the way the stool usurper spoke that made him hold his tongue. He stole a glance towards the double doors.

'Your buddy won't be coming back. Now, I want you to tell me everything he told you.'

'You're–'

'–someone acting in the interest of this country. Here–' The man in the open-neck flashed an ID card.

Collingworth read it. It looked official, but now he didn't know what or whom to trust.

The man's tone was tinged with exasperation and not a little urgency. 'I haven't got time for this, but if you need to double check, the address and phone number is right here.'

Collingworth read again. *Thames House, Millbank.*

'Your buddy is a Russian KGB agent. Educated at Eton, if you were wondering.'

'KGB? But I–'

'Just tell me what he asked you to do, what you did. What he wanted today.'

Collingworth cleared his throat. Five minutes later, he was finished.

'Thank you, DC Collingworth. Now, if I were you, I'd go home and stay home. And here, take these. Someone will be over in the morning to collect them.'

'What is it?'

'Official Secrets Act. Two copies. Sign both, please, and seal the envelope.'

Collingworth took the envelope without a word.

'And in future, try to avoid talking to strange men in pubs.'

'I thought–'

'We know what you thought. And if we hadn't stepped in, you wouldn't be thinking anything at all this time tomorrow.'

'You mean they were going to–?' Collingworth felt the blood drain from his face.

'Two birds with one stone. Nice and neat.'

Another guy appeared at the double doors, gestured urgently.

'Have a nice day, DC Collingworth.'

Collingworth didn't move for a long time, nursed his tonic water. He felt sick.

Half an hour later, his mobile rang. He had half a mind to ignore it, but it was insistent.

'DC Chris Collingworth.'

George McConnell's irate tones filled his ear. 'Don't you look at any of your messages? Briefing. Urgent. Started fifteen minutes ago. Get in here. That'd be now. Are you *there*?'

'I heard you.' Collingworth slammed his empty glass down, banged through the double doors.

Patronising little…

CHAPTER TWENTY-FIVE

'OK, gather round.' George McConnell polished his glasses as he waited for the team to settle. All present and correct – except for Collingworth. George had tried to keep his tone friendly on the phone but knew he had failed miserably. He only had to hear Collingworth's voice to feel a growing tension, his blood pressure rising. Lack of sleep probably didn't help, and neither the fact that he couldn't raise Brendan Moran despite several attempts. In Charlie's absence George was the senior most suitable to keep the ball rolling, and right now George was poised for a strike.

'OK, here it is. Following a lead suggested by DC Tess Martin, DC Odunsi and myself have spent a fruitful night sifting through one of Southampton's cold cases.' George clocked the reaction Tess Martin's name had caused. Wide eyes, sideways glances, a collective exhalation. A hand went up.

'DC Swinhoe.'

'Tess *spoke* to you? How–'

George held up his hand. 'Yes. Briefly, and with

difficulty, but she spoke.'

The mood in the IR perceptibly lifted. A buzz of conversation rose with it. George allowed their sentiments free rein for thirty seconds before he called a halt to the celebrations. 'All right, all right. Yes, it's great news. Early days, but it has to be a good sign. But the point is, Tess recognised a name. I was rambling on about the current case, and she stopped me. She'd heard the name before – Connie Chan. A cold case, from her Southampton days. If I read the newspaper article we found in the case notes, it'll give you a good overview, so pin back your ears.' George opened the folder, withdrew the photocopy, and started to read:

"A serial killer who murders vulnerable elderly people may have been active in Britain since the 1990s and could still be on the loose, according to an independent and confidential report.

The report, compiled by one of the most senior coroner's officers, raises serious concerns about two cases where widowers living alone were suffocated in their own homes. After re-examining the cases using modern techniques, the report finds that both cases were likely to have been murders and also identifies three other similar cases of elderly men killed in the northwest of England.

It suggests that the first two suspected murders — both in Knutsford, Cheshire — could have been the work of an offender unknown to the police.

This weekend Cheshire police said it was conducting a

review of the findings in the report, which was handed to the force last month. It has also alerted police in Greater Manchester and Cumbria where some of the other killings took place.

The 149-page report calls on the National Crime Agency and Interpol to review cases in Britain and Europe to determine whether there are more related murders. "This individual will not stop killing until someone or something stops him," the report says.

John Morris, MP for Chester, said police must act swiftly: "The implications don't bear thinking about if there is an offender responsible for a series of what were dreadful crimes."

The report, written by Steven Dalley, the senior coroner's officer for Cheshire, is supported by evidence from his predecessor at the time of the first deaths and a US-based crime-scene analysis expert.

The first two killings happened in 1991 and 1993 only two miles apart in Knutsford, the Cheshire town. These were originally thought by police to be murder-suicides. One victim was discovered lying on their bed and the other had been abandoned in the front seat of a car parked in a supermarket car park.

Similarities between the cases included the murder MO – suffocation by means of a scarf, or similar.

The report, which Dalley produced in his free time,

examined police files and crime scene photographs and points to "a number of inconsistencies which do not corroborate the original manner of death of being suicide".

It also identifies a further three cases — in 1995, 1996 and 2000 — that Dalley believes should be reviewed to see whether they are linked to the Knutsford killings. Two of the cases were in nearby Greater Manchester and the third was in the Lake District.

Denis O'Keefe, former chief prosecutor for the northwest, said: "We could potentially have a serial killer in our midst. There needs to be a proper review of these cases and others which carry similar hallmarks."

Cheshire police said: "We are in receipt of the report and it is being reviewed. This is a piece of research that has been undertaken by a staff member, independently. As with any case that has been closed, where new information comes to light it is reviewed and acted upon if appropriate. We have notified Greater Manchester police and Cumbria constabulary."

George finished and looked up. The silence was deafening. Another hand was in the air.
'DC Tomlinson.'
'Can we get hold of Steven Dalley? Sounds like he's committed to the case – he's exactly the guy we need, surely?'
'Surely, indeed.' George nodded. 'Unfortunately, that's not going to be possible.' He picked out another

photocopy from the folder, read aloud:

Daily Mail, Monday 2nd April 2005. Hit and run death. Steven Dalley, 43, from Frodsham, Cheshire was the victim of a hit and run driver in the early hours of Sunday morning. Mr Dalley was a long-serving member of the Cheshire coroner's office, acting as senior coroner's officer from 1995 to the present. He leaves behind a wife and two children. The driver and vehicle have yet to be identified.

Silence. Someone said 'Bloody hell' under their breath.

George went on. 'Zubaida Binti Ungu, native of Malaysia. Wanted by Malaysian authorities. Suspected of killing her uncle and absconding with his worldly goods. Arrived in the UK 1990 or thereabouts. Wanted in connection with the unexplained death of a seventy-four year old man in Bursledon.'

'She gets around,' DC Swinhoe observed.

'She sure does,' Bola Odunsi agreed. 'But what we need to know is, where the heck is she now?'

'This lady is very good at losing herself,' George said. 'Which is interesting, because she's a striking-looking woman. And the only person we know who's actually seen her in the flesh is–'

As if on cue, DC Chris Collingworth bumped through the IR door, took a seat at the back.

All eyes swivelled to the rear.

George resisted the urge to make a snide remark. 'DC Collingworth? A description of Connie Chan, if it's not too much trouble?'

Collingworth looked flustered, preoccupied. 'What? Oh, right. Well, she was a stunner. Oriental. Long black hair, tied in a loose knot. Mole high on her right cheek.

Perfect teeth. Around 5' 6"; puts on a good act, if she's the one we're after.'

'She is,' George said. 'DC Delaney? You have something?'

Delaney was an athletic-looking thirty-year old whose mission in life was to run as fast as possible to get there. Half-marathon, marathon, whatever, he'd be out in all weathers. A good detective, in George's opinion. Liked to get stuck in. Delaney's eyes were bright and focused, in contrast to George's which were in danger of closing unless he grabbed another shot of coffee, fast.

Delaney's words raced across George's lagging brain. 'Chan must have had lodgings nearby, if she was working at Chapelfields, right? Temporary, because she knew she wouldn't be staying long. So, not a tenant. Friends in the area? Doubtful. She sounds like a solo artist to me. So, what then? B&B, or a hotel somewhere nearby. Chan didn't get the King's Cross train. So, where did she go first? Has to be Reading station, right? I bet Marley was supposed to dump the car, get to Reading station to meet her, and then...' Delaney shrugged.

'To London, to King's Cross.' George nodded.

'So, assuming she found out pretty soon that Marley wasn't turning up, what's her next move?'

'Back to her lodgings.' Bola spread his hands.

'So where haven't we checked CCTV so far?' George appealed to the room.

'We covered Reading station,' DC Swinhoe said.

'Front *and* rear?' George stuck his chin out.

Bernice Swinhoe and Delaney exchanged a look.

'That'll be a no, then.' George made a fist, nudged his front teeth. 'And, correct me if I'm wrong, but there are several budget hotels to the rear, on the Caversham Road, are there not?'

Nods.

'Right, you two,' this to Swinhoe and Delaney, 'get to it. If she shows up on the recording, I want to know.'

DC Stiles had her hand up now. 'George, the newspaper report mentioned a US-based crime scene expert. Worth chasing?'

'Aye, I'll get onto Southampton first thing. Hopefully someone can supply a name.'

'Any word from the boss up north?' Collingworth called out as they began to disperse.

'I'll be in touch with DI Pepper shortly.' George raised his voice above the clatter of chairs.

'And DCI Moran?' Collingworth was making his way across to Julie Stiles.

'Not available as of now,' George replied. 'He'll be in contact soon, I'm sure.'

'Bad time to be out of the loop,' Collingworth said. 'Wonder where he's got to?' This with a wink to DC Stiles.

George took a breath. 'That's his business, DC Collingworth. You'd best be cracking on with the job in hand.'

'Makes you wonder, though.' Collingworth addressed the observation to Julie Stiles, although it was clear that his intended audience was George.

George tapped reserves of restraint he was unaware he possessed. 'DCI Moran has been through more crap than you'll experience in your lifetime, DC Collingworth,' he said slowly, for emphasis, tucking the photocopies back into the folder. 'He deserves some time to himself. A little peace and quiet. Let the man have his Sunday afternoon.

He'll be out walking his dog, enjoying his Sabbath rest.'

'R&R,' Collingworth smirked. 'That'll be right, eh Julie?'

Julie Stiles smiled coyly. 'I'd like some of that, too.'

'You can both forget that for now,' George said. 'We have a serial killer to catch.'

CHAPTER TWENTY-SIX

Moran heard the heavy steel door behind him open and then close with a bang as the wind caught it and slammed it into its frame. He was reluctant to upset the delicate balance of stability he had spent the previous few minutes achieving, so he didn't turn round immediately. He reasoned that Samantha would hesitate to shoot him in the back, would want some final word of absolution before she did what she had to do. The ship yawed, and he swivelled to face her, his back to the railing and his hands curled tightly around the metal tubing.

Her hair blew wildly as the wind caught it and he was struck once more by how attractive she was. She didn't look her age; her body could have belonged to a woman ten years younger. Her grip was firm, and the small automatic she held was unwavering, unaffected by the flurries and gusts being hurled at them by the North Sea squall.

'You figured it out, Brendan. As always.'

'Sorry if I'm getting a tad predictable in my old age.'

A stray wisp of hair stuck to Samantha's cheek and she

brushed it away. The pistol stayed where it was. 'This is hard for me.'

'Forgive me if any expressions of sympathy appear inadequate.'

The ship rocked again, and Moran experienced the illusion of the world being tipped backwards. His stomach see-sawed along with the motion.

'How did you know?'

'Flynn.' Moran had to shout as the noise of the wind grew stronger. 'Flynn is the only other person I told – that I recorded the conversation with Gallagher. I happened to mention it was a cassette. And so did you.' He shrugged. 'That's all.'

Samantha's feet were placed apart for balance. As the ship moved, she swayed with it. Sea legs, Moran thought; there's experience for you, right there. She was looking at him intently, as though she wanted to burn his image onto her memory.

Better keep talking, Brendan.

'And the more I thought about your disappearance, the credit card, how you'd been locked up for weeks for no apparent reason, well–' He tightened his grip on the rail as spray flew up, soaked his back. 'It didn't make sense.'

'I was supposed to do this before,' she said. 'I sent you out for a walk instead.'

'So what's changed?'

She shook her head. 'Nothing. Nothing about the way I feel, at least. But there's too much at stake. You're not going to part with the tape now, are you?'

'No.'

'Well, then. You understand.'

'What did they offer you, Samantha? Money? Property?

Kudos?'

'Moscow?' She laughed. 'None of the above. It's not about material gain, Brendan. It's a matter of principle.'

'I've heard that before somewhere.'

The gun was levelled directly at him. He couldn't get to the door in time, and even if he did she would shoot him before he was half way down the staircase. No one would hear. As long as he kept her in sight, faced front, there was a chance.

'How do you know I haven't left instructions to despatch the tape to Thames House?'

She cocked her head. 'I don't think so. I think you intended to give it to me directly. When you found me.'

He shrugged, nodded. 'You're right. That's what this whole setup was about. Clever. You knew I'd take the bait.'

'You don't like loose ends, Brendan. I've learned that much about you.'

A seagull cruised down to inspect them, hung on the wind for a moment, and was gone. No food, no stay.

'I'm disappointed about Flynn,' Moran said. 'One man I thought was dependable.' Disappointed didn't come close. He felt crushed by his mentor's betrayal.

'And he is, Brendan, so far as the Republican cause is concerned.'

'A closet extremist, all these years.' Moran shook his head sadly. 'I missed that one. I looked up to him. So I'm not always right.'

'Is he so wrong? He's willing to stand up for his cause. Not everyone can say that about themselves.'

'I have no problem with a cause. It's the methods I'd call into question.'

To his right, on a deck far below, Moran could see a knot of merchant seamen busy with some nautical task. They were absorbed in their work, too far away to be of any assistance, even supposing they'd be willing. 'Something must have happened to turn you from your original cause, Samantha. Something made you renege on your masters. What was it, I wonder?' He hesitated to use the word *traitor*, although the term seemed to fit the bill.

Samantha was keeping her distance. The automatic was still pointed at Moran's chest. If he rushed her, she'd get a shot in way before he made contact. The wind snatched at her voice, made her shout to get the words across.

'I was a student – Cambridge, if you want to know. One of my professors was more than he seemed. I knew there was something slightly mysterious about him. He was a headhunter for the intelligence service.'

'He had his eye on you?'

'In more ways than one, as it turned out.' Samantha flicked the unruly strand of hair away from her eyes, but the gun remained steady.

'He recruited you. And then he seduced you.'

She nodded, her lips twisting with distaste at the memory. 'I was young, impressionable. I looked up to him.'

Moran shook his head. 'Oh, no, no. Don't tell me this is all some kind of *revenge* trip? So what, he dumped you? You were devastated. How could a man you respected, a man you held in such high esteem mistreat you so badly? Is that it?'

'His wife found out. We got careless; he blamed me for the indiscretion; I left some article of clothing where I shouldn't have.'

'And naturally, he was never going to leave his wife.'

Samantha's compressed lips gave him the answer.

'So, you joined up but always intended, at some suitable point, to slip away from your spymasters, go over to the other side just to get your own back on the professor. Rather childish, don't you think?'

A shrug. 'Maybe. He's long dead, of course, but I won't pretend it wasn't hugely satisfying to imagine how he'd react if he knew. But there's more to it. You need to wake up, Brendan. Great Britain lost the 'Great' a long time ago. The country's a shadow of what it once was. The empire is over. It won't be long until the real world power makes its move, assumes its rightful place.'

'Russia? You really believe that?'

'If you only knew what I've been privy to, Brendan. It's only a matter of time. I know whose side I want to be on.'

'I think you're deluding yourself.'

'I don't think so. Have you any idea how easy it is to bring influence to bear in Whitehall? Especially where money is involved. Where do you think certain key political parties receive the majority of their donations from?'

'A covert network of Russian oligarchs, no doubt.'

'Correct. And a great deal of money buys many favours.'

'The enemy inside?'

Samantha's mouth formed a disdainful smile. 'Enemy? Saviours, more like. The UK is currently run by a bunch of privileged playboys. They deserve all they get.'

'In that respect, I might find myself agreeing with you.'

She raised the automatic. 'I'm so sorry, Brendan. I really am. I can't allow that tape to fall into the wrong hands. This is where it ends.'

At that moment, the ship plunged into a deep trough and Samantha was propelled forward into Moran's arms. He held onto her and, for a second they clung together like the lovers they had almost become. He caught her wrist in a firm grip, but the rain made her flesh slippery, and as the ship righted itself she tore herself away, staggered back. The automatic came up, purposefully this time, and she squeezed the trigger.

Moran felt a punch in his midriff and doubled over, slipped down the railing, legs splayed on the soaking deck. He couldn't catch his breath. It was like being badly winded, only exponentially so. He was vaguely aware of the *Rotterdam Comet* beginning a new plunge.

With nothing to hang on to, Samantha lost her balance and slid across the deck towards him; he felt her foot catch on his outstretched leg. Although his cheek was pressed against the deck, he had a clear view of what happened next. Samantha hit the railings hard and the automatic was thrown from her hand, went skittering across the deck and over the side. The railing, whether through negligence or sheer bad luck, gave way on impact with a scrape of tormented metal. For a frozen moment, like a still from a movie, Samantha held onto the unsecured tubing as the ship continued its downward dip. In the next second she and the railing had disappeared over the side.

Moran felt himself sliding and caught hold of the railing base, which had been partially torn from its mount. Two rivets remained. He hung on. His legs dangled over the abyss and he knew that, if the ship continued its current trajectory, he too would be swept overboard. He didn't have the strength to hang on for long. His chest was a breastplate of agony, and a fierce pulse was hammering in his temple, like Thor with his mythological hammer. Still he held on.

After what seemed an eternity, he felt the deck levelling out. As it reached the horizontal, Moran let go, began to crawl towards the stairwell. If he could reach the door, he might be able to force it open. At first, the ship's opposite roll assisted him and he made good progress but half way across he felt the familiar pull as, once again, the deck canted sharply beneath him. He grabbed the nearest object, a protruding air vent, wrapped his arms around it.

The pain in his chest intensified as he fought against gravity. When the ship flattened out again, he threw himself forward onto his hands and knees. Getting his feet beneath him proved even harder, but it had to be now, or he would be dragged back again towards the missing railing.

Lurching to a half-crouch he flung himself at the door, wrenched it open, tumbled down the first three stairs, slid on his back the rest of the way until his head was resting on the upright steel banister at the foot of the stairwell. He dragged in lungfuls of air, tried to calm himself. Gingerly, his hands began to explore his chest area. He stripped off his coat, found the straps securing the *Kevlar* vest and gently loosened them, slipped out of the garment and held it up for examination.

Just below the breastbone was a deep indentation, scarred at its edges by the heat and impact of the bullet. He pulled his shirt open, the buttons pinging and scattering on the floor. The bruise was already well-formed, the colours radiating outwards like a blurred butts target. He probed his ribs and groaned. Bruised, certainly, but hopefully, not broken.

It took another five minutes to reach the cabin. Moran stretched himself out on his bunk as the *Rotterdam Comet* continued its journey to London. No alarm had been raised, no panic or *man overboard* klaxon had sounded. Samantha had gone to her death silently, exactly as she had intended for Moran.

He closed his eyes.

No one asked any questions as he disembarked; no one even cast a curious glance in his direction. Merchant seamen went about their business, unloading, supervising quayside workers, arguing and swearing, whistling tunelessly as dockside workers did. Moran found himself walking along a service road next to a clutch of warehouses that looked as though they were in the process of restoration. His legs felt odd, like flesh-coated springs rather than bone-supported muscle. The pain in his chest was bearable, provided he took care not to make any sudden movements. The train station was a ten-minute walk, and Moran felt he could manage that.

He turned right, following signs to the railway, and very soon became aware that he was being followed. He stopped, turned, in no mood for evasion. An ordinary-looking man was walking smartly along the same route. Thirties, clean shaven, casual jacket and chinos. He looked vaguely familiar. Moran waited for him to catch up.

'Hello.' The man greeted him brightly. 'Sorry. Intended to meet you off the ship – had a few matters to clear up first. Took a bit longer than expected. Always the way. Good trip?'

Moran didn't need to ask for identification. The guy's whole demeanour was pure MI5.

'I've had better,' Moran told him. 'How can I help?'

'You've been jolly helpful already,' the man said cheerfully. 'Samantha not with you?'

'She lost her sea legs, I'm afraid.'

The man made a sympathetic face. 'I see. Ah well, I'll cross that one off my list.'

'You've been following me,' Moran said. He remembered now: the young guy in the car, always in the background, just out of reach, unseen at close quarters – except for his neighbour, Mrs P, who had reported his presence in Pangbourne.

'Bit strong. Keeping a watchful eye is a better way of putting it. Cigarette?'

'Not for me.'

'Very wise.' The agent lit up a Benson and Hedges and drew in smoke. 'Listen, I believe you might have something of interest to us.'

'Of course. You know all about it.' Moran felt a huge weariness come over him. 'And about Samantha's loyalty reshuffle, I'm assuming?'

'Indeed, indeed.' He exhaled smoke, nodded enthusiastically.

'But you let her off the leash, to see where it would lead you?' A plane droned low overhead on some unknown flight path, filled the area with the noise of its engines.

The guy raised his voice to compensate. 'She had to finish a little job for us, but then she went off the radar. Figured out what she was up to, and then lo and behold, up you pop again.'

'She tried to kill me.' Moran felt anger burning in his

throat. 'Was that part of your little job?'

'No, no, no! Not at all.' The man looked stricken. 'She was batting for the other side. We have no designs of that sort.'

'That's comforting. So it was only Liam Doherty's murder that was sanctioned by your lot?'

The man took another pull on his B&H. 'No. That wasn't part of her brief. Her new company issued that order. We wanted Doherty alive, as it happens. Look, I know it all sounds a little rough to a respectable police officer like yourself, but–' he shrugged. 'It's a dirty game. We try to keep one step ahead. Most of the time we succeed. Other times–' he shrugged again, 'one has to concede the odd wicket.'

'All for the greater good,' Moran muttered.

'Exactly so. Exactly. Now, I don't want to keep you. You have things to do, murders to solve, all that sort of thing.'

Moran sighed. 'The tape is with my neighbour. Mrs Perkins. I'll let her know you're collecting it.'

The man beamed. 'Splendid. That's the ticket.'

'Be nice to her.' Moran glowered. 'She's a good friend.'

'Of course, of course. Absolutely. Well, I shan't keep you. Thanks for your help, Chief Inspector.'

'You don't want to know what I found in Rotterdam?'

'At *Guust Vervoer?*' The man allowed himself a little chuckle. 'The trade route? Don't worry. We know all about it. And after we air the contents of your inspired recording, well, how can I put it?'

'MI5 win by an innings?'

'Spot on. I like that. Have a nice evening, DCI Moran.'

Moran watched the man walk away. He looked at his watch, acutely aware that he'd been out of contact with the team for way longer than he'd intended. Time to get back to work. He had a lot to catch up on.

Moran squared his shoulders and walked resolutely in the direction of Tilbury station.

CHAPTER TWENTY-SEVEN

'She's ready and waiting,' DS Luscombe said, holding the hotel door open for Charlie. 'Not too happy either, according to Jenny.'

'Happy or not, we're going to find out what she's hiding,' Charlie told him. 'I just got off the phone with DC McConnell. They've found some interesting intel about our Ms Chan.'

'Oh yes?'

Charlie held her coat over her head as they headed for Luscombe's car. 'God, doesn't it *ever* stop raining here?'

Luscombe looked at her with a twinkle in his eye. 'Not really, no.' He opened the passenger door, stepped aside. 'Maybe a wee bit in August. But then you have the midges.'

'And I thought it rained a lot in Berkshire.' Charlie buckled herself in.

Luscombe swung into the driver's seat. 'So, DC McConnell?'

'There's a cold case. A number of incidents – murders, going back to '91. We have a name for Ms Chan. Her real name.'

Luscombe nodded approvingly. 'Good work.'

'Zubaida Binti Ungu. Malaysian. Killed her uncle. Got a taste for it, came over here and refined her MO.'

Luscombe whistled softly. 'Well, well. At least we know who we're dealing with. That makes me feel a whole lot better.'

'I'll feel better when we get Mrs Brodie to spill.'

'You and me both. Anything else?'

Charlie shook her head. 'They've been through the contents of Mr Daintree's trunk. Nothing helpful, unfortunately.'

'The teacher.'

'Yep. The trunk was jam-packed with memorabilia – going back to the Seventies.'

'It's always worth a look. You never know.'

The remainder of the short journey to Luscombe's station passed in silence, but it was a comfortable silence in which the possibility of intimacy hung in the space between them like an unanswered question. Charlie felt as though she had known Luscombe all her life, even though, in reality, there was much she didn't know about the dour Scotsman. It was hard to concentrate on the job in hand, although George's early phone call had had the effect of sharply refocusing her attention on the case.

Jenny met them outside the pair of interview rooms. She looked Charlie up and down reflexively, and Charlie noticed that she took great care to address herself only to Luscombe.

'Just to warn you, she's not a happy bunny. You're liable to get an earful.'

'Thank you, Jenny. I'll take it from here.' Charlie gave

her a close-lipped smile. 'Could you arrange some tea for us, please?'

You're not undermining me, young lady ... whatever's been going on between you and DS Luscombe.

Ignoring Jenny's outraged expression, Charlie took a mental deep breath and went in.

'Good morning, Mrs Brodie.'

'*Good* morning? Well, I must say you have a ner–'

Luscombe interrupted Mrs Brodie's outburst with a raised hand and a calm tone. 'Just a few questions, Mrs Brodie. You're not under caution. We just need to get a few things straight.'

Mrs Brodie sighed. 'I've already answered your questions – on *two* occasions. What else do you want to know?'

Charlie sat down and folded her arms. She noticed immediately that, regardless of Mrs Brodie's abrupt manner, both eyes were red-rimmed – skilfully camouflaged, but still visible as such under close scrutiny. The harsh strip lighting wasn't helping the deception much, either. Charlie cleared her throat just as Luscombe hit the record button on the prehistoric tape machine. 'Let's begin with the young lady, shall we? Isaiah's girlfriend.'

Mrs Brodie's attempt at a blank expression didn't quite come off.

Luscombe hadn't sat down. He paced the floor behind Mrs Brodie. 'One of your staff members told us about her, Mrs Brodie. So why don't you save us a great deal of time and trouble and tell us what you know about Connie Chan.'

Mrs Brodie looked at her hands. 'Well, I can't say I

cared for the woman very much.'

'Why didn't you tell us this before?' Charlie asked.

'I don't know, really. I just didn't think. We're so busy–'

'Ach, come *on* Mrs Brodie.' Luscombe took the chair next to Charlie and looked Brodie in the eye. 'Stop shilly-shallying around. We're investigating a murder – no, *multiple* murders – so, time is of the essence. Do you get that?'

'Yes, yes. I do. Of course.' Mrs Brodie fiddled with her wedding ring. At close quarters Charlie could clearly see not only the redness, but also the lines around her eyes, the slight darkening of the thin skin beneath. This was a troubled woman, no doubt about it.

The door opened and Jenny came in carrying a tray. She set it on a table by the barred window and left without a word. 'I'll do the honours,' Luscombe said.

As Luscombe clinked about with mugs and milk, Charlie pressed on. 'You didn't care for her, you say. Tell me how you came to meet Ms Chan.'

'Through Isaiah, of course. She didn't work for us. She used to collect Isaiah after his shift. She talked to the carers, naturally. I didn't have a great deal to do with her.'

Luscombe set the mugs on the desk and sat down. Mrs Brodie eyed the tea suspiciously.

'Police standard issue. It won't kill you. At least, it hasn't killed me yet.' Luscombe kept a straight face. Charlie could see that Mrs Brodie was unsure how to respond. Frowning, she opted for a reluctant 'thank you.'

'Are you sure you didn't have a great deal to do with her?' Luscombe asked. 'You never spoke to her, passed the time of day?'

'We're so busy, I can't recall.' Mrs Brodie took refuge in

attending to her tea. She sipped the hot liquid delicately, grimaced and put the mug down.

'I did warn you. An acquired taste,' Luscombe said. 'I'm not altogether sure I've acquired it.'

'Where exactly is your husband, Mrs Brodie?' Charlie changed tack.

Mrs Brodie reacted as though she had been stung. Her face paled, and it took her a few seconds to regain her composure. 'As I told you before, he's away on business.'

'Something to do with a new home, we understand?' Luscombe prompted.

'A new project, yes. He wants to convert an old building. It's recently come into his – into our – possession.'

'Oh yes?'

'He likes to get a ... a *feel* for a building, you see, before the architects get to work.'

'And where might this building be, Mrs Brodie?'

'I don't see what this has to do—'

'Just answer the question, please, Mrs Brodie,' Charlie said.

'Sussex, if you must know.'

'And what sort of building are we talking about?' Luscombe went on. He took a sip of tea as he waited for Mrs Brodie's answer.

'I think it's ... I believe they were once school buildings.' She coughed, reached for the mug of tea, changed her mind.

Charlie turned to Luscombe. 'A quick word?' To Brodie she said, 'Excuse us a moment, please.'

The corridor was empty. Luscombe was looking at her curiously. 'What's up?'

'A school. It may be nothing, but...' Charlie chewed her

lip.

'Go on.'

'Our Mr Daintree was a teacher. Unpopular, by all accounts. He used to live in the south, before he moved here.'

'Then the daughter arranged for him to move south again – to the care home in Reading.' Luscombe said patiently. 'So?'

'Well, where did he live? Where in the south? And where exactly did he teach? I'm sure the guv said that Mrs Fowler – Daintree's daughter – mentioned that her father had spent a long time at a prep school in Sussex. I'm going to call George. If you want to carry on in the meantime…'

'Sure.' Luscombe looked slightly bemused.

'It's probably nothing. Indulge me.' She gave him a terse smile. 'I'll just be a few minutes.'

It took a while to run George to ground. 'Make it quick,' he told her. 'The guv's just arrived and he wants us all in the IR, pronto.'

She told him what she wanted.

'All right, I'll risk his wrath if you think it's important. Give us ten minutes,' George told her. 'The guv'll be all right if he knows it's come from you.'

'Thanks, George. Is he OK? I mean, how is he … in himself?'

'Not in the best of moods, but aye, he seems fine. Why?'

'I don't know … he just sounded a bit … *odd*, when I last spoke to him.'

'Well, he's here, in the flesh, so to speak, so I'd better get cracking.'

'Be quick.'

'Amn't I always?'

Mrs Brodie looked up as Charlie came back into the interview room, hesitated in mid-sentence. 'Carry on,' Charlie said. 'Don't mind me.'

'You were talking about your husband,' Luscombe reminded her.

'Yes, well, he's away a lot. He's a successful man. I don't try to keep tabs on him all the time. Why should I?'

'Why, indeed?' Luscombe agreed. 'Did your husband know this woman, Chan?'

'Certainly not,' Mrs Brodie replied, a small speck of colour appearing on her cheeks. 'What are you implying?'

'I'm not implying anything, Mrs Brodie,' Luscombe said patiently. 'I'm simply trying to establish a set of facts which will help us.'

Charlie took over. 'How often would you say Ms Chan came to see Isaiah at Chapelfields?'

Mrs Brodie considered the question briefly. 'A handful of times, I should say.'

'Did Isaiah's duties include any deliveries, or visits?' Charlie moved the interrogative goalposts in another direction.

A long hesitation. 'He may have used the van once or twice.'

'For … what, exactly?' Luscombe joined in.

'Collecting, running errands, that sort of thing.'

'Collecting people?' Charlie tilted her head to one side. 'Or medication? Or…?'

'Look, I can't remember everything the man did. Others would have asked him to perform various duties. He was there to help. A gofer.' A note of exasperation had crept into Brodie's voice.

A knock on the door. Jenny's head appeared. 'Phone call. DI Pepper. Urgent.' Her head disappeared again.

'Excuse me.' Charlie got up. 'Keep the tape running. I shan't be long.'

It was George. She listened impatiently to her colleague's rapid patter. A good copper, George, but he didn't half go on sometimes. 'And the name of the school?' she cut in.

She heard George riffling through sheaves of paper. 'Here we are. Eagle Court. It's near Petworth, in Sussex. Stockbroker belt,' he added, a note of disdain modulating the vowels and consonants of his soft Scottish brogue.

'OK, George. Look, you're going to kill me, but I need you to check that trunk again. Is there anything in there about the pupils? We're talking mid-Seventies, or thereabouts. School reports, photographs, maybe? I don't know … pupil admissions, sporting achievements. New arrivals.' She racked her brains. 'Prefects' lists?'

'What am I looking for?'

'It's a long shot,' Charlie admitted. 'But there may be some connection. Daintree taught at this school, right? Well, Mrs Brodie's husband has just bought an old school in Sussex. I haven't got the name yet, but I'm about to run this past her.'

George was silent for a moment. 'Sounds plausible. If she says *Eagle Court*, you're thinking…'

'Ex-pupil with grudge against ex-teacher gets his own back. Yes, that's exactly what I'm thinking.'

'And he buys the old place for … what reason, exactly?'

'He's rich and successful. He wants to expand, build further residential homes. An old prep school in the country – well that's a perfect location, right?'

'Right. And to put the past to bed, make some kind of peace with himself, and it. But hang on – that doesn't necessarily explain the other killings. They can't *all* have been teachers at the prep school.'

Charlie bit down hard on her lip. 'I know. You're dead right. But let's check, anyhow.'

She passed Jenny in the corridor. The DC walked right past her without a word.

Suit yourself, madam…

Back in the interview room, Luscombe was standing by the window, his back to the bars. Charlie took her seat as before. 'So, Mrs Brodie. I want you to think very carefully before you answer this question. Is the school your husband intends to buy called *Eagle Court*, by any chance?'

Mrs Brodie didn't need to articulate an answer. It was obvious from her expression. She almost winced at the sound of the name.

'I need to hear your reply,' Charlie said. 'For the tape, if you wouldn't mind. Is your husband's intended purchase *Eagle Court*?'

Mrs Brodie's mouth opened and closed. Her confidence had evaporated to the extent that Charlie decided to go with her hunch and pitch the big sub question. 'Did your husband attend *Eagle Court* as a pupil, Mrs Brodie?'

Luscombe's eyebrows were raised. He sipped his tea and watched from the wings.

'Yes,' Mrs Brodie said in a quiet voice. 'He did.'

CHAPTER TWENTY-EIGHT

'George? Are you joining us? The guv's asking for you.' Bernice Swinhoe's face was flushed as she delivered her message and waited for George's acknowledgement.

George looked up. The big room was empty, all hands having been summoned to the IR. 'Two minutes. You can tell DCI Moran that I'm sending something to Charlie – it's urgent and relevant. I'll be along shortly.'

'All right. Make it fast.'

Bernice disappeared and George lifted another stack of papers from the trunk. He had half the contents laid out beside him on the floor. Exercise books, stationery, folders, reports, financial documents, checklists, the flotsam and jetsam of a teaching career dating back to the Sixties. So far, there was nothing to indicate that the late Mr Daintree had anything to do with Duncan Brodie, and, so far as he could see, there was no further written memorabilia regarding Eagle Court.

The base of the trunk was visible now, just a few bits and pieces left. George's eye was drawn to the remaining items: a long cardboard tube and a soft-backed magazine.

He fished them out, placed the magazine on the carpet. On the cover was a pencil drawing of an austere, crenellated building, a coat of arms, and beneath it in typescript:

Eagle Court School Magazine 1976

George returned his attention to the cardboard tube. Something was rolled up inside. He prised the paper out with his forefinger and thumb, spread it on the carpet. A black and white school photograph, The same crest, name and date were printed in the centre at the bottom of the photograph: Eagle Court. 1976.

A couple of hundred boys stared back at him, standing almost to attention, each affecting solemn expressions. A row of stern looking teachers were seated in the foreground on a long bench. Next to the central figure, whom George assumed to be the headmaster, sat a middle-aged lady in a nurses' uniform. The school matron, probably. Next to her was a young girl, the only female in the photograph under the age of twenty, hands folded demurely in her lap.

George examined the photograph, squinted at each earnest face. Where were they now? What had their lives become? 1976 was another era, another world, without computers, internet, mobile phones, social media. A more innocent world, perhaps? But George had heard stories about boarding school, the things that went on. He remembered the guv recounting his experiences at Charnford Abbey, stories that had only reinforced George's opinions. Boarding schools were a world apart – especially back then – with their closed systems of rules and traditions, their own ways of dealing with misdemeanours, crimes and indiscretions, their own privileges.

And, perhaps, their own secrets.

George carefully photographed the image, five shots in all to cover the width of the original. He sent them all to Charlie's mobile, then turned his attention back to the pile of papers. There was just too much; he hadn't time to go through everything now. Reluctantly, he left the trunk and its time-capsule contents, and hurried off to the Incident Room.

'It's her.' Charlie jabbed a finger at the last of George's images. 'Agreed?'

Luscombe took the mobile, examined the image closely. 'I'd say so. Hard to be a hundred percent, but–'

'Let's see what she says. Over to you this time.'

Luscombe gave a brusque nod of acknowledgement and preceded Charlie into the interview room. Mrs Brodie's shoulders were slumped. She looked defeated, tired of keeping up her no-nonsense, 'everything's fine' persona. Luscombe restarted the tape, steepled his hands, gave her a long, analytical look.

'I think you have something to tell us, Mrs Brodie. And I think you'll feel better when you get it off your chest.'

Mrs Brodie gave a weary sigh. 'I've told you, I didn't have anything to do with this woman. I can't be accountable for her comings and goings.'

'Let's talk about Eagle Court.'

'But why? Is it relevant?'

'It might be,' Luscombe said. Rain blew against the window, rattled the pane in its peeling frame.

'You've told us that your husband attended the school. You've also told us that he intends to purchase the property with a view to creating another Chapelfields home.'

'Yes, that's correct.'

Luscombe leaned in close. 'But this is all getting rather cosy, Mrs Brodie, because it wasn't only your husband who spent time at the school, was it?'

Mrs Brodie toyed with her wedding ring, rotated it slowly.

'Or, perhaps, would it be truer and more accurate to say he 'did time' at the school? I wonder, did he experience difficulties there, by any chance? Bullying, or maybe abuse of some sort?'

Mrs Brodie moistened her lips, started to form words of reply, gave up.

'And you'd have known all about it, I shouldn't wonder, because you were also there. At the time,' Luscombe said pointedly. 'Weren't you, Mrs Brodie?'

Charlie handed Luscombe her mobile. Luscombe tapped the photos app, held the screen up for Mrs Brodie's perusal. 'That's you, right? In the centre, next to the nurse – or matron, is she?'

'My mother,' Mrs Brodie said quietly.

'We found this photograph in the late Mr Daintree's trunk,' Charlie explained. 'So that's all three of you, living at Eagle Court together at the same time.'

'Mr Daintree is murdered, having had his name down originally for Aviemore Chapelfields. And lo and behold, we now have your husband inspecting the old school buildings at Eagle Court with a view to purchase.' Luscombe sat back and folded his arms. 'Coincidence?'

'What happened at Eagle Court, Mrs Brodie?' Charlie prompted. Now was the time; Brodie's defences were shaky, beginning to teeter. The manageress' next question confirmed Charlie's suspicions.

'I'll be happy to put you in the picture, DI Pepper, but I'd rather not answer any further questions without legal representation, if you'd be good enough to allow me a telephone call?'

'Of course,' Luscombe smiled. 'If you'd care to follow me, you can use my desk phone.'

Mrs Brodie's brief arrived twenty-five minutes later, a thin, ascetic looking Scotsman in a brown pinstriped suit. He took his place in the interview room after the briefest of consultations with his client.

The tape rolled again. Luscombe recorded the formalities and gave the floor to Mrs Brodie, who paused for a moment before she began, as though preparing her mind to revisit painful memories.

'First of all, my requesting a legal representative in no way implies that I have anything to hide, or that I am guilty of any crime. I am simply protecting myself and our reputation. I hope that is clearly understood.'

Charlie nodded her assent. 'We understand. Go on.'

'I met my husband when I was very young – when *we* were very young, I should say. He was just a–' Mrs Brodie paused to blow her nose on a tissue. 'Excuse me.'

They waited patiently for her to continue.

The tissue disappeared into Mrs Brodie's handbag. 'Just a ... a schoolboy. Yes, at Eagle Court. My mother was the school matron. We lived in a cottage in the school grounds. I was sixteen at the time. My father left us when I was young, so it was just the two of us. Mother was always busy, and I was lonely.'

'And you used to talk to the boys? Was that allowed?' Charlie asked.

'Not really, no. But there were opportunities. The afternoons were all about sport. Rugby, cross country running, all that kind of thing. Manly stuff, to make men out of the poor, shivering wretches that they were. I was standing on the touchline one afternoon, watching the game, and the master in charge took offence at something that happened in the match. I don't know what it was, and neither does Duncan – my husband – but it was a trigger, a flashpoint. I couldn't believe what I was seeing. The man got hold of Duncan's ear and pulled it until he screamed in agony. This was a thirteen-year old boy, mark you. I could see blood pouring from the wound, but he was made to play on, to finish the game. After the game was over, the master called me over, told me to take Duncan to my mother because he'd injured himself in the match.'

'And this would be Mr Daintree?' Luscombe interrupted.

'Yes.'

Brodie's brief leaned over and whispered something in her ear. She nodded and took a deep breath before carrying on.

'I tried to cheer him up, but what could I say? What could I do? I had no power. I took him to Mother. She knew, I'm sure, that Duncan was lying, that he hadn't injured himself in the game at all. But in those days...' She shrugged, a gesture of futility. 'What could anyone do? Most boys were there because their parents worked abroad, or were too busy to have them at home. They assumed the boys were well-cared for. Well, why would they think otherwise? The headmaster was adept at painting a rosy picture, reassuring parents that their offspring would be looked after, nurtured, brought on in their learning, prepared for public school and a future professional life. That headmaster, he was worse than Daintree. The punishments he would inflict for the merest transgression.' Her hand went to her mouth at the memory. 'The abuse went on in the classrooms, on the sports fields, in the dormitories. Day by day, month by month, Duncan endured it.'

'And you were able to speak to him regularly, meet him in secret?' Charlie was scandalised by Brodie's recollections, but she couldn't allow herself to be overly sympathetic. Her intuition told her that something deeper was about to be revealed.

'Yes. We became close. I was his confidante. He was a shy, nervous boy – more so as the term went on. He only had a stepmother to look after him in the holidays, and she wasn't that interested. He'd never had any love shown to him, you see.'

Luscombe had been listening attentively. Now he spoke up. 'So, you watch from a distance, comforting where you can, all the time wishing there was something more you could do to help. But then presumably Duncan Brodie leaves the school. What happened next? How did you hook up later?'

'We left the school when my mother retired. I was twenty by then, and I don't think my mother considered it safe for me to be under the same roof as a few hundred lustful adolescent boys. I took a part-time job in a hospital, just secretarial work, and then one of the consultants asked me to help him with his private practice, at a psychiatric hospital.'

Luscombe nodded. 'Go on.'

'Well, you've probably guessed. I was walking along the corridor one morning, and there was Duncan in his dressing gown. He looked different, I mean older. He'd aged ten years in half that time. I had coffee with him, reprised my role as chief cheerer-upper, and that was it, really. We started going out when he felt well enough. He was discharged six months later, and a year after that we were married.'

'A heartwarming story, Mrs Brodie,' Luscombe concluded. 'I'm sure you must take a great deal of credit for your husband's recovery and his subsequent extraordinary success.'

'He's a bright man.' Brodie rose to her husband's defence. 'Very capable. A good brain, but so…'

'Damaged?' Charlie said.

'Of *course*.' The testiness was back. 'You can't go through something like that in your formative years and *not* be compromised in some way.'

'Compromised enough to consider murder?' Luscombe brought the investigation into sharp focus.

'I can't believe he'd stoop to that. But, oh, who can say? It's possible, I suppose. Oh God, do you *really* think…?'

'We need to speak to him, that's for sure.' Charlie said. 'But you say he's out of touch right now?'

'I can't get hold of him, no.'

'Is that unusual?' Luscombe asked.

She sighed. 'We had a bit of a tiff before he left last week. I haven't spoken to him since.'

Luscombe leaned forward. 'Really? About what exactly?'

'A small disagreement about finances, that's all. Duncan

can be a little impulsive.'

'And you're the Chapelfields chancellor?' Charlie probed. 'The brains behind the investments?'

'Perhaps. I'm good with numbers, Duncan less so. People are his thing.'

'I'd like your husband's mobile phone number, please, Mrs Brodie. His car registration too, if you wouldn't mind.'

'Yes, of course.'

Luscombe wasn't finished. 'You've told us that your husband didn't know Connie Chan, Mrs Brodie. Are you quite sure about that?'

'As sure as I can be. He's not often here, so how would he have come into contact with her?'

'Mrs Brodie.' Charlie evoked as much gravitas as she was able. 'Where would your husband choose to stay if he was revisiting Eagle Court, as you've suggested?'

A long sigh. 'I have no idea. Some hotel nearby, I would have thought. A nice one, mind. He likes his comfort. Now, I have cooperated in every way, and answered your questions to the best of my ability. Chapelfields doesn't run itself. I really need to get back to work.'

'All right, you may,' Charlie told her. 'But don't leave the area, please.'

'Interview terminated at 14:03,' Luscombe said, and flicked the tape machine to *off*.

'Why let her go? She's not telling us the whole story, I can feel it,' Luscombe said to Charlie as they headed back to the team's office.

'Probably not,' Charlie agreed. 'I'd like Jenny plus one to keep an eye on her, if you could arrange that? If she talks to anyone, makes any calls, takes any detours, I want to know about it. Oh, I could use a sandwich and a coffee too? I need to touch base with DCI Moran – chances are they've made progress we need to know about – before we decide what to do next. Back in a mo.' Charlie headed off to the loos.

'Don't want much, do you?' Luscombe called after her.

'I'm easy to please, most of the time,' Charlie replied over her shoulder. 'You just have to treat me right.'

She felt his eyes on her.

I'd say that was dangerously close to flirting, Charlie…

CHAPTER TWENTY-NINE

'Let's hear it,' Moran invited the team. 'Update from the Reading station CCTV? DC Swinhoe?'

'Yes, guv. We found her last night. A woman matching Zubaida Ungu's description showed up the evening of Daintree's murder, headed up the Caversham Road, by the station rear entrance. We lost her at the roundabout but she made a right turn.'

'Good. And then?'

'DC Delaney and myself had a look, guv. First hotel we tried, bingo.'

Bernice Swinhoe was clearly pleased with their result. Moran felt the warm satisfaction of knowing that the team could function – and perform – well in his absence. He nodded appreciatively. 'Good work. What did you find out?'

'It's the Star Hotel, guv. Owner remembered the POI. Called her a 'looker'. Didn't engage in any small talk, just gave the minimum details – Connie Chandra was the name she wrote in the book – *but* he did overhear a subsequent telephone conversation.'

'Did he indeed.'

'I got the feeling that he was, er...' Swinhoe paused awkwardly.

'Sniffing around?' one of the male detectives suggested.

The IR erupted in laughter. Moran let it happen. The team had been hard at it all weekend; they deserved a little light relief.

'All right, all right. We get the picture.' Moran waved his arm to quieten them and felt a surge of pain across his midriff. When he'd awoken at six after a fitful sleep and examined his injuries, he'd found that the bruise had spread further up his abdomen during the night, and had turned a bluish purple colour. He didn't think any ribs were fractured but it was hard to tell. A&E wouldn't do anything for ribs anyway, so he just had to get on with it. Hopefully there wasn't any internal damage that had yet to make itself apparent.

When the noise had died down, DC Swinhoe went on. 'So, he heard her say – Mr Giles, I mean, the hotel manager – he heard her booking a room. He wasn't sure where exactly, but there was mention of a station that sounded like Billing something.'

'Billing?'

Swinhoe made a face. 'That's what he said. I guess that's all he heard.'

'Dirty so-and-so probably had his ear glued to her door,' DC Collingworth suggested. 'Till she sussed him out and caught him at it.'

'Billingsgate?' someone suggested.

'That's a fish market,' DC Delaney pointed out.

More laughter. 'Thank you,' Moran said. 'We'll assume fish are off the agenda, but perhaps someone can follow that up? Can't be too many stations beginning with 'Billing'. Ah, DC McConnell?'

George found an empty seat. He looked out of breath and slightly harassed. 'Sorry, guv. DI Pepper needed some intel pronto.'

'Apple for teacher,' Collingworth stage-whispered with a smirk.

George replied with a look that would have frozen the Gobi Desert.

'Did you get anywhere with the US-based crime scene expert from the report, George?' Moran asked.

'Nope. Couldn't reach anyone with a clear memory of the guy. Cumbria thought he might have been from New York, but they've just re-jigged their archives and–' George rolled his shoulders. 'No dice – no one remembers it. Team members've moved on, retired, died … it's history now.'

'Looks like we're on our own, as per usual.' Moran's mobile vibrated. 'One moment–'

He saw who was calling and raised his hand to the room. 'That's it for now. Get to it and keep me posted, please.'

As the team dispersed he accepted the call. 'Charlie? How goes it?' He grimaced at a sudden stab of pain as he turned to leave the IR. Bernice Swinhoe caught his expression, gave him an odd look that she modified to a concerned smile. He shook his head as if to imply that it was nothing – he was fine.

'You there, guv?'

'Most of me, yes. Go ahead, Charlie.'

'Well?' Luscombe held out a full, steaming mug.

'Thanks.' Charlie took the mug and drew breath sharply. It was scalding hot.

'Sorry, boiler's only got one temperature: max.'

They were alone in the team's small open plan. Charlie shook her head in a disparaging gesture. 'As long as there's caffeine, I'm happy.' She set the mug down on her allocated desk. It looked bare, with its Eighties-style Trim phone and scattering of used biros and old, curling folders. 'No luck with Duncan Brodie?'

'No reply – straight to voicemail.'

'So, switched off, or in a dead zone?'

'Could be either. I'd recommend your team contact Sussex constabulary, get searching for him.'

Charlie considered the suggestion. 'You're right. I'll set the wheels in motion.'

'And maybe a bite to eat after that?'

Charlie collected herself, made a conscious effort to relax. Her head was aching dully, a problem she'd noticed was occurring more and more frequently during working hours, especially after interviewing. She ran her fingers through her hair. 'That sounds like a great idea.'

'Nice pub I know, just a few minutes drive.'

'Perfect.'

As Luscombe directed the car out of Aviemore, Charlie rested her head and closed her eyes. The throbbing in her temple was receding, a response to either the caffeine or the two paracetamol she had taken; honestly, she didn't much care. Luscombe had sensed that she needed an hour to unwind. Perceptive as well as good-looking. She smiled to herself.

'What are you grinning about?' Luscombe shot her a

sideways glance.

'Just a private thought.'

'Fair enough.' He turned onto the main road and accelerated. 'Your lot get hold of Sussex?'

'I've left it with George. He'll sort it out.'

'Good.'

'Where are we headed?'

'A wee place called the Boat of Garten. Ten minutes. You'll like it.'

Luscombe's ten minutes was spot on. He pulled into the car park of a grand stone building which announced itself as *The Boat*. The rain had petered out and blue patches had begun to appear in the brooding greyness. The Cairngorms rose majestically in the distance, an undulating line above the treetops. Charlie stepped out of the car and took a deep breath. The air felt clean, unused, fresh from the mountains.

I could get used to this…

'Are you coming in, or what?' Luscombe jangled his keys. 'It'll be a wait for the food, so best get the order in asap.'

'Coming.'

The pub was half-full, lunchtime service almost ended. They found a vacant table by a picture window and Luscombe procured a menu. Charlie chose a round of avocado, hummus, spinach and cucumber sandwiches, while Luscombe went for Highland cheddar and roast ham, with leek and potato soup and a bowl of chips on the side. He went to the bar to order, and returned with a Diet Coke for Charlie and an orange juice for himself. He set the glasses down and settled in his chair.

'So. Our friend Mrs Brodie – what's your take?'

'Still holding out.' Charlie sipped her Coke. 'There's something not right, but we'll have to wait for Duncan Brodie's side of the story before we find out exactly what.'

'OK,' Luscombe said. 'But d'you think he's the kind of guy to risk all for revenge?'

Charlie shook her head. 'I don't know enough about him. From what I've seen – and that's not much, just the odd TV interview – he seems straight enough. Self-effacing, I'd say, but you never know.'

'He went through a hell of a time at that school,' Luscombe said. 'At that age, too. Resentment sticks, don't you think?'

'So you're suggesting what? That he hired Connie Chan to do the deed?'

Luscombe made a face. 'Why not? There's every chance he knew the woman, even if Mrs Brodie denies it. Exactly how he discovered Chan's area of expertise is less clear.'

Charlie's phone buzzed. 'Hold on. Sorry.' She answered the call. 'George, what's up?'

George's voice was faint. Bad connection. She jammed the phone against her ear and caught the tail-end of the first sentence. '…a lead on Chan. We think she bought a ticket to Billingshurst.'

'Where the hell is Billingshurst?'

Crackle, crackle…

'Bad line, George, can you shout?'

'Sussex,' George's voice yelled faintly. 'Three miles from Eagle Court.'

Charlie's heart leaped. 'Fantastic. Well done. What's the state of play regarding Sussex back-up?'

'Ah,' George replied. 'The SSU was disbanded five years ago and they've got manpower issues just now.'

Charlie groaned. 'Meaning they're not playing ball?'

'The guv's talking to one of their senior guys,' George said. 'They might be able to get uniform over to the school for a quick look, but we've just heard there's been a massive shunt on the M25. Traffic's chaotic and alternative routes are filling up nicely. Fog, they say. It's a wee bit misty here, but you can't see your hand in front of your face in Sussex, so they tell me.'

'Oh, that's just perfect.' Charlie pushed a hand through her hair.

Soup finished, Luscombe was watching her patiently, chewing thoughtfully on a mouthful of sandwich.

'We'll sort something out, probably the best thin—' George's voice vanished and the phone went dead.

Charlie chucked the phone down on the table in frustration. 'Damn.'

'Problem?'

She prodded at her salad garnish but her appetite had vanished. She put down her cutlery, looked out on the wide landscape, arms folded, rigid with frustration. 'She's *there*. At the school, or damn close to it. Looks like she and Mr Brodie have arranged a bloody rendezvous.'

'Seems clear cut, in that case.' Luscombe tapped his temple. 'They've known each other – in the Biblical sense – for quite some time, is my guess. Mrs Brodie reckons they've never met, but come on; he and Chan are in this thing together, and not just as partners in crime. The guy's never home, always away on business. He could have been up to all sorts. I'm speculating, but you have to admit it's plausible.'

'And Mrs Brodie probably knows about them, or at least suspects.' Charlie's mind was tripping over itself with theories. 'So Mrs Brodie tells us where he is – the school – anticipating that he's on a meet with Chan?'

'She's torn. She wants to protect him, but part of her wants to bring him down, too.'

'It makes sense.' Charlie chewed a nail. 'It really does.'

'So they should pick 'em both up.' Luscombe finished his last chip and pushed his plate away regretfully. 'The Sussex lot.'

'But George says they're short on manpower. And it's not a priority for them, is it? It's not their problem, technically.'

'Not their problem?' Luscombe bristled. 'They'd better arrest the pair of them PDQ, or my boss'll be wanting to know why.'

Charlie bunched her fingers, covered her mouth. 'I've got to get down there.'

Luscombe eyebrows arched. 'What?'

'I can be at Gatwick in a few hours – well, why not? The school can't be more than thirty minutes from the airport. Does your phone have a signal? When's the next flight?'

'Are you serious?'

'Yes. You can keep tabs on Mrs Brodie. Right now, Chan is the prime suspect and I want her and Duncan Brodie in custody.'

Luscombe was looking at his phone. 'Aha. Free wifi. Hold on a sec.'

Charlie paced up and down. The pub was emptying fast, groups of tourists departing for their afternoon ambles. She felt a bolt of envy. What must it be like to be carefree, nothing on the agenda except fresh air, the beautiful Highland scenery, the prospect of a cozy hotel, a leisurely evening meal, a comfortable room, a long, luxurious sleep? Repeat all of the above the following day. When had she last had a holiday? She honestly couldn't remember.

'There's a flight in an hour. I can get you there. If you insist.'

'I do.' Charlie retrieved her handbag. 'Shall we?'

Luscombe tucked his phone away. 'You'll be missed,' he said.

'I can always come back,' she heard herself say. 'When this is over.'

Luscombe gave her a brief nod, took out the car keys and made for the exit.

CHAPTER THIRTY

The Swan Hotel was originally a sixteenth-century building. The tar-blackened timber of its frontage proudly proclaimed that fact, as did the small leaded windows and the cantilevered second storey that overhung the entrance porch. The hotel had been privately run for many years until, eventually, the economic climate had taken its toll and The Swan passed inevitably into the hands of a hotel chain. Despite this unwelcome change, it stuck to its high standards. Many of the experienced staff were retained and the hotel continued to run smoothly and efficiently. It was the best hotel for miles around, and Petworth itself was a pleasant, if rather anonymous, town.

All good reasons, Duncan Brodie had reasoned, for booking a few extra days and taking time to ponder the wisdom of his decision. He glanced at his Rolex, tutted, picked up his phone and glasses, closed his bedroom door carefully behind him, and made his way to the lounge.

She was waiting for him by the fireplace, reclining on a two-seater settee beneath a portrait of Capability Brown – in honour, Brodie supposed, of the famous gardener's contribution to the landscaped vistas of nearby Petworth House. As Brodie approached he was struck by two things: first her sheer beauty, and second, the stroke of favourable providence that had brought them together.

'Hi.' She greeted him with her perfect smile.

'Hello yourself,' Brodie said, bending to kiss her on the lips. As he did so he kept his face close to hers for a moment, allowing her features to fill his eyes. He recalled Dudley Moore's film, simply entitled '10', the diminutive late comedian's score for a perfect conceptual woman. Well, this lady would score twelve, if that were possible. She was quite simply off the scale beautiful.

'Did you order?'

'I did,' she replied. 'Tea for two with scones, cream and strawberry jam.'

'Spot on,' Duncan Brodie nodded enthusiastically. 'Just what's required.'

She laughed, a tinkling, musical sound that he found entrancing and hypnotic in equal measure. If he were a comedian, he'd make jokes all day just to get her to reprise that laugh.

'Enjoy your morning?' Brodie enquired, slipping into the soft cushions of the settee next to her and encircling her shoulder with his arm. 'Sorry I couldn't join you. Phone calls, things to organise. It never ends.'

'I had a *lovely* morning,' she replied. 'I walked around the shops, bought a new jacket, a sandwich and a coffee for lunch at the cutest little place – you must see it – came back, had a little beauty sleep, and here we are.'

'Good, good.' Brodie nodded.

'Is something bothering you?' Her brow furrowed. 'You seem a bit distracted, Mr Brodie.'

'Mm? No, not really. Well, maybe a little. I apologise. It's always the same before I commit to an investment. Have I done the right thing, you know. Is it wise? What could I do as an alternative, to make the money work better for the company? That kind of conversation bounces around in my mind. Sorry, I don't mean to appear preoccupied.'

She took his hand. 'You are a clever man, very wise. Look at how successful you are. I am sure that your investment is a good one. But tell me more about it. I would like to hear, really I would.'

'Well, I don't want to bore you.'

'Bore me?' The laugh came again, sent shivers of delight up and down his spine. 'You will not bore me, Duncan Brodie. I promise.'

And yet, he hesitated to share his concerns. This wasn't a normal purchase. This was Eagle Court, the location of his youthful traumas. But he'd survived the privations of the school's Draconian regime, hadn't he? He'd put it behind him. The past was the past, and best left there.

'Uh oh.' She nudged him teasingly. 'I've really lost you now.'

'Sorry. I'm here, honestly I am. I'm all yours.' He smiled reassuringly.

A waiter appeared with the tea order. A minute passed in silence as the silver service was laid out and they were invited to choose from a selection of cakes from the trolley.

'Scones *and* cake. I shall get fat, lose my figure.' She opened the teapot and gave the dark liquid a stir with the provided long-handled spoon. 'But I can't resist these lovely English customs.'

'Special cream tea,' Brodie agreed. 'One of the things

us Brits do well, and this particular hotel, exceptionally well.'

He watched her small hands working with assured delicacy, applying cream and jam to the scones, first for him and then for herself, pouring the tea, arranging the plates and sugar bowl in a pleasing pattern before them on the low table. Once again he found himself marvelling at his good fortune. How had the stars aligned with such benign mathematical precision that he had found himself in the same hotel at the same time as Ms Connie Chan? And moreover, that she had been instantly attracted to him, approached his solitary table at dinner that first evening, introduced herself and, before he'd known what was happening, invited herself into his bed?

Such good fortune had been more than Duncan Brodie could have hoped for, his great wealth notwithstanding. The most pleasing thing, for him, was that she hadn't known who he was. She'd never heard of him, being a newcomer to England. And that meant she must be genuinely attracted to him, rather than his money, or his fame. After so long with Fiona, he'd found that there'd been an outstanding question in his life, unanswered until now. That question was: 'Am I worthy in myself? Am I an attractive personality?'

When he'd taken the first tentative steps in his entrepreneurial journey so many years ago, he now realised that he'd failed to prioritise time for personal reflection, Fiona having taken up most of his mental space during the few hours of downtime he'd allowed himself. He'd lost himself somewhere along the line. Who exactly was Duncan Brodie these days? He needed to find out. Perhaps the row he'd had with Fiona the previous week had been precipitated by just that desire; he was breaking out, finally discovering himself, cutting himself free. It was at once both frightening and exhilarating. And Eagle Court … now, of all times. It was meant to be, surely? A cathartic end and a new beginning, all rolled into one…

'Hellooo?' Connie Chan wiggled her fingers. 'I'm still here, you know.'

He looked at her and grinned. 'I know,' he replied, 'and I'm so glad you are.'

After a moment of silent intimacy, she raised her pencil-thin eyebrows. 'Well?'

'Mm? Oh, the investment. If you insist, then, I'll tell you. I'll tell you the whole thing.' He picked up his teacup, took a sip, and began.

She listened attentively, her expression moving between fascination, concern, horror, and admiration as the story unfolded. Around them, the hotel moved into its early evening phase. Guests came and went, bellboys hurried to and fro, carrying suitcases, wheeling trolleys and sack barrows; the lounge ceiling lights burned into life and soft music crept into the room from hidden speakers. When he'd finished, she said nothing for a long time. Eventually, she stirred and said, 'That's quite a tale, Mr Brodie. I don't know what to say. But the school, is it far? And it is empty – unoccupied, you say? I would very much like to see it.'

'Of course. I'll probably be popping over in the morning. You're very welcome to come along.'

She frowned. 'I'd like to see it sooner. Why not tonight?'

He was a little taken aback. 'Well, I mean, there's no rush. It'll still be standing tomorrow.'

She leaned across and took his hand. 'I want to make

that connection with you,' she said earnestly. 'I want to feel it, understand it.'

He puffed out his cheeks. 'Well, all right. I don't see why not.' He glanced outside. 'It's a little foggy, but that won't hinder us. It's only a twenty-minute drive. How about we pop out shortly? I'll show you around, and then we can stop at a pub for dinner afterwards.'

'That sounds wonderful,' Connie Chan said. 'I'll go and get changed.'

CHAPTER THIRTY-ONE

Moran checked the time. Four o'clock. Mrs P would be sitting down for her habitual afternoon cup of tea. She was never out at four.

He'd arrived home the previous evening, collected Archie and told his neighbour that someone would be calling the following day to pick up the package he'd left in her care. Mrs Perkins had nodded.

'That'll be fine, Brendan. I'll be in all afternoon. And how was your weekend away?'

'Unusual, Mrs P, would be the way I'd put it. But I'm back safe and sound.'

Mrs Perkins was, Moran knew, insatiably curious, but to her credit, she rarely probed into his activities, especially the kind of activities associated with his job. For that, he was grateful. She was discreet. Also in her favour, Archie loved staying over at her house. He looked down at the excited little dog, pacing the hallway with furiously wagging tail, torn between returning to his permanent home and the prospect of extra time with his exciting friend, Mrs P, who always took him for long walks by the river or into the woods at Sulham to sniff out deer or rabbits.

'Will you call me when it's been collected, Mrs P?' Moran asked as he clipped Archie to his lead.

'I'll be sure to.'

'Thanks again.'

'Think nothing of it, Brendan. There was one thing I was wondering, though.'

'Oh, yes?'

'Did you find your duck?'

Moran smiled to himself. On the ball, as ever, Mrs P had referred to Samantha Grant, regarding her abduction a few weeks back, as a duck between two drakes, the Russian duo who'd played the role of her kidnappers. 'Let's just say she took to the water on a permanent basis.'

Mrs Perkins had folded her arms. 'Well, as long as that's a tidy solution, I'm glad. Now you'd better get Archie his dinner. He'll be hungry after his swim.'

That had been last night. Since then, no phone call – and now, no reply from her landline. Mrs P didn't believe in mobile telephony. He ought to pop over, check that all was well.

Moran looked up as his office door swung open after the most perfunctory knock. DCS Higginson, in full uniform, assigned himself the visitor's chair without invitation and placed his hat carefully on Moran's desk.

'Sir. How can I help?'

'You have a suspect, I understand?'

'Yes, sir. We believe the lady in question is on her way to, or has recently arrived in, Billingshurst – a small station in Sussex, near Petworth.'

'And you can't raise my opposite number in Sussex?'

'Not so far, sir, I'm afraid. They have a lot on their plate today, so I'm told. Traffic down that way also have a major incident on the M23 to contend with.'

'Yes, I heard. Major RTC on the M25 as well, near the M23 junction. Fog. Worse down there than here. We have to apprehend this POI, Brendan. We can't let her slip through the net again. I've seen the history. Makes grim reading.'

Moran sighed. 'I can't help but agree, sir. I'll keep trying Sussex.'

'Anything I can do, you'll let me know?'

'Sir.'

Moran watched Higginson stride from the room, straight-backed, uniform crackling in its finely pressed creases. The boss'd carry the can for this one, for sure – and Higginson clearly wanted the can to be brightly painted, a success trophy.

Moran went to the internal window, drew the blind. A thin mist was blurring the fading, wintery light. Headlights were on, traffic crawling. He returned to his desk, eased himself into his chair. His ribs were so tender he'd hardly slept. He took a deep breath and winced.

What had happened on the boat had shaken him, taken the wind out of his sails. He was too old for this kind of thing. He remembered the automatic, how it had jerked slightly as Samantha pulled the trigger. The hammering blow to his chest.

He'd been lucky. It could have gone the other way. It was hard not to go through the list of what ifs. What if he hadn't thought to don the Kevlar jacket? What if she'd gone for a head shot? What if the barrier hadn't given way? Samantha had been a professional. She hadn't wanted to kill him, he firmly believed that, but professionals were trained to get the job done.

Moran dragged his mind back to the present. Chan was, in all likelihood, and for reasons yet unknown, heading for a meeting with Duncan Brodie. Which implied a degree of collusion. Or did it? Sure, the guy had suffered a bad few years at school, but then again, Moran's schooldays had hardly been a walk in the park; Blackrock had been renowned for its discipline in those days, and for all he knew, still was.

But, there's a thin line between discipline and abuse, right? In fairness, he conceded, Blackrock had always stayed on the right side of that line. If that hadn't been the case, though, would he have considered murder as a revenge option? The answer to that question depended much on character, and from what he knew of Duncan Brodie, the guy was personable – if a little bland – generous, a philanthropist of note, a successful entrepreneur, a businessman with a conscience. It didn't sit right.

He checked his watch. Four thirty-five. Mrs P.

He called, let it ring for a minute, two minutes.

No answer.

He had to be sure. It would take forty minutes to get to Pangbourne and back, allowing for rush hour traffic – and fog.

As he put the phone into his pocket it vibrated. He stabbed the answer button. 'Charlie. What news?'

'Guv, I'm boarding a flight to Gatwick. Should be there by six-thirty.'

'You're flying into *Gatwick* – in this muck?' Moran glanced outside. 'I hope your pilot knows what he's doing.'

'They ummed and ahd for a bit but they're going for it.

I've got to get down there, guv. She's in Sussex somewhere, for sure. The school, or–'

'I know. But you'll be on your own, Charlie.' Moran tried to keep the alarm out of his voice. 'The roads are a nightmare – you'll be lucky to get out of Gatwick, let alone anywhere near Petworth.'

'If Sussex can't oblige, what are we going to do? This is the closest we've got to picking her up. And you're not going to get there, with the traffic, weather and all, are you, guv?'

An idea occurred to him. 'There's always the chance of a chopper. I'll see if I can swing it – Higginson'll sign anything off, the mood he's in.'

'They're calling the flight, guv. Got to go.'

'Tell me when you've–'

There was a bleep and the line went dead.

He pocketed the phone and went to find Higginson.

The DCS had said *anything*, hadn't he?

CHAPTER THIRTY-TWO

'It's worse than I thought.' Duncan Brodie peered through the Lexus' tinted windscreen. 'Where are the damn fog lights?' His fingers scurried across the instrument panel. 'Aha. That's a bit better.'

'It's nearly dark,' Connie Chan said. 'That will help.'

'How'd you figure that?' Brodie shot her a sideways look.

'The half-light is the hardest time to see, even in the mist. I don't often go out at this time.'

Brodie chuckled. 'Why ever not? You're a strange one, right enough.'

'Listen to this, Duncan Brodie. *The dead come without a history in this shifting rain, and leave no trace in our habitation, our private landscape. In the light of morning, upon a fallen hillside and mud about the hedges in a suburb without memory, they will bring no change of heart and no hint for new rooflines. Word of the terrible dragon's descent upon a neighbouring hill will pass into the breaking prism of the rain, leaving house and suburban roads in the cold and wet and nothing to plague the dreams of precocious children. In the rain's passing, I stare upon the quiet, the mild hysteria of lallang, green under street lamps.'*

'That's rather beautiful – a little sombre, maybe,' he said. 'Who is it?'

'Wong Phui Nam,' she replied. 'A Malay poet. I like his work very much.'

'And what is *lallang*?'

She laughed. 'It's a type of grass, very common in Malaysia. A wetland grass.'

'Well, you learn something new every day.' Brodie squinted at the road ahead. Dim, shrouded headlights passed on the other side of the road, like ghosts following some predetermined track through ancient forest.

'It's very spooky, in this fog,' Chan said. 'I'm glad I'm with a big, strong man.'

Brodie felt a burst of protective pride, but modesty directed his response. 'Oh, I don't know about that.'

'But you are,' Chan said admiringly. 'A successful businessman needs to be strong, forceful.'

'Mentally, perhaps. But I'm no gym fanatic or sportsman, I'm afraid.' He felt a cold thrill of memory, the rugby fields of Eagle Court, the freezing cold afternoons, the fear. He coughed. 'I haven't participated in sport since school, as a matter of fact.'

'*As a matter of fact,*' she mimicked. 'You Englishmen. So funny with your expressions.'

He smiled indulgently, tucked the vehicle behind a cautious fellow traveller, allowed the car in front to feel the way forward. 'Well, I think that's enough about me. Tell me more about yourself. You haven't mentioned your family, your career.'

'My family? Ah…'

'I'm sorry – have I trampled on a sensitive issue?'

She sighed. 'My mother died in childbirth. And my father died when I was still young.'

'I'm sorry. That's tough.' He glanced at her but her face was turned away. 'No siblings?'

'No.'

'Well... how about your job? How do you earn a living?'

Now she turned her head towards him. 'I murder old men for their money.'

'What? Ha ha! Seriously.'

'Yes, seriously.'

'Now you're playing with me.'

'And you are a lovely toy, Duncan Brodie.'

'Wait.' He spotted the familiar sign looming through the fog. 'We're here. Look at the state of those gates – I had to prise them open the other day. I'll just open the right hand one a little further– it was a bit of a squeeze last time.' He parked next to the stone gateposts and, leaving his hazard lights blinking, got out of the car and tugged the obstructive iron gate open a few more inches. The other was non-functional, broken-hinged. He stood back and assessed his efforts. That should do it. Plenty of room now.

He rejoined Connie Chan, and eased the car cautiously through the gap. His heartbeat accelerated the way it always did when he got close to Eagle Court. He remembered the dread with which he'd used to return after spending half-term with his stepfather. Half-terms had hardly been full of love and excitement, his stepfather being a reticent, ascetic man, but at least it'd been an opportunity to escape for a few days.

They passed the familiar 10 MPH signs; the drive

swung to the right and there were the twin gates, one to enter, one to exit, the drive itself arcing around in an inverted U to lead parental traffic in and safely out.

Brodie entered via the left gate and drove slowly up the slight incline to park four-square in front of the main school building. 'We'll need a flashlight. The power's off.'

'OK,' Chan said. 'It's all right, Duncan Brodie. I'm not afraid if you're with me.'

Outside the protective carapace of the Lexus, Brodie felt the damp air invade his lungs. He paused before walking around the car to open the door for Connie Chan. He felt the need to remind himself that he was an adult, and he could leave this place any time he chose. No one was going to harm him, make demands on him. He was with a beautiful woman, a fun companion. He was buying Eagle Court in order to make something good out of something bad. There was a sense of karma about the whole prospect.

'Come on.' He held the passenger door open. 'I'll show you inside the main school building. The school is split in half. Old House, over there – can you see the bell tower?' He pointed down the incline. 'And here, where we're standing, School House. Originally a stately home. Some sugar magnate built it in the early nineteenth century.'

'Ah,' Connie Chan said. 'And those little huts?' She drew her coat around her slender body, pointed to the low line of rooftops that ran north south beside a row of tall maple trees.

'Originally built for the Canadian army. They were billeted here before Dieppe – a Second World War raid. They lost over three thousand men.'

'So, unlucky for them, this place.'

'Yes. But let me show you inside.'

Brodie inserted the key into the impressively solid front door. It swung open at his gentle push. He turned on the flashlight, lit the way, and they entered the building into a wide reception area. Doors led off left and right to other rooms. 'The library,' Brodie pointed to the right. 'And along this passageway the refectory, and a staircase up to the dormitories.'

'All little boys, sleeping together in a cosy room? It's so sweet.'

Brodie thought of the cold nights, the barely-suppressed weeping from his neighbour's bed, the insistently tolling bell that would awaken them at six. 'It wasn't quite like that,' he said.

He led the way along the corridor. It smelled musty, unlived in. 'The changing rooms are in there.' He pointed to a doorless area, the flashlight glinting on rows of coat hooks. 'And just in here, the communal showers.'

'You all had showers together?' Chan asked.

'Yes. In batches, like battery hens. We were herded in, given a squirt of shampoo by the supervising teacher, ten minutes maximum, then out.'

He shone the light into the cave-like room. The shower nozzles were rusting, much of the pipework stained green and blue with corrosion.

'Yes, I think this will do,' Connie Chan said.

Brodie frowned, half-turned to ask for an explanation. 'Do for wha–?'

He felt a crushing impact on his head, an explosion of pain that made him stagger, fall to his knees. He tried to make sense of it. Had the ceiling fallen in? Was Connie all right? He tried to speak, but another blow crushed him face down onto the concrete. A black cloud filled his head, gradually sucked all the light away until he knew nothing more.

CHAPTER THIRTY-THREE

Moran cursed himself for a fool – not for the first time since he'd left the station. He'd underestimated the weather conditions, big time. Traffic was stacking up on all routes in and out of town, and his forty minute estimate was proving to be grossly inaccurate. Four-thirty already and he had just under an hour to get to Pangbourne and back to Prospect Park in time for the helicopter to pick him up. Even then, it would only pick him up if the pilot considered it safe to do so – and that, looking at current conditions, seemed increasingly unlikely.

The main road into Pangbourne from Reading was host to two sets of roadworks, the second of which was responsible for this final, frustrating holdup at temporary lights. Moran banged the steering wheel with both hands as the lights changed to red with five or six cars still ahead of him.

The more he thought about it, the more sure he was that he'd endangered Mrs P. He'd broken his own rule and confided in a stranger, the spook on the docks. But the guy had known all about Samantha, her divided loyalties.

Yes, but so do the Russians, Brendan...
He'd been exhausted, battered, bruised.
Excuses.
He'd let his guard down...
How could he have been so stupid? Maybe he *was* losing it. He'd wanted a sabbatical, but the wiser option, surely, would be to bow out gracefully. Call it a day.

The lights changed and the traffic crawled forward.
Come on...
The sequence clicked to red, one car ahead.

She'd be all right. He'd knock on the door, and she'd answer. He'd politely refuse an offer of tea, get back in the car and head for Prospect Park. Why hadn't he taken an official car? He could have put the blue lights on, be past the roadworks by now.

Green. The guy in front stalled.

One second, two seconds ... the car edged forward.

Then he was through, twenty metres from his turning.

Moran found a space on the road and parked badly. The curtains were drawn in Mrs P's front room. He rang the bell. Waited. Nothing.

Rang again.

His heart sank. She was *always* in at this time.

Maybe the garden? In this weather ... doubtful.

He peered through the front-room window. Empty.

'Is that you, Inspector?'

He turned to see Mrs Perkins, one hand on her gate latch, Archie straining eagerly on his lead.

'I hope you don't mind, darling, but I took it upon myself to pop out for a bit. I do *love* this weather. I know it sounds eccentric, but it reminds me of my childhood in London. The pea-soupers. And then I thought to myself,

Constance, why not take Archie with you? Inspector Moran won't mind. You don't, do you?'

'Not at all, Mrs P, not at all.' Relief swept through him.

Archie was wagging his tail excitedly. This was an unexpected treat – an extra walk, and his master at the end of it, too.

'Mrs P, I wondered, have you had any visitors? Someone may be calling to collect the package I asked you to hang on to.'

'Nothing so far, darling. Will I need to ask for ID?'

Moran reconsidered. 'I think perhaps it might be better if … I take the package back, if you don't mind?'

'Mind? It's your business, Inspector. Hold on and I'll fetch it for you.'

Something else occurred to him. 'Hold on, Mrs P. Maybe that's not a great idea.' He wasn't thinking clearly. If an unwelcome visitor *did* call and Mrs P denied possession of the tape, things could turn nasty. 'On second thoughts, it might be better if you hang on to it. I'll assign an officer to keep an eye. He'll be unobtrusive, don't worry. And I'm sure everything's fine,' he added. 'Just a precaution.'

'Well, that sounds rather dramatic. Am I to give the caller what they ask for?'

It was a simple question, but Moran's mind was as fogged as the surrounding streets. Charlie's safety was nagging at him, the competing urgency compromising his judgement. Perhaps he should just have Mrs P taken into protective custody? No, too drastic. Not fair either, to spring something like this on her. *Come on, Brendan, make a bloody decision…*

'If and when you receive such a visitor, Mrs P., tell him

– or her – that Inspector Moran will personally deliver the package, sometime over the next twenty-four hours. My officer will be on hand to make sure you don't have any trouble.'

'Of course. That's fine, darling. Now, can I offer you tea?'

Moran pulled the car into the lay by opposite Prospect Park. The helicopter was airborne, incoming – ETA, ten minutes. The fog had lifted over the town and NPASS had rubber-stamped the provision of a Eurocopter AC135.

Moran made the call to secure Mrs P's protection and followed it with another to Charlie. The call went to voicemail. If they'd let the flight go ahead, she'd be landing anytime now. He left a message, ordered her to wait before taking any action.

George had confirmed with a hotel in Petworth, the Swan, that Brodie was in residence, but that he'd left the hotel sometime over the last hour with a friend. The friend had been described by the hotel receptionist as petite, pretty, and of Eastern origin. The receptionist had provided Brodie's car registration, and DC Swinhoe had traced the vehicle heading east along the A272.

Eagle Court was on the A272.

Time to call this in.

He tried Charlie one more time. Still voicemail.

A thrumming vibration, growing louder by the second, alerted him to the AC135's imminent arrival. He left the car and walked into the park, scanning the sky. A powerful light pierced the gloom like a sharp knife slicing through cake, and the yellow belly of the helicopter came into view. He waited until it settled, bouncing gently on the soaking grass, and came to rest, before ducking his head and making for the opening door as fast as his aching limbs could carry him.

CHAPTER THIRTY-FOUR

Duncan Brodie was dreaming. He was being hanged on a scaffold, surrounded by a baying crowd. The noose was tightening gradually, by small degrees. He opened his mouth to protest but there was something blocking it, some material. He gagged at the smell.

And then he was wide awake. Not dreaming.

Living a nightmare.

He tried to focus on his immediate surroundings. The showers, Eagle Court. What had happened? He remembered parking the car, opening the door, walking along the corridor to the changing rooms, to the shower room, but then...

'You're awake. Good. I'm getting hungry. We should begin.'

Brodie shook his head, tried to clear the fuzziness. Bad idea. It felt as though his head had become detached from his body, as though someone had lined up a croquet mallet and connected it squarely with his temple. The pain made him nauseous, but he knew he daren't vomit – he would choke.

'This is nothing personal, Duncan Brodie. Nothing to do with you at all, actually.'

Connie Chan's voice went on as though she were chatting to him in the Swan's restaurant. His puzzlement overrode his discomfort and he managed an interrogative grunt.

'What's that, Duncan? I can't hear you very well, I'm afraid.'

He was close to panic. What was she doing? And why?

'Your wife. That's your problem, isn't it, Duncan? You want to break free, prove yourself. You're tired of her, exhausted by her needs. I can read it in your eyes. Well, women are nothing if not intuitive, Duncan.'

Brodie listened, rigid with terror. Chan was busy as she spoke, preparing something he couldn't quite see, his head being restrained by whatever was around his neck. His hands were tied behind his back. He flexed his wrists, but there was no leeway. Connie Chan had him trussed like a chicken.

'You laughed when I told you my occupation. I don't tell many people what I do, Duncan, so I guess you are privileged. You won't tell anyone, though, will you? No, of course you won't. Your wife, though. She's a nosy bitch, isn't she? She should have minded her own business.'

Brodie tried to force the gag out of his mouth. If he could just speak, reason with her...

'Is that uncomfortable? I'm sorry. I don't want any noise, Duncan. Not that anyone would hear you anyway.'

He gave up. He couldn't free his voice. He heard Chan's small hands deftly working away at some hidden task, the completion of which was clearly intended for his discomfort or, worse, his despatch, and this thought fanned the flames of panic. The compulsion to lose it completely was overwhelming. He tried to calm himself. There must be a way. Was he attached to the piping? It was rusted, he remembered. There would be weaknesses in the metalwork. But, without his hands, he couldn't test the ancient plumbing's robustness. If he moved his head the cords around his neck simply tightened, so that was no good. Chan had begun to hum to herself as she worked. Now she interrupted her tune to impart further revelations.

'My Isaiah. I didn't love him, exactly, but we were good together. Maybe it's the closest I've come to closeness, if you understand me? I don't mind sharing that with you. Maybe that's how you once felt about your wife? A good arrangement? Was that how things were, Duncan? Yes, I think so. But she's worn you down, hasn't she?'

Brodie closed his eyes. This wasn't happening. He wasn't tied, helpless, in the very shower room where as a pre-pubescent boy he had joined the other members of his dormitory for their daily ablutions, shivering as the cold water played over their pale bodies. This was a nightmare, and he'd wake up shortly, find himself comfortably enveloped by the warm duvet of the king-size bed in his hotel room, perhaps even with Connie at his side, breathing slowly and evenly in her sleep. This was a nightmare, that was all. Of course it was.

But Chan cut disdainfully into his fantasy. 'So, your Mrs Brodie,' she said, 'she's smart, I'll give her that. She figured what Isaiah and me were doing. The day after I killed McMillan, she was waiting for me – when I came to see Isaiah at Chapelfields.' Connie chuckled and the hairs on Brodie's head stood to attention.

'She says, I'd like a word – oh, I know she doesn't like me, Duncan. I can tell. A woman's instincts. But that day she looked like she had something specific to tell me. So I popped into her office, just as she asked me to. And she gave me a big surprise, I can't deny it. She says, oh, I know what you've done, you and Isaiah. And she proceeds to tell me. You ask Isaiah to give you the key safe code, she says, after he's made a visit and dropped off an application form. Isaiah has a good look around when the old fellow isn't paying attention. When he finds money, or valuables, it's game on.' Connie Chan laughed. 'Game on. Another lovely English expression. I'll bet you use that sometimes, Duncan. Maybe even when you decided to buy Eagle Court it was game on, was it?' There was a moment's silence as she concentrated on some detail of her task before continuing.

Brodie's ears were doing their job, feeding the information to his brain, but he was struggling to take it in, the pain and discomfort in his neck and hands becoming too much of a distraction to be able to focus on Connie's monologue.

'I know, your wife says. I *know*, and I can give the police all the information they need to have you arrested. I followed you, Connie, did you know that? You were careful, sure, but not careful enough.' Connie Chan made a soft, self-disparaging noise in her throat. 'So, I was too blasé. And this, Duncan, is where it gets interesting. Oh, listen, shall I let you talk? Just for a bit?'

Chan ripped the gag from his mouth, and Brodie sucked in air. He felt lightheaded at the sudden intake of oxygen. 'Why are you doing this?' he managed.

Her shoulders slumped. 'Such a vacuous question,

Duncan. I'm disappointed. You're a clever man, so why don't you have a think and figure it out?'

'She was blackmailing you,' he croaked.

He sensed Chan quieten, perhaps to consider a suitable response. He tugged gently at the cords around his wrists, assessing their efficacy. It hurt, but he was beginning to realise that getting out of this pain-free wasn't going to be an option. It seemed that he had more chance of working his hands free than his neck. If he could free them he could maybe reach up, grab the piping, take the pressure off his neck, use his legs somehow...

Chan's answer was straightforward enough, however unlikely the dry confirmation seemed to him. 'Yes, she was.'

'Then what did she want? Blackmailers always want something, right?' Brodie tried to imagine his wife seated at the office desk in Aviemore, setting out her terms, Chan perched opposite, listening attentively. Had that scene really taken place? Could Fiona do such a thing? It seemed ridiculous.

'Of course they do. It's very simple, Duncan. She wanted me to do it again. But this time, she was going to choose the victim. You know, I love the serendipity of this – there's a lovely word.'

'What are you talking about?' Brodie had found that by dint of repeated wrist flexions, he could make a little more space each time. The cords were cutting into his wrists and it would take a while, but eventually he might be able to slide a hand free. If Chan didn't notice what he was doing.

'Serendipity. An unplanned, fortunate discovery. That's what it means.'

He felt her breath on his neck.

'Here we are, back in your childhood prison. And you remember it all, Duncan, don't you? You remember the teachers, the gentle ones, the strict ones. And the sadists, the real bad guys.'

Brodie shivered. Where was she going with this?

'You remember Mr Daintree?'

She bit his neck – he felt her sharp little incisors draw blood. He yelped, more in surprise than pain, and she stepped back, laughing. 'Just a nip, Duncan.'

Daintree ... that name...

'I remember Daintree. What of him?'

'He wanted to come and live with you,' she sang. 'In Chapelfields. Now, wouldn't that have been nice?'

He felt a cold thrill run through his body, from the apex of his skull to his toes. Now it made sense. Of course he remembered.

Chan went on, still in a sing-song lilt. 'So, I kill him, like she wants. But my Isaiah, he is killed too, because of what she asks us to do. Because of her *whim*.'

'That has nothing to do with me.' His wrists were sliding more freely now, his blood providing the necessary lubrication. 'I'm sorry about ... Isaiah.' Who the hell was Isaiah?

'Tit for tat, though, that's what we're doing here, Duncan. My Isaiah has gone. And so Mrs Brodie's darling Duncan must follow.'

'You're sick. Crazy.'

'Reverting to insults, Duncan, after we've had such a nice time together?'

With a final *slip*, his hands came free. It was so sudden that, for a split-second, he froze. His hands went to his neck, grappling for the unseen metalwork which supported the cords that were strangling him. He pulled himself up, took some pressure off. He heard Chan's exclamation of surprise, but before she could intervene, Brodie lunged with the desperation of a doomed man, and his legs encircled Chan's slim torso. She pulled away, cursing him in some unknown language. His legs were losing their grip, he could feel his muscles weakening as she twisted and wriggled to free herself.

No, no, no…

He let go abruptly, drew his legs into his body, lashed out with all the power of his quads. He felt his feet connect with Chan's upper body and she reeled back, cracked her head on the mould-coated institutional tiling, slid to the concrete and lay still.

Brodie's heart was beating like a mad timpanist. He had to free his neck. His hands scrabbled at the knots that held the truss together. His fingernails splintered as he wrenched and tugged, and finally, just as he had reached the point of despair, he felt the noose loosen sufficiently to allow him to slip his head out. He sank to the floor, panting hard. Chan's head had left a smear of blood on the wall. Beside her lay an open wallet containing a selection of small knives, the largest of which, a slim, black-handled flick knife, was still resting in the palm of her outstretched hand. Brodie's eyes scanned left to right, recording the scene with a kind of fascinated horror. Chan's high heels lay discarded next to a rusted bucket – she obviously like to work bare-foot – while her designer jacket was hanging on the nearest hook just outside the shower, where the shower supervisor used to stand all those years ago, issuing squirts of Vosene on request.

Brodie made himself get up. He looked down on his lover's prone body, his emotions see-sawing between disgust and bewilderment. Chan wasn't moving.

But Brodie could move. He staggered to the changing room entrance and clung briefly to the doorframe as his legs threatened to give way. Then he broke into a limping shuffle towards the front entrance.

CHAPTER THIRTY-FIVE

Charlie fumbled in her purse and found two twenty pound notes. She pressed them into the taxi driver's hand. 'Thanks. I'll be fine from here.'

The driver looked doubtful. They were parked in an area set back from the road beside two stone gateposts. The gates themselves had seen better days; one had become detached from a hinge and lay askew from its partner like a recalcitrant drunk on a night out with a more sober buddy; the other was partially open and, judging by the fresh score marks on the ground, it had evidently been no easy task to shift it. The faded nomenclature worked into the iron of the skewed gate could still be read:

Eagle…

There were no houses on this stretch of road, just a solitary phone box perched on the verge a hundred metres further on.

The driver voiced his concerns. 'Are you sure, miss? On a night like this?'

The fog was beginning to lift, but it was nevertheless,

Charlie conceded, a filthy night to be out and about.

'I'm sure.' She gave him a confident smile and added, more for her own reassurance than his, 'It's fine, really – I'm a police officer.'

'Well, if you say so. I wouldn't let my missus wander about in a place like this, mind you, but...' he shrugged, 'you're the boss.'

'Thanks. I appreciate your concern.'

'You need me again, give this number a call. It'll come straight through to the cab.'

Charlie took the proffered card and tucked it into her pocket. 'Cheers. I will.'

She watched the minicab's rear lights fade into the murk. The sense of isolation made her wrap her arms around herself as she stood before the forbidding gates.

Come on, Charlie girl. What's the worst that can happen?

First thing: check in.

She found her mobile, called up Moran's number. Nothing. George was next on the list. After a few rings she was greeted by the familiar voice. 'McConnell.'

'George. I'm at the school. Where's the guv?'

'On his way in a chopper, believe it or not. He should be with you sometime in the next–' There was a pause as George made a quick calculation. 'Twenty minutes, I'd say – provided they don't run into a tree, or a hill, or overhead power lines, or... hell, I can't believe they got authorisation to fly in –'

'–All right, George, I get it. But, as far as we know, Brodie and Chan are still here – the car hasn't been picked up again since the original trace?'

'Nope. But there's always a chance they left and took another route. No guarantees that we'd pick 'em up again, not in this muck. Then again, they haven't checked out of the hotel, so…'

'So they're probably still here.'

'I'd wait for the guv if I were you, boss.'

'I'll be fine, George. Just stay on the end of the phone. I'll let you know when we've got this wrapped up.'

Charlie signed off, took a deep breath, and went through the open gate.

Brodie reached his car, fumbled in his trouser pocket for the keys. They weren't there. He tried the nearside door. It was locked. Of course it was. He always locked the car.

He leaned against the Lexus and tried to compose himself. The only way out of here was the car. No point even thinking about walking; the school was in the middle of nowhere, surrounded by woodland, the drive a half-mile stretch to the main road. His leg hurt with a fiery pain. He bent to inspect it and his fingers came away bloodstained. One of Chan's blades had found its mark. It wasn't deep, so far as he could tell, but it hurt.

There was nothing for it; he had to retrace his steps and find the keys. Then … then get the hell out, call the police at the first opportunity. An image of the bright hotel lounge, an officer or maybe two seated at the table, listening sympathetically to his account, a stiff Scotch in front of him. A rueful shake of his head. A close call, yes, indeed. How could he have known the woman was mentally ill? How indeed? The imaginary police officers nodded their respective agreement.

The front door yawned like a mocking mouth, daring him to enter. For an instant he thought he heard voices, young voices bantering, cat-calling as they filed towards the refectory for supper. The gruff voices of the supervising masters, the occasional yelp as a cane lashed out, made contact with a bare leg. He shook his head to dispel the ghosts. *Pull yourself together, Duncan ... Find those keys. Then you're safe.*

He went in, inched along the corridor towards the changing rooms. If he had his phone on him he could have used the torch, but it was locked in the car and the flashlight was still in the shower room. No matter; his night vision was improving. He scuffed the floor in a left-to-right, sweeping motion as he went – it would be all too easy to miss the lost keys in the stygian darkness of the corridor.

There.

He could see the dim outline of something on the floor a few metres ahead. He rushed to the spot, got down on his haunches, his hand closed over the object.

Yes!

He *had* them. Now, get the hell out of here...

That was when he heard a noise – the brittle clink of metal on concrete and, a second later, the soft, stealthy shuffle of bare feet on linoleum.

Brodie's composure collapsed. He backed along the corridor, turned, lost his balance, fell sprawling. The keys fell from his hand, spun away into the darkness.

'Is that you, Duncan?'

Chan's voice, musical, a song of seduction, rising and falling in the blackness.

'We have so much to do together, Duncan. You'll see. Don't run away, I have something for you...'

Brodie picked himself up, scrabbled for the keys. Where were they? How could he not see them?

259

In the way of all dropped objects, the keys had fallen and bounced to some obscure location. There was a darker rectangle on his left – the stairwell leading up to the dormitories. Perhaps they'd dropped onto one of the lower treads? His fingers probed, danced from left to right. Nothing.

Next step.

Same. God, where *were* they?

'Duncan?'

Her voice was closer, too close. He shrank into the shadows, took three steps up the stairwell, pressed his back to the crumbling plaster.

A shadow passed across the stairwell, so close he could almost reach out and touch her. Brodie held his breath, flattened himself against the wall, tried to become one with the fabric of the building.

'Are you *here*, Duncan? You're not hiding from me, are you? Oh, what have I found? What do we have *here?*'

Jangle, jangle...

Brodie's stomach yawed, sweat erupted on his brow.

OK. Now what?

He couldn't go down.

So, let's go up...

He placed a foot carefully on the next step, prayed that it wouldn't make a sound.

And the next.

He reached the top, drenched in sweat.

Come on, Duncan, where are you? Think ...

It came back to him. He'd been a dormitory captain here, once, in another life. He was standing on the landing, the toilet was on his left and dormitory seven on the right. Matron's lounge dead ahead.

And there was a fire escape directly from the lounge, he was sure there was. He remembered being fascinated by the green railings, the skeletal iron steps leading down the side of the building to safety; he had once asked one of the matron's young assistants if he could open the fire door, have a go on the fire escape. She'd said no, of course. A Swedish girl, Brodie recalled, Miss Olssen…

He held his arms in front of him like a blind man, felt for the door handle he knew must be there. It was. He turned it, gently pushed, froze as it creaked before opening fully. He held his breath until he was sure he was still alone on this level, that Chan hadn't crept up the stairs behind him.

Now, the window. He crossed the room, feeling his way until his hands met glass.

Bolted shut. Security lock.

Brodie clenched his fists.

Don't panic.

He was safe for now. As long as he could keep out of sight, hide, even until the morning if necessary, all would be well. He'd be able to make a dash for it, somehow. Find a telephone, call for help.

Chan might give up. She was injured, maybe bleeding. Perhaps she'd pass out … or maybe she'd simply go away…

His sensory faculties fluttered, a fly's twitch in a spider's web, a heartbeat before the gentle footfall and hiss of Chan's breath on his neck told him he'd been outmanoeuvred.

An arm encircled his neck, something cold pressed into his ribcage. 'Oh, Duncan. I'm so disappointed in you.'

Jangle, jangle…

'Were you looking for these, by the way?'

Charlie plodded up the drive, wondering how far she'd have to walk before she arrived at the school buildings.

The drive forked left, and she went with it. She was soon rewarded by the sight of a silhouette against the misty backdrop, the shape of a dark, foreboding building. Ahead, the drive split into two further gates separated by a decorative wall and a short stretch of grass. The way in, the way out.

Charlie took the gate closest to the main building. As she entered, she registered a number of prefabricated huts dotted around the grounds.

The drive delivered her to the impressive school frontage. Charlie's heart gave a small skip as she saw the silver shape of a Lexus parked right outside.

Gotcha, Mr Brodie…

But what could she do to detain the entrepreneur, should he decide to take off?

Close the gates, for a start. She backtracked and swung the rusted ironwork across the gap, walked to the exit and repeated the process. The latter required freeing from a tangle of nettles and brambles that had wound their way around the gate's hinges and lower cross-section. With a mighty effort, she tugged it free and swung the gate across. It wasn't much, but it might hold Brodie up for just long enough.

Charlie brushed moss and flakes of rust from her trousers and headed towards the Lexus. What were Brodie and Chan doing here at this time of night? Why not visit in the morning when natural light would reveal how much work would be required to restore the old building?

The Lexus' exhaust was cold to the touch; they'd been here a while. She walked to the end of the building where an archway led into a neglected landscaped garden. The dim outlines of untended borders were still discernible, as was the centrepiece, a sculpted pond fed by some kind of ornamental fountain, long since dried up.

All was still.

Charlie retraced her steps until, once again, she found herself by the front door. She stood back and looked up. Eagle Court had been a classic stately home in its pre-school days, and it certainly looked the part. It was imposing, almost gothic in design, with its arched windows and crenellated tower high above. What must it have been like to live here as a schoolboy? Especially under the regime Fiona Brodie had outlined. Charlie repressed a shudder. Memories of her own schooldays were warm, happy, home-based. What kind of parents sent their children to a place like this?

Charlie walked to the opposite side of the building. A narrow gap led to another prefabricated outbuilding parallel to the main house, which looked as though it may have functioned as a study hall or meeting room. She peered through a filthy window but could only see a few items of scattered furniture. Two long trestle tables, upended in a corner, a tall dais propped up against the far wall.

She continued along the side of the building. A concrete structure dead ahead caught her attention and she went to investigate, peered gingerly into the open entrance. A toilet block, the rows of undersized cubicles tailor made for under-twelves. Her nose wrinkled in distaste. This was nothing more than a prison camp for children.

She turned around to walk back to the car. Brodie would have to return to it eventually, and it would be reckless to search the main building on her own. Better keep out of sight, wait for Moran. He should be here by now. Unless the weather was causing major issues for the chopper. In which case … in which case, she would deal with whatever needed dealing with.

She found her way back to the Lexus, leaned against its sleek wing. *Worth more than my annual salary*, she thought. *One day, maybe…*

The silence was shattered by a loud crash, as if a door had been violently thrown open against an exterior wall. A howl of anguish split the air, tailing off in what sounded to Charlie's shocked ears like a wild animal's snarl of rage. Then the sound of footsteps, running hard…

Towards her.

CHAPTER THIRTY-SIX

Brodie didn't move a muscle – Chan was pressing the blade against his jugular, so it would have been unwise. Beyond the window, the geometry of his failed escape route – rusted, angular twists covered by peeling green paint – curled seductively to earth. Despair washed through him from head to toe. His limbs felt watery, pliable, as though his bones had been replaced by some alternative, sub-standard composite. His right thigh was throbbing dully.

The voice whispered softly in his ear, like a lover's entreaty. 'Shall we go back to the showers, Duncan?'

He allowed himself to be led towards the stairwell. But he wasn't going to let her truss him up again. He'd rather risk all, than that. It was just a question of how and when.

'Why kill me, Connie?' His right foot felt for the the first step. 'It doesn't make any sense.'

The knife pressed harder into his flesh. 'I don't like to be crossed, Duncan. I don't like to be used. And I'm upset about Isaiah. He didn't deserve an end like that.'

'What happened?' They were half-way down the

staircase now.

'An automobile accident. His car was hit by a lorry.'

'I'm sorry to hear that.' Crazy, incongruous conversation.

'Why, thank you. Turn left, please.'

There was a door leading to the outside world just before the changing room block. Was it bolted? It had often been left unlocked during the school day to accommodate pupils' various comings and goings. Only a select few, the prefects, had been allowed to enter by the front portal. This door was a convenient side entrance to the refectory, changing rooms, dormitories. It had been referred to by masters and pupils alike as the 'common door'.

But was it locked? And if so, would it resist a determined shoulder?

It wasn't just a chance; it was his *only* chance. Beyond the common door lay the showers, and he wasn't going to let that happen.

Just a few more steps.

'You have alternatives, Connie. You can stop all this. There are people who can help you.'

The knife dug savagely into his neck. 'Help? There is no one to help me. There never was. I learned that very early in life, Duncan, so don't talk to me about *help*.'

They were almost level with the common door. It was now or never.

He jerked his elbow back into Chan's body, ducked his head forward to escape the knife, fell against the common door with all his weight. It stayed put, secure in its frame.

Try the handle you idiot ...

His hand fumbled for the knob, turned it, pushed.

The common door flew open, and he threw himself through. He felt the knife graze his back, a sudden, shocking burning sensation. Then he was running towards the car.

Oh God, she still has the keys…

He was running, but his legs were struggling to cooperate. Here was the blind corner where one of the boys had almost been run over by a master's car as he chased a friend to the rugby field. The wooden sign was still there, faded now:

NO RUNNING!

Hysteria welled in his throat. Where could he go?

Wait. There was someone by the car. *Who…?*

Brodie didn't care. Another human being had entered his nightmare. They would help. Of course they would. He flung himself forward, Chan's banshee-like screams ringing in his ears, lost his footing, fell spreadeagled at the feet of the new arrival.

Charlie saw immediately that the man was injured. His trousers were bloodstained, as was his shirt collar. But the man, presumably Duncan Brodie, wasn't her priority, not right now. Her priority was the woman with the knife – no, two knives, one in each hand. They were all Charlie had eyes for, those two silver blades, moving this way and that as the woman assessed the new situation, decided on her best angle of attack.

Charlie heard herself tell the man that it was OK. Everything would be all right. Time seemed to slow and her mind filled with images of the break in at her apartment, not long after she'd arrived in her new post at Thames Valley – the assassin lying in wait, the cosh she'd only narrowly escaped from, the trail of blood as the would-be killer was impaled on the glass shards of her front door.

The last time.

And now, here she was again, facing a murderer.

Chan feinted right, went left. Charlie read it correctly, sucked her tummy in as the blade whickered through the air, glided harmlessly past. A miss.

'Stop. I'm a police officer.' Charlie held up both hands, the time-honoured signal of non-provocation.

Chan's eyes flickered with – what? Excitement? Anticipation? Yes… definitely, she was getting a buzz out of this. She was moving gracefully from side to side, probing Charlie's defences, waiting, watching. There was something of the martial arts in the woman's movements, small as she was. Somewhere on the periphery of Charlie's subconscious she heard Duncan Brodie moan in pain. It was a fleeting distraction, but Charlie saw Chan's eyes dart to her original prey, just for a micro-second. It was enough. Charlie went in with her fists, dodged the left-hand knife, felt a sudden sting as the second grazed her shoulder, felt her fist strike Chan's cheek with a slapping crunch.

Chan's chin jerked up and Charlie followed her assault with an attempted uppercut, but Chan was too fast – she jerked her head back, slid out of reach and Charlie's fist swept harmlessly through clean air. She ducked, anticipating the descending blades, allowed her initial impetus to carry her out of harm's way.

Chan was still off-balance and Charlie charged at the woman's midriff, using all her weight. They fell together, Charlie grabbing the sinewy arms tightly at both elbow joints to prevent Chan gaining an angle of attack. Something fell to the tarmac with a clink. A knife? No, a set of car keys. Was Brodie in a position to act on instructions? Chan was wriggling in Charlie's vicelike grip, cursing, spitting.

'Get the keys!' Charlie yelled at Brodie. 'Get in the car!'

She heard Brodie scrabbling about on the ground but Chan had grabbed her left ear in her teeth, was biting down hard. Charlie gasped. She used her only available weapon, her skull, flicked her head to the left, felt Chan's cheekbone crack at the impact. She let go of Charlie's ear with a howl. Charlie released Chan's elbows, rolled away, got to her haunches.

The Lexus' lights beeped on. Brodie was pulling at the door handle. Chan shrieked, lunged at him. Charlie tackled her but Chan's arm came down and Charlie felt the knife enter her shoulder like a hot needle. She fell to her knees. Her arm wouldn't obey her, it was getting number by the second. She felt a wave of nausea wash over her.

Brodie had made it into the car, closed the door behind him. Chan was attacking the passenger side window like a berserker, using both knives and hammering into the glass with repeated blows. Charlie's vision blurred. Somewhere in the distance she heard a repetitive thrumming, maybe her own heartbeat, maybe the blood pounding in her temple…

She had to stop Chan, protect Brodie. She crawled forward, reached out with her good arm, heard the Lexus' engine purr efficiently into life and then die abruptly as Chan crashed through the passenger window. Charlie lifted her arm, the wrong one. The pain made her gag,

her head spin.
    The lights went out.

CHAPTER THIRTY-SEVEN

'That's the spot,' Moran yelled into his microphone as the helicopter hovered five hundred feet above the grass. Eagle Court's old playing fields made an ideal landing strip for the Eurocopter. They'd already spotted a car parked outside the main building, and the heat source device Moran's opposite number in the front was operating revealed the presence of three bodies – two static, one moving erratically in their direction. Moran hoped it was Charlie.

The pilot chose his spot and the aircraft settled gently on the turf. The rotors slowed, the racket gradually decreased and Moran was able to remove his headset. They were later arriving than he'd wanted to be, but he was thankful that the fog had lifted enough to make the intervention possible.

Moran stepped clear of the aircraft, bending low instinctively even though the rotors were still. The most recent plot of the moving body had veered east, towards the dilapidated shape of an old cricket pavilion.

'Want me to check the status at the main building,

Chief Inspector?' The accompanying police observer, Ed Maynard, a genial sergeant from Abingdon, joined Moran on the overgrown games pitch.

'If you would,' Moran confirmed. 'I'll take a look over at the pavilion. Give me a shout if you need to.'

'Right you are, sir.'

Maynard moved off at a jog. The pilot was busy talking to control, confirming their position, fiddling with the instrument panel, doing what pilots do after landing. Moran left him to it, pausing only to reach into the fuselage to retrieve a heavy duty torch from beneath the rear seat.

The darkness of minimal light pollution along with the slowly dispersing fog made the going slow, Moran's torchlight only serving to reduce his field of vision as it reflected against the surrounding mist. Whoever was on the move must have heard the descending helicopter – it would have taken a serious measure of hearing loss to miss it. Now that the runner had changed direction, elected to avoid a confrontation with the helicopter, Moran was sure it wasn't Charlie. This left only a couple of possibilities, either of which were potentially dangerous.

'Police. Show yourself,' he called into the void. His voice came back to him flattened by the suffocating effect of the fog.

The pavilion was almost totally derelict, the frontage rotted and windows cracked or absent. Gaps left by two missing boards ran the length of the edifice beneath the roof, giving the impression that the structure was smiling sadly, wistfully recalling afternoons of white flannels and sausage rolls. A teetering scoreboard stood to one side with sad, numberless holes for eyes, like a loyal straight man guarding his ailing comic.

Moran was about to move on when he heard a series of clunks from inside the structure, as though an item of furniture had been moved or some other heavy object displaced. He stepped gingerly onto the first of the two steps leading up to the pavilion's shallow deck. Ahead, two interlocked, once partly glazed doors led into the main body of the building. Now they were empty rectangles of darkness. Moran went forward, played the beam of his torch in and around the interior. Not much to see.

Wait.

In the far corner, from behind what might once have been a trestle table, now upended, his torchlight picked out a trouser leg, ridden up to reveal white flesh and a shoeless bare foot.

'I'm coming in. Police.' Moran announced, for his own benefit more than anything else. He moved across the floorboards cautiously, fearful that one might give way under his weight, but also alert to the possibility of sudden aggression.

There was no movement from whoever was slumped in the corner. If mischief was intended, they'd have made a move by now. He relaxed a fraction, advanced slowly, shone the torch into the gap behind the table.

A woman was sitting curled up, her back to the wall. She looked Asian, exotic. Her long, glossy black hair was caked with blood. As Moran's light reached her face he saw the angry, purple bruise just parallel to her right eye. A trickle of blood ran from its corner to her chin, but the woman made no effort to wipe it away. Her eyes were vacant, almost pleading.

'I'm not going to hurt you,' Moran said gently. 'I'm

going to call an ambulance, get you some medical assistance. Do you understand?'

The woman nodded, but the next instant her eyes widened in panic and she lunged forward, grabbed his trouser leg. Moran's instinct was to pull back, treat the gesture as potentially offensive, but then he saw that she was crying, her tears creating watery tracks on her bloodstained cheek. 'Please,' she looked at him beseechingly. 'Please don't tell my uncle I'm here. Please don't let him hurt me.'

'A little blood loss, no major arterial damage, should be fine in a week or so, if a little sore in the meantime,' Moran announced. 'That's the doc's verdict. And you are one lucky officer, DI Pepper.'

'I don't feel particularly lucky,' Charlie replied. 'In fact I can't feel much at all. Whatever they gave me is coating everything in woolly sugar.'

They were sitting in a Triage A&E cubicle in Crawley General Hospital. The bustle of a busy emergency department contrasted starkly with the sinister silence of Eagle Court. Despite traffic and weather conditions they'd made a fast transfer from the school grounds, thanks to Moran's flying associates.

'How's Brodie doing?' Charlie grimaced as she shifted to a more comfortable position, propped herself up on the institutionally hard pillow.

'Still in ICU, so we won't know for a while. Same with Chan. Severe concussion, they tell me. Suspected fractured skull. I don't know what you hit her with, Charlie, but it sure knocked the stuffing out of her.'

'My head.'

'Sorry?'

'I hit her with my head.'

Moran bent forward to inspect Charlie's skull. Sure enough, his searching fingers found a bump the size of a small egg. 'Good God.'

'No underlying damage, apparently.' Charlie sighed. 'My skull is clearly thicker than hers.'

Moran chuckled. 'Skull thickness is no reflection of brain power. Although I might question your decision to wade in,' Moran said, a touch playfully, 'especially given my explicit instructions to wait for backup.'

'I didn't have a choice, guv. The action came to me, not vice versa.'

'Sure. Well, you can save it for the report. All in good time.'

'Please tell me there's not going to be another enquiry?' Charlie made bunny ears with her fingers and winced as her shoulder complained. 'I don't think I could cope with that. I mean–' She started to well up. 'I'm sorry, guv, it's just that, last time, you know…'

'I know. It's all right, Charlie. I'll deal with it.' He put his arm on her good shoulder. 'It's a clear case of self defence.'

'Her word against mine, though. Like last time.'

'Brodie saw what happened. He'll back you up.'

'Sure, if he survives.'

'Look.' Moran sat down on the ICU examination bed. 'Don't worry about it now. We still have a lot of unanswered questions. And as far as tonight is concerned, I'm going to recommend you for a commendation, not an enquiry.'

Charlie chewed her lip. 'Thanks, guv. You don't have

to—'

Moran held his hand up. 'Enough for now. Drink some water, rest.'

'All right. You win.' Her head flopped back. 'One thing I don't understand, though.'

'Namely?'

'Why did Chan attack Brodie? They were in partnership, right?'

Moran stood to one side as a nurse materialised from behind the curtain, deftly took Charlie's temperature, made a note, departed.

'Jury's out on that for now,' Moran told her. 'Your friend Luscombe is paying Mrs Brodie a visit even as we speak. I suspect we'll get the full story via that channel in due course.'

On his way out, Moran wrestled with Charlie's question. Did Brodie and Chan have a falling out? What was Chan's motive for harming Brodie? They were staying at the Swan, in Petworth, he recalled. It wasn't that far. Might be worth a visit, a few questions to the right staff members. Moran found his mobile and called a taxi. Damn the expense. He'd lived with too many puzzles of late and as sure as eggs were eggs, he wasn't going let this one add to his tally of sleep-deprived hours.

CHAPTER THIRTY-EIGHT

It was a pin-sharp morning, the sort of morning that makes arriving at work less of a chore than usual. Charlie blinked in the strong sunlight as she emerged from the underground car park and headed for the lift.

Her shoulder was still aching but it wasn't stopping her from carrying on as normal.

What's normal, Charlie? Fighting a deranged knifewoman; all part of the service, ma'am...

She pushed through the doors into the open plan.

Applause. *Loud* applause.

Her colleagues had formed a semicircle, and there was George at the front, goading the team on like a wild-haired conductor, exhorting them to louder demonstrations of congratulation.

Charlie didn't know what to do. It was embarrassing. She held up her good arm to quieten them but this only made their clapping even more enthusiastic.

As the noise gradually died down, she addressed the sea of grins. 'Thanks, you lot. It's good to be back. No big deal. Just did my job.'

As the crowd dispersed, Moran beckoned from his office door. Charlie moved self-consciously through the room, through liberal smatterings of 'well done, ma'am' and 'great job, boss' asides, several pats on the back, and, worst of all, admiring looks from two of the younger team members, until she gratefully entered Moran's inner sanctum and closed the door behind her.

'Have a seat, Charlie. How's the shoulder?'

She plumped herself down. 'I can cope. They only kept me in overnight, thank God – I've had a gutful of hospitals.'

'I'll bet.'

She smiled a sheepish smile. 'I'll see if I can stay clear of the medical profession for the next twelve months. So, what's the latest? How's Brodie doing? He'd been discharged from ICU by the time I left.'

'Surgeon is confident he'll make a complete recovery – that's just come through, Bola took the call.'

'And Chan?'

'Conscious. Not saying much. Sussex have an armed guard on her side ward.'

'But she'll be all right?'

'I've been assured that she hasn't suffered any permanent damage. So, you be assured too, Charlie.'

Charlie looked over Moran's shoulder to the window where a rectangular frame of azure sky was bisected by a thin contrail from some intercontinental airliner moving at what seemed to be, from her perspective, a snail's pace. 'I'm glad. No, relieved.'

'We have quite a bit more on Chan – or Zubaida Ungu, to use her real name. George has been digging – turns out she has rather a sad history.' Moran let out a weary sigh before continuing. 'When I found her, Charlie, – at Eagle Court, I mean – she was just a frightened girl. That knock on the head seemed to regress her, transport her back to her childhood.'

Charlie nodded. She wanted to understand the woman. 'She'll be thoroughly assessed, won't she? Whatever persona she's adopted, she sure is one very disturbed individual, take my word for it.'

'Of course,' Moran said. 'I'm not suggesting she's an innocent. It was just unexpected, that's all.'

'You're lucky she didn't try to carve you up, too.' Charlie tried to smile, but Moran didn't look as though he'd been fooled.

'She's safely in custody, Charlie. You did a great job.'

'Did I? She got the better of me.' Charlie felt herself welling up, put a hand to her mouth. 'She could have killed Brodie, and I just–'

'Enough.' Moran raised his forefinger, mock-sternly. 'Take it easy for a few days, that's my advice. You've done the team proud, DI Pepper – you've just witnessed their reaction first-hand. George told me he's chuffed to work for such an inspiring boss. And coming from George,' Moran spread his hands, 'that's pretty impressive stuff.'

Charlie grimaced. 'Bloody creep.'

They both laughed.

'George and me are overdue a catchup, anyway,' Charlie said. 'But how long before we get to speak to Duncan Brodie?'

'A day or so. But we have to tread cautiously – or politically, I should say. We need agreement on who's taking the lead on this. Higginson's on the case. We'll have to wait and see.'

'So, it could all be handled by Police Scotland?'
'Possibly,' Moran conceded.
'Guv, I have to say that I take a personal inter–'
'I know, I know. It's not signed and sealed yet, Charlie. Let's be patient for now. Oh, by the way, I made an interesting discovery concerning Brodie and Chan's relationship.'

Charlie tried to calm herself. She wasn't prepared to let the case walk all the way back to Scotland without her involvement. 'Oh yes? Go on.'

'According to the maître d' of the Swan in Petworth, Brodie and Chan only met while Brodie was staying at the hotel. She approached him one evening while he was eating. It was a setup on Chan's part, by the look of things.'

'She lured him to the school to kill him? But why?'

Moran joined his hands together. 'All will become clear when we can speak to them both, I'm sure.'

'Take a look.' George proffered a document with a black and white photograph clipped to the top corner.

Charlie inspected the photograph. It showed a young girl, aged around twelve or thirteen, Charlie estimated, seated outdoors at a plastic white table. She was looking at the camera, but her eyes were looking right through it. There was a crudely manufactured doll lying on the table, and the girl had thrown a half-hearted arm across it, perhaps at the instigation of the photographer. The setting was a garden in which a number of exotic plants and trees formed a leafy backdrop against a whitewashed wall. The girl's expression wasn't hard to decipher; her mouth was a silent pout of indifference, or perhaps unhappiness, and her eyes were devoid of emotion.

Someone had inscribed a name in black ballpoint in the top right hand corner of the photograph:

Zubaida Binti Ungu

'All from the original case files,' George said. 'I'll leave you to have a read.'

Charlie read the summary document. It was a bleak story. Zubaida was the daughter of a wealthy Malaysian businessman. The first seven years of her life had been idyllic; the family had lived in an exclusive suburb of Kuala Lumpur. Servants, pool, chauffeur-driven car, the lot.

This had all come to a tragic end one night as her parents returned from a company dinner. Their car was hit by a drunk driver; it left the carriageway, turned over, burst into flames. No survivors.

Zubaida was adopted by an uncle, and until his wife died suddenly from some unspecified ailment, all was well. Then the abuse began. Zubaida must have confided in the mother of a school friend, because there was an archive report expressing concern. Nothing was ever followed up, or at least no documentation could be unearthed to suggest that the complaint had ever been taken seriously. The uncle's reputation for inappropriate behaviour in relation to members of the opposite sex was, if not documented, then certainly hinted at.

When Zubaida was sixteen her uncle was found in his bed, apparently asphyxiated, and Zubaida simply disappeared. The murder had been carefully planned; no forensic evidence could been found to implicate the teenager, although she remained the prime suspect. Malaysian police suspected that she had fled to a boyfriend somewhere in the city, persuaded him to put her up for a while, obtained a passport at some later point, and left the country. The uncle's bank account had been cleared out.

Charlie exhaled, pressed the heels of her hands into her eyes, briefly saw stars, and continued reading.

Zubaida popped up again two years later in France in connection with an unsolved case – an elderly man's suspicious demise. Zubaida had been working as an au pair with a family in Canet Plage, and the elderly man was a family friend. He had taken a special shine to Zubaida, although the family didn't know her by that name. To them, she was Zazu, reliable, kind to the children, fun-loving. After the family friend's mysterious death, Zazu handed in her notice, much to the family's chagrin, and was neither seen nor heard from again.

The family friend had been something of an eccentric, his house a veritable museum of valuable antiques and antiquities. It was all uncatalogued, so the gendarmes had no idea what, if anything, might have been missing from the collection. Six months later, a rare sixteenth century bracelet appeared in a Paris auction, and achieved a record sale price in a tensely fought bidding war. Such was the interest generated that its provenance was methodically traced back to Canet Plage, and eventually to the eccentric collector. The auctioneer remembered the vendor well – a strikingly pretty Malaysian woman. young, very well spoken.

Next sighting, England, UK…

Charlie had read enough. She paper-clipped the photo to the summary document, slid it into the folder. It was time to tell Luscombe what she'd found, or rather not found, at Crawley General Hospital.

CHAPTER THIRTY-NINE

Luscombe nodded to Fiona Brodie's brief, received a blank expression in return.

OK, pal. We all know what your job is...

Fiona Brodie herself seemed composed, if a little irritated by DC Jenny Armitage's earlier summons. Luscombe kicked off with the customary caution, then handed over to Jenny.

'Do you have any idea why we've asked to speak to you this morning, Mrs Brodie?'

'Something to do with my husband, I expect. You're aware that he has been hospitalised?'

'We are, Mrs Brodie. You'll be anxious to visit, I'm sure, but this won't take long.'

Mrs Brodie sighed. 'I'm not rushing down to Crawley, if that's what you mean. I have a home to run, and by all accounts Duncan is stable and out of danger.'

Jenny frowned. 'You don't seem that concerned. It was a particularly violent attack. He could have lost his life.'

'Well, he didn't, and for that I'm grateful. Can we get on, please?'

The brief shot his client a sideways glance which Luscombe interpreted as less than empathetic.

'Of course. You're a busy woman, as you say.' Jenny smiled sweetly.

Sugar before the castor oil, Luscombe chuckled to himself. *That's my Jenny…*

'So, can I start by going back to something you mentioned a wee while ago, in our previous interview?'

'Yes, if you think it's at all relevant.' Mrs Brodie looked at her watch.

'The psychiatric hospital, where you caught up with Duncan after leaving Eagle Court? That would be the Hawkhurst Infirmary, correct?'

'I don't recall the name of the place precisely – it was a very long time ago.'

'Yes, it was,' Jenny agreed. 'But you gave us the name of the consultant, a Mr Frederick Marsh? And the only hospital of that discipline he would have been involved with at that time was the Hawkhurst.'

'Very well, then. There's your answer.'

'The thing is,' Jenny tapped her pencil on her cheek, 'I didn't find a Duncan Brodie on the in-patient records for the year you specified.'

'Wrong year, probably,' Fiona Brodie said. 'Try the one after. My memory…' another shrug. 'You know how it is when you get older.'

'I expect I will do, when the time comes.' Jenny reprised her smile.

Luscombe covered his mouth to hide his expression.

'Well, as it happens, Mrs Brodie, we did check the next year, and the one after that. In fact, we checked the records over an entire ten-year period. And we still couldn't find Duncan Brodie.'

'An oversight, I expect. It takes a certain discipline to keep an accurate records system.'

'That would be one of your top skills, Mrs Brodie?'

The brief leaned forward, 'Is this strictly relevant? My client's skills regarding record-keeping are neither here nor there.'

'We'll move on,' Jenny said.

The brief sat back in his chair, satisfied.

'I'll tell you what we did find, though, Mrs Brodie.'

A resigned sigh. 'I'm sure you will.'

'We found *your* name in the records for 1979. Miss Fiona Campbell. Campbell is your maiden name, is that correct?'

Mrs Brodie's brow furrowed. She turned to her brief but received only an impartial expression in return.

'For the benefit of the tape, please, Mrs Brodie?'

'Yes. That is my maiden name.'

'And what would your name be doing on the in-patient list, I wonder?'

'Just an error, a stupid clerical error. They probably confused the visitors' book with the in-patients register. Or something. *I* don't know.'

'Well, I don't think that's the case, Mrs Brodie, because I spoke to Mr Marsh, your consultant.'

'My—'

'Yes, that's right, Mrs Brodie, *your* consultant. He's long retired now, of course, but we had a nice wee chat on the phone. He remembers you very well. Sends his best wishes, and hopes you've made great progress since your stay in Hawkhurst.'

Mrs Brodie examined the tabletop, ran a manicured

finger across a fine crack in the varnish.

Jenny pressed on. '*You* were the in-patient, Mrs Brodie, not Duncan.'

'I don't see what on earth this has to do with anything. May I ask what point you're trying to make?'

'My point is, Mrs Brodie, that *you* were the one who suffered abuse at Eagle Court, not Duncan. He might have had a rough time, sure – it was no picnic for the pupils, by all accounts. But what happened to you was of a different order, wasn't it? I mean, there you were, a young, vulnerable female living in a predominantly male environment–'

'This is ridiculous,' Mrs Brodie interrupted. 'Totally irrelevant.'

'But I have to disagree, Mrs Brodie,' Luscombe broke in. 'It's highly pertinent. If you'd be kind enough to continue to answer DS Armitage's questions, I'd be grateful.'

Mrs Brodie glared at her brief, a silent instruction to challenge Luscombe's interjection, but the solicitor was busy scribbling something on his pad and her entreaty went unnoticed.

Jenny continued. 'You were friendly with some of the boys, of course. That's only to be expected. I imagine they rather enjoyed having an attractive young girl living among them.'

'We had our own accommodation,' Mrs Brodie said, stiffly. 'The school cottage. It was called 'Old House'. We were entirely separate from the boarders. There was nothing inappropriate about our situation or location.'

'I'm sure there wasn't, Mrs Brodie. But although it might have been out of bounds for the boys, that wasn't the case for staff members. They would have been able to pop in and out on school business – fairly regularly, I would imagine, your mother being the matron.'

'Of course.'

Jenny joined her hands together, leaned forward. 'And that would have included Mr Daintree, wouldn't it, Fiona?'

Silence.

'Please answer the question, Mrs Brodie,' Luscombe said quietly.

A nod.

'For the tape, please, Mrs Brodie,' Jenny prompted.

'Yes.'

'Yes...?'

'*Yes*, Mr Daintree did visit. From time to time.'

'From time to time,' Jenny repeated. 'And these visits became quite troublesome, didn't they, Fiona?'

Mrs Brodie's lips were compressed into a thin line. Her face had paled beneath the foundation.

'And in those days it wasn't so easy to object, was it, Fiona? Mr Daintree was respected in the school. Feared, even. An old-school disciplinarian, his daughter called him. No one would dare question his integrity, his motives, his … predilections?'

Jenny's voice went on relentlessly. 'You tried to tell your mother, but she had her job to consider; it was her living, her calling – a lifestyle choice. She'd given everything to the school. It was her home.'

Fiona Brodie's eyes were lowered now. No eye contact.

'Eventually,' Jenny continued, 'your mother conceded that the only way out of the situation was to resign from her position as matron, just to get you to a place of safety.

But by then, the damage had been done. Your mother was ill by then, too, but she had the good sense to understand that you needed help, some serious counselling to help you come to terms with what had happened.'

Luscombe realised that he had been holding his breath. The atmosphere in the small interview room seemed to have contracted, sucked in upon itself, like a star being swallowed by a black hole.

'But Mr Daintree was never charged, was he, Fiona? In fact, he was never even accused of any misdemeanour. You didn't make a formal complaint. Maybe it was just too much to bear, after what had happened. Maybe you just couldn't face the questions, interrogations, court appearances?'

'It was a long time ago,' Mrs Brodie repeated, a dry, hopeless statement.

'But then, out of the blue, Chapelfields receive an application from one Mrs Fowler. Her elderly father has moved to Scotland – but he's not managing so well on his own any more. She wants him in Chapelfields, where he'll be cared for. Mrs Fowler is a busy woman, runs her own business. Hasn't got the time to be a full-time carer. You remember speaking to Mrs Fowler, Fiona?'

'For the tape, please,' Luscombe reminded her.

'Yes. I remember.'

'So, here's the name again, after all these years, popping up like a Halloween monster. You must have had a bit of a shock when you realised who Mrs Fowler's father was, Fiona? When the name 'Daintree' was spelled out for you?'

Mrs Brodie moistened her lips.

'But then … goodness me, a change of plan! Mrs

Fowler decides that a better idea would be to move her dad down south. After all, she lives in Berkshire, so it makes sense to apply to a home in her own county. And lo and behold, there's another Chapelfields in the town of Reading. Perfect.'

Mrs Brodie's brief shuffled his papers, crossed one leg over the other.

'But not so perfect for you, Fiona, because you've already hatched a plan. You've already figured out what Isaiah Marley and his exotic girlfriend have been up to. You've already been bold enough to make Connie Chan an offer – one she can't really refuse, because you've told her that if she doesn't help you you'll go to the police with the evidence you've collected. And as record-keeping, attention to detail and so on is something of a primary skill, Fiona, I imagine you managed to collect a fair bit – photographs, times of Isaiah's deliveries, whatever. What matters is that you figured out what they'd been up to. And you offered her money, didn't you, Fiona? An extra carrot, to get a little job done for you.'

'DC Armitage is showing the suspect evidence folder P1A, item 1,' Luscombe said.

Jenny pushed the bank statement across the table. 'A large sum of money was debited from your account ten days ago. We've traced the recipient to an account in France. Account holder is one *Ms Z Binti*. Can you explain the purpose of the transaction, Mrs Brodie?'

'I ... I can't recall–'

'You can't recall? Let me help you, Fiona. You paid a woman, known to you as Connie Chan, to murder Mr Daintree after he'd relocated to Reading. Unfortunately, it all went wrong after the deed, and Isaiah was accidentally killed. Chan wasn't happy about that. She blames you, and she decides to take it out on your nearest and dearest. Only, perhaps, Duncan can't really be described in those terms any more, Fiona, can he? Has everything gone a bit stale? Was he thinking about *leaving* you?' Jenny raised her voice by the merest sliver of a decibel. 'And I wonder, were you hoping that Chan would finish him off properly, so you could play the innocent, blame Duncan for Daintree's murder?'

Fiona Brodie was staring fixedly ahead. Her mouth was open a fraction but nothing was coming out.

'You spun us a heart-rending story about Duncan, how he was abused at Eagle Court. That incident at the rugby match, the damage to his ear. Needed quite a few stitches, didn't it? Well, let me tell you, Fiona, that a colleague of ours has had a good look at Duncan's ear. An injury such as the one you describe would have left a scar, for sure. Guess what? Not a dicky.'

Mrs Brodie's brief leaned back and closed his eyes.

'DC Armitage is showing the suspect evidence folder P1A, item 2,' Luscombe said.

'A mobile phone, Fiona. What we call a burner. Cheap, disposable. We found this in a room at the Swan Hotel in Petworth. The call history is interesting. There's a number of missed calls from one particular mobile – yours. We found the burner in Connie Chan's room, Fiona.'

There was a short silence, broken only by the tick of the radiator as water was pumped through from some unknown cistern elsewhere in the building.

'What did you expect me to do?' Mrs Brodie said eventually, her voice barely a whisper. 'You don't know Daintree. You can't know what he did to me. No one will ever understand.' She shook her head. 'No one can ever understand how alone I felt. How dirty. How used.' She looked up and now her mouth twisted into a sad little smile. 'I'd do it again, you know. I hope he burns in hell.'

'I think that will do,' Luscombe said. 'Interview terminated at eleven-twenty-six.'

CHAPTER FORTY

'You've just been attacked by a madwoman, you're in hospital, and all you can think about is Duncan Brodie's ear?' Luscombe's voice rose to an incredulous crescendo. 'Good God, DI Pepper, you're a case of pure vintage, all right, no mistake.'

'Is there a reason for your call, DS Luscombe?' Charlie tried not to laugh, but the tone of her voice was all smiles.

'Just to say that Fiona Brodie fessed up a wee while ago. Your intel helped us along, so thanks for that. And Jenny did a fine job.'

'Ah yes, Jenny.'

'And what's that supposed to mean?' Luscombe asked innocently. 'Jenny Armitage is an excellent detective.'

'I'm sure she is.'

'And that's all,' Luscombe said. 'She's a respected work colleague.'

'Right.'

'How are you, though? Seriously?'

'Shoulder's a bit stiff. Otherwise, I'm fine. We're waiting to see how Chan's going to be handled. We've got three constabularies barking down the phone at our boss – they all want a slice of her.'

'I'll bet they do,' Luscombe said.

'So … what are you up to next? How's local crime in Aviemore?'

'Oh, you know, pretty average. Enough to keep us in a job.'

'That's good. I was wondering…' Charlie made a face to herself.

'Uh huh?'

'I thought I might take some leave, have a change of scenery.'

'Anywhere in mind?'

Charlie grinned widely. 'They say the Highlands are nice this time of year.'

'A little on the dreich side today, I'm afraid.'

'I'll let you have the flight times later,' Charlie said. 'You can bring a brolly.'

There was a moment's silence at the other end. 'I'll pick you up in the Rolls then, shall I?'

'If you insist.' Charlie laughed aloud. 'I'd settle for a horse and cart, if it makes it any easier.'

'Whatever ma'am is comfortable with,' Luscombe assured her. 'Your carriage will be waiting.'

'What are you grinning about?' Moran looked up as Charlie knocked and came in with an evident spring in her step.

'Nothing, guv. Just arranged a few days off.'

'Well, you've certainly earned it.'

'Thought you'd like to know – Fiona Brodie's confessed.'

Moran slapped his desk. 'That's *great* news. Let's hope we get to have a crack at Chan – Zubaida, I should say – as well.'

'Higginson still negotiating?'

Moran nodded wearily. 'The woman's left a trail of destruction behind her – ten year's worth at least. And that's just the stuff we know about.'

Charlie pursed her lips. 'As you said before, her background…'

'Bad, sure, but it doesn't excuse a record-breaking serial-killing spree.'

'No. No, of course it doesn't.'

'I can hear the 'but' loud and clear.' Moran's smile was not unsympathetic.

Charlie sighed. 'It's been playing on my mind. Not just Chan, but Fiona Brodie too. Both lives wrecked by what happened to them, by something they couldn't control.'

Moran nodded. 'They're not the first, and they won't be the last.'

'It's just … I don't know, it's not–'

'–Fair? Uh huh.' Moran steepled his fingers. 'So … exactly how long have you been a serving police officer, DI Pepper?'

Charlie groaned. 'OK. Point taken. I think I need that break.'

'With my blessing,' Moran said. 'Go on, push off. And if you see DC Collingworth, ask him to pop in, would you?'

'Sure.'

Charlie was half-way out the door when he called after her. 'And give my regards to DS Luscombe.'

Moran was still smiling when Collingworth's tentative

knock made him look up again.

'Ah. DC Collingworth. Come in, please. Shut the door behind you, would you?'

Collingworth's body language as he made the short journey between the door and Moran's desk called to mind a condemned man's final approach to the scaffold.

'Have a seat.' Moran's invitation was genial, and Collingworth nervously did as he was told.

'I expect you've been a bit fretful recently, Chris.'

Collingworth appeared a little startled at Moran's use of his Christian name. He managed a short reply. 'Been busy, guv. A lot going on.'

'Yes, and I hear you've been very helpful. Getting stuck in, mobile traces and the like, some good research on Duncan Brodie's background. You found the asylum – perhaps we shouldn't call it that these days – the *hospital* where Fiona and Duncan Brodie ran into each other again, that right?'

'Yes, guv.'

'Good work. Nice to see a healthy spirit of co-operation between ourselves and Aviemore. DCS Higginson will be pleased.'

'Thank you, guv.'

'Just wanted to clear something up, Chris. About the RTC, the Cleiren shunt.'

'Oh, yes?'

'Yes.' Moran put his pen down, allowed his spine to sink into the supportive leather of his new chair, and joined his hands together. 'The credit card you found in the artic? I've spoken since to Sergeant Ruiter – you'll recall he was overseeing the forensic investigation?'

'Ruiter, ycah. I spoke to him.'

'That's right, he remembers your visit. Funny thing is, he swears on his wife's life that they'd been over the shell of that truck with a fine-toothed comb – his expression. All that was there to be found, had already been found.'

'He was surprised when I pulled the card out, I remember that.'

'Careless of them, to miss something obvious, you think?'

'I suppose, yeah. Easily done, though.'

'Easily done.' Moran scratched his chin.

'You know, Chris, I'm aware that there may have been a few rumours doing the rounds recently concerning my time in the *Garda*.'

'Rumours, guv?'

'Relating to associations, affiliations, that kind of thing.'

Collingworth made a noncommittal gesture.

Moran went on. 'It's just that, I wouldn't believe everything you hear. Especially from the man in the street, if you understand my meaning.'

'Man in the street,' Collingworth repeated.

'Or in the pub, even.'

'The pub,' Collingworth parroted.

'You see, I know the landlord pretty well. We go back a long way.'

Collingworth's face was stone. He knew what was coming, just not exactly how it was going to end.

'He keeps an eye on what's going on,' Moran said. 'All part of the craft of the pub landlord. It's not all glasses and pulling pints.'

'It was a mistake, guv.'

'Oh?'

Collingworth nodded vigorously. 'I made a fool of

myself. It was stupid. I risked my career, and now I've blown it. I'm sorry – I got involved in something I didn't understand.'

Moran looked Collingworth up and down. 'That might be the most sensible thing I've ever heard issue from your lips, DC Collingworth.'

Collingworth looked confused, so Moran kept talking. 'I've been in this game a very long time, son. And you'd be right in thinking I've learned a few lessons of my own by this stage of my career. But, you know what?'

Collingworth shook his head dumbly.

'I still muck things up, often very badly. These last weeks, for instance, I've had to relearn a very old lesson, a lesson that's particularly relevant when it comes to the rather … shadowy world in which we've recently found ourselves.'

Collingworth looked as though he might issue some kind of denial, but then thought better of it and kept his mouth shut.

'Would you like to hear the advice I had to repeat to myself?'

'Yes – I mean, absolutely, guv.'

Moran leaned forward and folded his arms on the desk. He looked Collingworth directly in the eye. 'This is appropriate for any number of circumstances you might encounter during routine investigations, but it's particularly appropriate when we find ourselves rubbing shoulders with…' Moran lowered his voice, 'the shadowy world in question. You understand me?'

'Sir.'

'OK. Here it is, the first rule: *Trust no one*. Got that?'

'Yes, guv.'

'Repeat.'

Collingworth cleared his throat. 'Trust no one – guv.'

'Good.' Moran sat back in his chair.

'What's going to happen now? I mean, are you going to–'

'You're going to get on with the job, DC Collingworth, *without* further distractions, I trust.' Moran beamed. 'And who knows? You might even find yourself in a sergeant's post before too long.'

Collingworth sprang from his chair. 'All *right*. I mean, thank you very much, guv.'

After Collingworth had left, Moran spent a few minutes reflecting on the wisdom of his decision. He was a pretty good judge of character, and his judgment was that Collingworth had learned his lesson. Time would tell if the lesson was going to stick.

We shall see, DC Collingworth…

The mention of Sergeant Ruiter reminded Moran that the forensic overseer had left a message to phone him. He tapped the number and Ruiter answered instantly.

'It's DCI Moran returning your call, Sergeant. How can I help?'

'I'm beyond help, have been for years,' Ruiter said drily, 'but this might help you. Or it might not.'

'Let's have it,' Moran said. 'Whatever the result, eh?'

'Okey dokey.' There followed the sound of rustling paperwork as the sergeant searched for the relevant place in his notes. 'Your artic shunt. Like I told your man, we've been over and over it, but this popped out from forensics yesterday. They were dragging their heels while they repeated some test or other. All to do with the brakes.'

'The brakes?'

'Yep. Turns out there were microscopic traces of explosive residue in and around the brake mechanism.'

Moran was baffled. 'There were traces of explosive inside the truck – we knew that much already. So what's the implication? That someone set out with the specific intention of causing the brakes to fail?'

'That's your department, DCI Moran. I'm just passing on the info. Forensics speculate that the charges could have been set off remotely. A pro job – you know, state-of-the-art device that leaves little evidence behind? So they reckon, anyhow. It'll all be in the report, which'll be on its way to you shortly. State-of-the-art carrier pigeon.'

'I see. Thank you Sergeant – I may need get back to you on this.' Moran's mind was whirring. Someone had wanted to make sure Cleiren totalled his truck right where it happened: on the M4, on Moran's patch. The question was, which of two possible perpetrators would stoop so low?

CHAPTER FORTY-ONE

Moran wearily unlocked his front door, stepped into the hallway, picked up his post, dumped the pile onto the hall table, and greeted Archie with a quick ruffle of the spaniel's tufty head. Checked the lounge, kitchen. Went upstairs, repeated the same for the bedrooms and bathroom. Caught himself reaching for the long pole that unclasped the attic trapdoor latch. Stopped himself.

Come on, Brendan. Enough …

Went downstairs, put the kettle on, took out the bread and butter to make a jam sandwich.

It was no good. He had to know. He grabbed his keys, went to the front door.

'Hold on a little while longer, boy,' he told the little Cocker who had reappeared with a ball jammed firmly in his mouth, tail windmilling like a propeller. 'I just need to check on Mrs P. Won't be a second.'

There was no response to his knock. He waited for a bit. Knocked again. Still nothing. He bent and opened the letter box flap.

'What on earth–?'

The hallway was bare. The big dresser had gone. On the wall to the left was a clean space where a full-length mirror had hung. Moran let the flap go with a clang. He went to the front window, cupped a hand over his brow, squinted. Empty. Not one single piece of furniture, nor carpet. Bare boards.

He returned to his house. It made no sense. He picked up his letters, sifted through the usual junk mail, circulars, pizza offers, until he got to the last item. An envelope simply marked: 'DCI Brendan Moran'. Hand-written and hand delivered.

Now what?

He slit the envelope open, took out a single folded sheet of paper.

Hello Brendan

Sorry I wasn't able to put you in the picture in person before the move. Don't worry, everything is fine and the item you were concerned about is safely in the right hands.

I do feel that I owe you an explanation. Would you care to meet up tomorrow morning? How about Streatley? At the top of the hill there's a sign across the road from the car park which reads 'The Holies' – I'll take a stroll up there, rendezvous say 8.30? Lovely views. Do bring Archie – he'll love it. Lots of rabbits, moles and goodness know what else.

Kind regards,

Constance P.

Moran reread the note before placing it carefully in his

coat pocket. He was too tired to even consider what might have prompted Mrs P's abrupt relocation, or where she might have gone. Tomorrow was another day, and Mrs P herself seemed keen to save him the trouble of attempting to unravel this latest conundrum on his own. He returned to the kitchen to finish making his sandwich, and ate it with an accompanying cup of strong breakfast tea, watched intently all the while by Archie, who had carefully positioned himself to address any morsels Moran might be careless enough to drop.

The sun was bright in Moran's eyes as he left the car park, which was already half-full, and crossed the road. There was the sign Mrs P had mentioned – 'The Holies'. Archie tugged at his lead, already scenting the wildlife, and pulled Moran up the incline into the woodland. The hundred odd acres of The Holies was now owned by the National Trust, and the chalky grassland was home to a number of rare flowers and insects. Somewhere up here, Moran recalled, was the remains of a Bronze Age hill fort. And no wonder the ancients had selected this spot – the views of the surrounding landscape were breathtaking.

They made good progress along a flint and gravel track, continuing along the path and through a robust kissing gate, Archie taking the easier route beneath the woodwork and accelerating up the slope in pursuit of a bolting muntjac.

The trees gradually thinned, until dog and man were delivered onto a wide, grassy coombe dotted with stemless thistle and wild thyme. A low bench presided over the expanse in the centre of which, sitting demurely with her hands recumbent on her lap, was Mrs Perkins. Archie spotted her immediately and gave up on the muntjac. Here was something more familiar and much more accessible. The spaniel dashed across the grass and pushed his nose against Mrs P's coat, tail thrashing furiously.

'Hello Archie. You found me.' Mrs Perkins smiled indulgently. 'Let's see if I have a treat for you.' She reached into her pocket and produced a thin paper bag. 'Nicely now, no snatching.'

Moran joined Mrs P on the bench. 'Morning.'

'Hello Brendan.'

'They've moved you on, then. Job done.' Moran was taking in the view. It was extraordinarily clear, miles of hedgerow-delimited fields, smoking chimney stacks, clusters of houses nestling in the dips and cracks of the rural landscape. He'd slept well – surprisingly so – and his clarity of thought had been, if not entirely reinstated, at least ameliorated to some degree.

'You've been thinking it through.'

Archie was sitting at full attention, waiting for the next tidbit.

'I can only get so far, but yes, I think I have a rough idea. The thing is, just when I think I've worked it out, another layer presents itself and I'm back to square one. A bit like trying to peel a large onion in the dark with a blunt pair of pliers.'

Mrs Perkins made a face. 'I don't think I've ever been compared to an onion before. That's a first.'

Moran laughed, 'No offence. I'm just a simple policeman trying to do my job.'

'None taken. And for what it's worth, you do it very well.'

They lapsed into a companionable silence. To the

north, the landscape unrolled before them like a mosaic tapestry, the needlework of numberless hedgerows separating the greens and browns, criss-crossing the panorama like the work of a careless seamstress. Leaves rustled in the westerly breeze, unseen wings fluttered in the undergrowth. Archie's ears twitched, and the spaniel cocked his head. Too many scents, too many choices…

Presently Moran said, 'You were right, this is quite a view.'

Mrs Perkins sighed. 'Beautiful, isn't it? I could sit up here forever. One feels … *above* the world and its problems.'

'Yes. It's very peaceful.'

'I'm officially retired, you know.' Mrs Perkins fed Archie his next scrap. 'But from time to time I receive a little message. It's understood, you see. Once you're in, you're never really out.'

'You don't find that rather – unsettling?'

Mrs Perkins gave a short laugh. 'I suppose some might, but I like to keep myself occupied. Keep the grey matter ticking over.'

'Yes,' Moran agreed. 'I'd probably feel the same way.'

'Look, Brendan, I don't want to you to feel that our friendship is all a … well, a sham. Not at all. I've genuinely enjoyed your neighbourliness, walking Archie, all those things. I hope this business doesn't leave a sour taste. I should be sorry if that were the case.'

'It's all right, Mrs Perkins. I'm getting used to it.'

'Well, let's hope you'll be intrigue-free from now on, darling – *patience*, Archie.' Mrs P rummaged in the paper bag. 'Just two left. There you are. Good dog.'

'Let's rewind,' Moran said. 'Samantha Grant killed

Liam Doherty in my house. Shortly after that, she was taken by persons unknown.'

'Our friends from the East, yes.'

'Samantha told me that MI5 wanted Doherty terminated, that he was too much of a risk.'

'He represented a risk to us, yes. But more so to Moscow, and especially to Joe Gallagher.'

Moran nodded. 'I figured that much. So Samantha was acting on behalf of the Russians. But what about her abduction?'

'Staged,' Mrs P said. 'For my benefit – and yours. But we already knew what she was up to. She was good, Brendan, but not beyond a careless slip or two. She'd probably have been offered in an exchange, some time in the future.'

'Ah, one of theirs for one of ours?'

'Precisely. And then she'd have been in a perfect position to continue acting as a double. And they'd have got a man back.'

'Except she didn't know you were onto her.'

'Indeed.'

'I learned an interesting snippet of news yesterday evening,' he said, 'about the RTC, the *Guust Vervoer* truck.'

'Oh yes?'

'The brakes had been rigged. Explosive charges.'

'That was them, not us. Ruthless lot, aren't they?'

'They wanted Cleiren's artic to crash *exactly* where it did, because they knew I'd be dealing with the aftermath, make the link with *Guust Vervoer* and from there to Samantha.'

'That's how we read it, yes. Typical belt and braces approach. Although, from what I understand, Cleiren lost control even before the charges went off.'

Moran frowned. 'You're aware they knobbled one of my team? Got him to plant Sam's credit card in the wreck?'

'Yes, we were onto that. My guess is that other links – *carrots,* we could call them – to lead you to Samantha that had been planted in Cleiren's truck were destroyed by the fire. Samantha and Cleiren were something of an item, by the way – a fast worker, that woman. Cleiren no doubt had a photo, or a scribbled love letter, or something of that nature somewhere in the cab. That's why they selected Cleiren's artic – there should have been plenty of Samantha for you to discover. Unfortunately for them, the fire destroyed all of it. Your man was plan B.'

'Let's talk about the tape.'

'You weren't to know, Brendan, but when you gave it to me for safekeeping, you were effectively giving it directly to Thames House. It's a done deal. Action is being taken, even as we speak.'

Moran fell silent. A kestrel hovered, tracking some unfortunate shrew or vole. As they watched it stooped, struck, and sailed away with its breakfast hanging limply.

'One other thing. I'm assuming your lot intended to apprehend Samantha when we arrived at the Port of London, but there was no reception committee waiting. She might easily have slipped your net even then, got herself on board some another ship.'

'Unlikely,' Mrs Perkins said. 'You only saw the fellow you spoke to because he wanted you to see him. We were well represented, trust me. But as things turned out, the operation was unnecessary.' She fed Archie his last treat, and the spaniel gulped it down. Mrs P screwed up the paper bag and stuffed it in her coat pocket. 'Off you go, Archie. Have a run around.'

They watched the little dog sniff the earth as he caught a scent, trotted off to investigate, nose to the ground.

Mrs Perkins said, 'I'm glad you've come through this, Brendan. And I'm sorry you were dragged into it.'

'I seem to have a nose for trouble,' Moran said drily. 'It's always been a problem.'

Mrs P had risen from the bench. 'I'd better be off, darling. Things to do, you know how it is with a house move.'

'I'll not expect a Christmas card.'

Mrs P laughed. 'I won't be so far away, Brendan. I'm sure we'll bump into each other from time to time.'

'I'm not sure if that's a comfort or not.'

'I'll leave you to work that one out. Goodbye, Chief Inspector.'

Moran sat for a while longer, watching Archie scurry hither and thither. He knew what Mrs P meant, about feeling above everything on this plateau. In the distance the two wooded hills known as Wittenham Clumps presided over the landscape like silent guardians. It wasn't hard to imagine the hill forts of bygone days, the stern, vigilant eyes looking out from their vantage point, alert for an approaching enemy. Had it been easier then, Moran wondered, to tell friend from foe? Before men had perfected the art of subterfuge, deceit, mendacity, betrayal?

A breeze ruffled the leaves in the surrounding trees, as though in answer to Moran's unspoken question.

Not at all, they whispered. *It was always this way.*

CHAPTER FORTY-TWO

'George? I took a call for you – I left a message on your desk.'

George took off his jacket, hung it on the back of his chair. 'Oh, right. Thanks, Avani.' He gave the recently seconded DC a wave of acknowledgment, picked up her scribbled note. He recognised the number instantly. High Nelmes. The note read: *Call manager urgently.*

'Avani?' he shouted across the office. 'Did they say what it was about?'

'No, not at all, actually. But she sounded a bit stressed, I think.'

'Tell the guv I'll be back later.'

George took the stairs two at a time. Damn the lift. He bleeped his car unlocked and gunned the engine. Traffic was bad, the IDR still jammed with commuters. 'Come *on*.' George nosed the car forward, blocked a patiently queuing Corsa, drew a silent, hostile stare from the driver. No matter, he'd made a space. Ten frustrating minutes later he was at last able to open the throttle and point the car towards Cold Ash, the well-worn route to Tess' residential home.

As he drove, George's imagination filled in the gaps. Tess was dead. Or perhaps worse, had suffered some catastrophic stroke. No, a heart attack. That was more likely. Her heart had been erratic since the poison had been administered. Or maybe an accident? An overdose?

George banged the steering wheel as a tractor emerged from a gateway a few hundred metres ahead.

He ground his teeth for the next half-mile, following the farmer along the narrow country lane, half-tempted to use the blue light. Eventually the tractor turned off, the farmer gave a laconic wave of thanks, and George steamed on past.

As he approached the familiar Nelmes entrance, with its security box, ivy-clad gateposts and well-tended frontage, he slowed to a sedate 10 miles per hour. His heart was thudding heavily under his ribs. He couldn't go in, couldn't face it, whatever it was. It was a mistake to have come. He should have just made a call, got it over with quickly. He parked the car and turned the engine off. There were the hedgerows, beyond which lay the lake, his thinking place. Everything looked the same. But something had changed. Well, there was nothing for it. He might as well go and find out the worst.

A receptionist he recognised looked up as he came in. 'Hello, DC McConnell. Have you come to see our Tess?'

George wanted to reply but his throat felt constricted, his mouth dry. He nodded to the girl.

'Go right on up,' she said with a smile. 'You might get a pleasant surprise.'

George climbed the staircase with winged feet, his mind in a whirl. What did she mean? She didn't look upset, or worried, or–

He saw a wheelchair being wheeled along the corridor from the direction of Tess' room. A carer was chatting away to the person in the wheelchair. The carer saw him first.

'Ah,' she called out. '*There* you are. We saw you parking from the window. Tess was wondering if you were *ever* going to come up, so we decided to come and meet you instead.'

George reached the top of the staircase and waited, scarcely daring to believe. As the wheelchair drew closer he saw Tess, smiling – no, grinning – the way she used to when she was winding him up, or telling a joke, or–

The wheelchair stopped, dead in front of him.

'Hello, George.' Tess' voice was husky, as if speech was a newly-learned art form, but her eyes were sparkling and her smile was wide and focused. 'You took your sodding time. I hope you haven't brought more of those wretched satsumas. I *hate* satsumas.'

George hardly dared open his mouth. When he eventually managed to speak, he heard himself say, 'I'll bring grapes instead, then. Bloody ungrateful, I call it.'

Someone had left a copy of *The Times* in reception. Moran picked it up, scanned the front page.

'All bad, as usual,' Denis Robinson, the duty sergeant, said from behind his screen. 'I don't bother reading the papers any more. Life's hard enough as it is.'

'You're a cheerful soul this morning, Denis.' Moran looked up and smiled.

'Nothing good in there, Brendan, like I said. They reckon this budget is going to wreck the economy for years to come.'

'Do they indeed,' Moran said, but now he was only half-listening, because his eyes had lit upon a column at the foot of the front page.

Irish Minister exposed as terrorist sympathiser

Joseph Gallagher, the current Irish Minister for Trade and Industry, is being questioned by senior Garda officers concerning his alleged involvement in historical and current terrorist activities...

Moran scanned the article to its conclusion.

...It is understood that a retired senior Garda officer is also helping investigating officers with their enquiries. His name cannot be divulged at present for legal and statutory reasons.

'Public services were badly off before,' Robinson was saying. 'And what about the NHS? Been hanging on by a thread for who knows how long? No better for us lot, either. Same old story, every year.' Robinson shook his head sadly.

Moran folded the paper and set it down on the table. 'Well, thanks for the cheery welcome, Denis. Have a good morning, yourself.'

Moran took the lift. He'd promised himself he'd use the stairs in future, any exercise being worthwhile. But today, sod it.

'Morning all,' he greeted the room as he went in.

Bernice Swinhoe stage-whispered on his way past. 'The boss is waiting for you, guv. In your office.'

'Thanks, DC Swinhoe.'

That was all he needed. An ear-bending from Higginson. Moran braced himself before he opened his door.

'Morning, sir. What can I do for you?'

'Have a seat, Brendan. 'Not good news, I'm afraid.'

'No? Oh, well, I'd better hear it, anyway. Oh, before you tell me, have you heard about Tess Martin?'

Higginson's face cracked a smile. 'Yes, now that is excellent news, indeed. She looks to have turned a corner. DC McConnell tells me she's talking, even walking a little. Marvellous to hear.'

'It is, sir. Now then?'

Higginson sighed, tapped the brim of his cap, which he held on his lap as though cradling a baby. 'Well, you're not going to like it. I expect the news'll be breaking very soon.'

Moran felt a cold hand race along his spine.

'It's Chan, I'm afraid. *Zubaida.* She escaped from Crawley Hospital. Sometime in the early hours.'

'But they had a twenty-four hour guard–'

'They did. But Chan apparently exchanged places with a nurse. The nurse is ... currently being treated, but–'

'She's not going to make it.'

'It doesn't look good, no,' Higginson admitted. 'Strangled, I believe. A belt.'

Moran could find no words.

'Sussex are on the case, of course, but by now…'

'She could be anywhere.'

'Exactly.' Higginson stood up. 'It may not fall to us, Brendan, but I thought it might help if you gave Sussex a buzz, as you've personally encountered the suspect.'

'Of course. I'll call them now. Does ... does DI Pepper know about this?'

'You're my first port of call, Brendan. I'll leave it to you to brief the others.'

Moran nodded. Charlie was going to love this. 'I'll make sure they're informed directly, sir.'

'Good man. Well, keep me posted. And, ah yes, Brendan, I wondered–?'

'Sir?'

'This… sabbatical? I don't like to ask, but it might be prudent to–'

'–Hold fire for the time being, sir? Of course. Probably a bad idea, in any case.'

The Chief Superintendent nodded briskly. 'Good to know you're still on board, Brendan. Hate to think we might lose you.'

Higginson sat his cap on his head, and with a curt nod he left Moran to his thoughts.

The noise of traffic filtered in through his half-open window. The hiss of air brakes, the hooting of impatient taxi drivers, the roar of motorcycle engines. The world was turning as usual, people going about their normal activities, secure in the knowledge that tomorrow would follow the same pattern, and the day after that. But there were monsters out there, too. And it was Moran's job to catch them, so that ordinary lives could continue in their usual, predictable patterns.

But where did they come from, these monsters? Who created them? Moran rose and went to the window, looked out on the scurrying pedestrians, the cyclists, trucks and cabs. Those same people, ordinary men and women, members of the public he was employed to protect; they all had the potential to create monsters, given the right circumstances.

Moran sighed. *And so do we all, if we're honest.*

He returned to his desk. Better call Sussex, as Higginson had suggested.

Before he could pick up the phone, it rang.

Moran paused, sent up a silent prayer, reached for the handset.

Here we go again…

Glossary

SECTU
South East Counter Terrorism Unit

RBH
Royal Berkshire Hospital

IR
Incident Room

IDR
Inner Distribution Road

PACE
Police and Criminal Evidence Act (1984). An Act of Parliament which instituted a legislative framework for the powers of police officers in England and Wales to combat crime, and provided codes of practice for the exercise of those powers

NPASS
National Police Air Support Service

RIPA ('Ripper')
Regulation of Investigatory Powers Act (regulates the powers of public bodies to carry out surveillance and investigation)

POI
Person of interest

The DCI Brendan Moran Series – have you read them all?

Black December

DCI Brendan Moran, world-weary veteran of 1970s Ireland, is recuperating from a near fatal car crash when a murder is reported at Charnford Abbey.

The abbot and his monks are strangely uncooperative, but when a visitor from the Vatican arrives and an ancient relic goes missing the truth behind Charnford's pact of silence threatens to expose not only the abbey's haunted secrets but also the spirits of Moran's own troubled past . . .

Black December is an atmospheric crime thriller that will keep you on the edge of your seat until the stunning climax. This is the first in the DCI Brendan Moran crime series, one of the new breed of top UK Detectives.

'...gripping, with a really intriguing plot.'

Creatures of Dust

An undercover detective goes missing and the body

of a young man is found mutilated in a shop doorway. Is there a connection? Returning to work after a short convalescence, DCI Brendan Moran's suspicions are aroused when a senior officer insists on freezing Moran out and handling the investigation himself.

A second murder convinces Moran that a serial killer is on the loose but with only a few days to prove his point the disgruntled DCI can't afford to waste time. As temperatures hit the high twenties, tempers fray, and the investigation founders Moran finds himself coming back to the same question again and again: can he still trust his own judgement, or is he leading his team up a blind alley?

'...non-stop action and convoluted twists. Another brilliant read in the Brendan Moran series...'

Death Walks Behind You

DCI Brendan Moran's last minute break in the West Country proves anything but restful as he becomes embroiled in the mysterious disappearance of an American tourist. Does the village harbour some dark and dreadful secret? The brooding presence of the old manor house and the dysfunctional de Courcy family may hold the answer but Moran soon finds that the residents of Cernham have a rather unorthodox approach to the problem of dealing with outsiders...

'...a pleasure to read – gripped from start to finish...'

The Irish Detective - digital box set

The first omnibus edition of the popular DCI Brendan Moran crime series. Contents includes the first, second and third in series, plus an exclusive CWA shortlisted short story 'Safe As Houses'...

Silent As The Dead

A call from an old friend whose wife has vanished from their home in Co.Kerry prompts DCI Brendan Moran to return to his Irish roots. The Gardai have drawn a blank; can Moran succeed where they have failed?

Moran's investigation leads him to a loner known locally as the Islander, who reveals that the woman's disappearance is connected to a diehard paramilitary with plans to hit a high profile target in the UK.

Time is running out. Can Moran enlist the Islander's help, or does he have to face his deadliest foe alone?

'Superb storyline with plenty of twists and turns…'

Gone Too Soon

Moran is called to a burial in a local cemetery. But this is no ordinary interment; the body of a young woman, Michelle LaCroix, a rising star in the music world, is still warm, the grave unmarked. A recording reveals the reason for her suicide. Or does it?

Why would a young, successful singer take her own life? To unlock the answer, Moran must steer a course through his darkest investigation yet, as the clues lead to one shocking discovery after another…

'…endlessly twisty – an explosive finish…'

The Enemy Inside

DCI Brendan Moran's morning is interrupted when a suicidal ex-soldier threatens to jump from a multi-storey car park ...

Moran soon regrets getting involved when an unexpected visitor turns up on his doorstep to confront him with what appears to be damning evidence of past misconduct.

Can the Irish Detective clear his name, or must he come clean and face the consequences? One thing seems certain: by the time the night is over, his reputation may not be the only casualty...

'...a cracking, fast-paced thriller.'

The Irish Detective 2 digital box set

The second omnibus edition of the popular DCI Brendan Moran crime series by CWA shortlisted author, Scott Hunter. Contents includes the fourth, fifth and sixth in series,
plus an exclusive short story 'Inside Job'...

A Crime For All Seasons (short stories) - FREE via website

From the midwinter snowdrifts of an ancient Roman villa to a summer stakeout at an exclusive art gallery, join DCI Brendan Moran and his team for the first volume of criminally cunning short stories in which the world-weary yet engaging Irish detective reaffirms that there is indeed a crime for all seasons…

'…great characters, plot lines and dialogue. More please!'

For more information – www.scott-hunter.net

Printed in Great Britain
by Amazon